The Third Arm

The Third Arm

Kenneth Royce

HODDER AND STOUGHTON
LONDON SYDNEY AUCKLAND TORONTO

British Library Cataloguing in Publication Data
Royce, Kenneth
  The third arm.
  I. Title
823'.9'1F   PR6068.098T/

ISBN 0 340 25009 7

1

"WE'LL SET HIM UP. Conveniently. All you have to do is shoot him."

"Kill him?"

"Wounding him won't be any good. We need a body. One whose identity we can change."

Ross Gibbs shook his head slowly. He was not horrified at the suggestion; not even surprised. He had become almost immune to Bannerman's ideas. The lank, city-broker image of the man made his dialogue bizarre; the lean, serious face, with its air of quiet concentration, a mask for the grotesque. George Bannerman could speak of killing like any other subject. With the inevitable rolled umbrella now lying flat on the bare table the whole scene seemed unbelievable.

"No," said Gibbs. At twenty-eight he looked older. Privation, disillusion and fatigue on his young face. He was out of uniform, the cheap civilian suit ill-fitting and uncomfortable. Discomfort was something he had learned to endure. "You're asking me to commit murder."

"To execute. The man himself is a murderer."

"It would still make me one."

"No. An executioner. There *is* a difference. He needs putting down before he kills again."

"I couldn't do it. Not in cold blood."

"We have to do something convincing to get you accepted. What you've done so far is not enough."

"You didn't mention this at the beginning."

5

"That was over a year ago. Things change. Its worked so far, but not far enough." Bannerman had stopped ageing at forty-five, as if the clock had stopped for him at that point. He eyed Gibbs shrewdly. "I'm thinking of you. I'm worried about you."

Gibbs caught a trace of sincerity. Bannerman was never demonstrative. "I think what I've done is enough. They do accept me."

"Only in your present context. We *are* talking about the Provos Ross. The Provisional Irish Republican Army. You seem to have lost sight of it. Outlawed by both London and Dublin Governments. Killers, torturers, thugs. A small minority who murder, maim, disrupt because they want Ireland, all of it, for their rule of terror. Bader Meinhof, Red Brigade, Provos; what's the difference?"

"For chrissake, you think I've forgotten? There has to be another way."

"Would it help if the man were a Provo? A proven killer, a known terrorist?"

"Proven to whom? A jury?"

"The Royal Ulster Constabulary would convince you."

"Where Provos are concerned the R.U.C. have been known to be prejudiced. If they could prove it legally he'd be behind bars fast."

"I assure you they would satisfy you. I have a man in mind. A renegade. A loner. He would not be missed by anyone."

The dreadful thing about Bannerman was his unfailing persistence. He did not become passionate, nor raise his voice. He simply worked quietly until he got his way. Gibbs lost a little patience. "I'm not killing anyone like this."

"Then Ross, you are dead yourself. Unless I relieve you of your duties. A wasted year."

Gibbs was as upset by that as Bannerman knew that he would be. Many risks taken in vain. He tried to reason. "Even if I agreed, those same police who just might convince me that a man is an unconvicted killer would be duty-bound to find his murderer."

"Don't be naïve. You know they wouldn't. And if they did I would stop them."

"It's justice we're fighting for."

"Legal justice won't beat the terrorist. Everyone knows it, including the extreme idealists, many of whom *are* terrorists. They *use* legal justice like a riot shield. Only the milk-and-water, rabble-rousing verbalists believe in that kind of justice. But what they preach never touches them. Their way of life is not inconvenienced. There's a real reason for my asking, Ross."

Gibbs gestured wearily. "There always is."

Bannerman watched Gibbs, probed beyond the first pleasing impact. The freshness of face was waning, the eyes narrowed with tiredness. Strain had tightened the skin. "The pack is said to be heading for London. We don't yet know how many. Mohammed Nuzzale will be one. We believe Raul Orta is being resurrected. There will be others."

"Orta?" Gibbs straightened. "He's taking a chance."

Bannerman smiled briefly. "It's never worried him." He could see that Gibbs was almost hooked, gave him time to accept the necessity to kill to protect himself and others.

"If Orta's out of hibernation it has to be big."

"Precisely."

"I know someone who knows Nuzzale. It should be possible to infiltrate."

"Only if they need you, and then only if you bear the right credentials. They will want blood on your hands. Whose, precisely, will not matter provided it's someone they approve; a traitor or an enemy."

Bannerman let it hang for a while. Then he added, "Your present hand isn't strong enough. Let's see what we've got. As a Captain in the Special Air Service you came here two years ago. You work out of Londonderry with Sergeant McKechnie. You're employed at the local shipbuilding yard on the estuary. Your ploy of letting one or two Provos off the hook and then making more positive contact has taken a good half of your time here. Inevitably they've wanted more from you. Acute distrust of the S.A.S. dies hard with the boyos. They loathe the very concept of the Special Air Services. The name itself is misleading. They see it as a military undercover organisation that moves among them using strange methods and arms and sophisticated equipment. They detest the very clandestine nature of it. And they fear it. Yet, you've so far survived the hot seat. To have a spy in the S.A.S. had a schizophrenic effect on them; they needed you and hated you at the same time. It wasn't until you placed some incendiary bombs in Belfast that they began to relax."

"I was careful where I placed them," Gibbs defended quickly.

"It would have made no difference. They would have been

planted anyway. So we have the result of knowing our enemy over a large area. The time to pounce is the day you leave. That day was imminent until we found a more important role for you."

Again Gibbs interrupted, "Don't take me for a fool. The day was never imminent. You could have pulled them in long ago. Right from the beginning you saw this as a springboard. So people have gone on dying."

Bannerman tapped the umbrella with the flat of his hand. "Don't give me too much credit. I hadn't the remotest idea a year ago that the pack might gather in London. No one had."

"So I must join them."

"You can't push yourself. How can you be expected to know that London is a target? Ross, the invitation must come from them."

Gibbs gave Bannerman a long curious look. Invitations like that didn't come by order. "You *know* they need me?"

"No. I believe they have made enquiries. You are known. The Provos have most probably been your reference."

"Well, then. What's all this about killing?"

"You need better credentials for the international pack. The S.A.S. tag will always be with you; they'll want a corpse, Ross, before they believe you."

"Then we'll do a mock killing. Keep him on ice after the act."

"There will be too many mouths to silence. A wife, sweetheart, mother. The natural reactions of those emotionally involved. Too many people need to be rehearsed. Too many problems, too much to go wrong. We need a body. A real one. And if the killing doesn't stand up under the toughest scrutiny they'll kill you. Not too pleasantly."

Gibbs rose thoughtfully, and put his hands in his pockets. "I'm still not killing anyone. Not like that. Not for you, nor anyone."

"The safety of the State?"

"You'd have to prove it to me."

Bannerman nodded, rose at the other end of the table. His round shoulders came as a surprise as he straightened. He reached for his umbrella. "All right. You'll have to leave it with me. I must protect your flanks as best I can. There's a likelihood of your being approached. Be ready for it; but don't show that you are." Bannerman lifted his umbrella in salute like a guardsman's sword.

Gibbs smiled wryly. "You want me to smell the carrot before nibbling it? I've played that game before."

"Not in this division, Ross. I implore you, be extra careful."

"Okay."

"I'll work on a substitute scheme. Get it through your head that it will have to be totally convincing. Your usage hasn't been left entirely to the knowledge of the Provos; they are necessarily tight-lipped about it. I've been extraordinarily careful in passing the word. I've had to feel out every step two or three times before placing it down. Don't spoil it for me."

"You mean you'll be the one to stop the bullet if I make a balls up of it?"

"No need for that. I'll be in touch. If you change your mind about a target send a top priority."

"Don't expect one."

"Just be careful. It matters to me."

Gibbs believed him.

*   *   *

George Bannerman caught the plane back to London at Alder-grove Airport, Belfast. He now wore a heavy topcoat against the biting early January winds, thick gloves and a Homburg hat. He had fiercely rejected a bodyguard even though many in Ulster would have liked to have seen him dead. At London's Heathrow Airport his special taxi was waiting to drive him back to Whitehall where Sir Henry Winter waited for him.

Winter's spacious, well-furnished office was in marked contrast to the meeting place of Bannerman and Gibbs, illustrating the difference in operational comforts between administrator and field man. The light through the big windows softened the winter gloom. Outside it was hardening towards a new ice age.

Winter gestured with his pipe towards a chair. The ex-admiral of the fleet viewed Bannerman suspiciously. They didn't like each other. In Bannerman's eyes Winter fell short, a caretaker head on a short-term assignment to clean up after a rather nasty public scandal. He should never have left the navy, in Bannerman's view. Winter sat sucking the filthy pipe which he claimed had gone right through World War II with him. Both bowl and stem had been replaced several times but it somehow retained its original identity.

The admiral's dislike of Bannerman was partly due to his own temporary appointment. He had been unable to connect Bannerman with the scandal, which annoyed him; he was secretly convinced that he was. Bannerman cut corners. His loyalty was not in question, and one had to accept the ruthlessness that went with the job. But there was more to it. Bannerman's deviousness could side-swipe both friend and foe. It didn't matter to him, provided he attained his object. Casualties were inevitable.

If there was dislike between them there was also a begrudging respect. Bannerman could just about tolerate Winter's blunt honesty; at least he left no one in doubt. And Winter knew Bannerman to be unusually dedicated and efficient. It was still sometimes difficult for them to communicate to each other that they were both on the same side.

Winter glared cagily behind his smokescreen. He was a square man; short and stocky with a stone-cast head mounted by wispy grey hair brought forward to cover the spreading baldness.

Bannerman adopted his careful pose. He could feel the con-strained antagonism pouring across the leather-topped desk. "It may be possible to slip Gibbs in. It won't be easy. Recklessness will finish him and wipe out a year's effort for us."

"You see it in that order?"

Oh Christ. The bloody old fool. "The two issues are complemen-tary."

"We don't want to lose him."

"Naturally not. It's a touch-and-go situation. If, through con-tacts, we push too hard, it's self-defeating. My feeling is that they need him, or someone like him. His experience is extremely valuable, particularly on his own soil."

"If we knew their plan we'd know if they needed him."

Good grief. "If we knew their plan he would not need to risk his neck."

The pipe sent a warning signal. "You know what I mean, George."

Bannerman wasn't sure. "Any further word from Craven?"

Winter didn't miss the new bite. The pipe lifted to reveal the rough face. "You resent the fact that the first tip-off came from him?"

"It didn't. The Israelis informed me direct."

"He's a closer tie with them, wouldn't you say?"

"We have better sources. Not only the Israelis."

"And Craven hasn't? Your dislike of him is showing."

"I can't stand the man. I'm not alone. The Company has been trying to get rid of him for years and all the time he's worked his way further up the tree."

"Almost to the top, George. He's lopped off a good many branches on the way."

"Oh, he's frightened a lot of people, all right."

"You two have something in common."

"God forbid. I'd resign if I felt that."

"You both get on with the job. Achieve the object."

"I don't use bulldozers and battalions to do it. Why the sudden discourse on Craven?"

"I thought you knew. He's coming over here."

Bannerman stared across the desk, not fooled by Winter's benign expression; the admiral was enjoying himself. "Why?"

"He sees it as partly his problem. I suspect, too, that he wants to keep the pack off his own doorstep."

"Not at our expense."

"We can't refuse him. The Company have been helpful."

"So have we."

"Let's not debate the various merits. We're small league these days, George."

"You mean we operate one competent man where they employ a committee." Bannerman surrendered with a raised hand. "I'm sorry. This is becoming childish. I expect soon to have Gibbs at considerable risk. I don't want Craven coming over here with his size eleven hobnails, treading over everything we've done. I don't want his amplified advice. His colleagues must be glad to lose him for a while."

"You can handle him, George. You've done so before."

"It's the time factor. I'll have to delegate someone to take care of him. Unless you'd do it for me?"

"He knows I'm a figurehead. He won't take kindly to delegation, George."

"When's he coming?"

"I don't know precisely. I doubt that he does. He's merely voiced an intention."

"To give us time to dust the red carpet."

"I didn't realise you disliked him quite so much."

Bannerman uncrossed his legs. "Paul Craven is a pain in the arse. He always will be."

Winter almost broke his pipe stem as he jerked it from his mouth. He had never once heard the polished Bannerman utter a crudity of any kind, nor for that matter show much emotion about anything. "Is there something between you two? Something I should know?"

Bannerman rose. "Is that all? For the moment?"

Winter placed his pipe down carefully. "No, it's not. I asked you a question."

"It's one I decline to answer. With respect. It's quite personal."

"Not in this game, it's not. Tell me."

"No, sir. It really has no bearing. My opinion of Craven is firmly based on fact. If you want me to go through the motions of meeting him I will. I won't let you down."

Winter abstractedly tapped the pipe into a cut glass tray. "You really feel so intense about him that you are polite to me?"

Bannerman added nothing more.

*   *   *

It was almost three weeks later that word reached Ross Gibbs that he was wanted in London. The word came from the higher command of the Provisional I.R.A. in Derry. It was not an instruction. That was impossible. He was still a serving officer in the S.A.S., and acceptance of the invitation would mean desertion from the British Army. It also meant a loss to the Northern Irish terrorists. He insisted on a day or two to think it over, and there was no objection to this.

When he came up with his answer it was both reasonable and plausible. There was a limit to the amount of time he could fool his colleagues and the security forces in general. Both he and the Provos had known this for some time. Perversely, the longer he succeeded in apparent betrayal of the British the more suspicious the Provos might become. If the security forces tumbled to him then Bannerman would have to move fast to protect him and restore a status quo. And that would mean sharing a confidence with certain people where none was shared at the moment. That alone was always an increased risk. The timing for a move was right.

Gibbs had no idea what he was needed for in London. His training was highly specialist. His reference, as Bannerman had pointed out, was clandestine action with the Provos and the breaking of an oath necessary to prove an anti-British aim. Bannerman was right; it suddenly looked thin. An anti-Brit attitude might not be enough to satisfy the international pack. Yet they needed him. He'd have felt happier had he known why. To have a highly trained Englishman operating on his own soil was an obvious advantage, but that could have been sounded out in a different way.

He accepted the invitation on the basis that time and luck must soon run out for him in Ulster. There was no dissent and he made his preparations to depart. He was left with the feeling that certain of the Provos would not be sorry.

2

MOONLIGHT SLIPPED THROUGH the gap in the flimsy curtains and crept like the beam of a fading torch across the sergeant's face. McKechnie slept so quietly that with the ghostly light waxing his features he appeared dead.

As Gibbs eased his legs down the bed creaked. It always did. He rose from it swiftly, looking back across the darkened room to the moonbeam lengthening down McKechnie's bed.

Gibbs remained still for several seconds before reaching under the pillow for the Browning. He leaned forward to gather up his clothes from the wooden chair. A straight bend from the hips to retrieve his shoes. McKechnie hadn't stirred. Gibbs used short steps towards the door so that he could immediately lift a foot at the first suggestion of noise. The linoleum was ice cold on his bare feet.

He reached the door, did not turn at once but stayed still with his back to McKechnie. He looked round. The moonglow had spread fractionally. The sergeant's eyes were still closed, his breathing quietly even. Gibbs placed his free hand on the door knob and slowly turned it. He opened the door and edged round it on to the draughty landing. His bundle of clothes was slipping from under his arm. Coolly, he stood still, adjusted the bundle, tightened his grip on the shoes and carefully, noiselessly closed the door behind him. He allowed himself a slow, controlled exhalation of breath.

There were still the stairs to descend, every one of them ancient wood that should long since have shrunk to its limit but somehow never had. Mrs. McCarthy was snoring in the next room but Gibbs was more concerned that he might wake her three children in the room to his right.

The journey down the stairs was agonisingly slow. It was pitch black. In the hall the murky square of opaque glass in the front door gave him direction. He knew where every piece of furniture was in this confined space; the hall table with the potted plant, the tall pedestal with its broken leg glued; the coat stand. He stood in the centre of the tiny hall and began to dress without moving position. It was difficult, done by touch and instinct while he listened for the slightest sound from the bedrooms above. And it was freezing cold, icy air finding the many gaps through the front door. He dressed over his pyjamas, knowing he would need their extra insulation once outside. Clothed, he groped for his shabby topcoat on the stand. He could identify it by touch from a tear on one of the pockets. He slipped the Browning in the torn pocket. All this could have been made easier by the use of a flashlight. But he knew the risk of the glow showing through the glass panel and of it being seen outside. He turned up the collar of the overcoat and produced a pair of worn, woollen gloves, holes in some of the fingers. Carefully, he pulled back the bolts, unlatched the chain and slipped the door catch.

He gasped as he opened the front door, the cold air whipping the back of his throat. A heavy frost sparkled under the moonlight along the street and clung to the slates of the old terraced houses. Gibbs shivered, huddled in the thin, worn coat and thrust his gloved hands in his pockets. He went down the hill. Even with care his shoes still crackled on the frost. He looked back up the hill once.

The city walls stood out like a child's fort, the bastions and one of the seven gates visible. A tiny, ancient fairyland that had spilled over beyond its walls a very long time ago. The silent innocence of it was bewildering. As he continued down the hill Gibbs plotted his bolt holes in case he should need one quickly.

When he reached the bottom of the hill he gave one last valedictory glance up it. Londonderry. But he had long learned to think of it as "Derry", and to refer to it as such. Actually he preferred the older, Gaelic name for it. It meant an oak wood, a meaning long lost since the sixth century. He moved on, disturbed by the long, exaggerated shadow he cast ahead. He tried to reduce his height by shrinking more into his coat. At corners the shadow was a danger. He gripped the gun butt in his pocket.

Gibbs headed for the sea and the small boatyard. He took a circuitous, planned route that brought him downstream of the Foyle towards the river mouth. He suffered a bitter, cutting wind blowing from the Atlantic across north Donegal in the Republic just a few miles over the estuary. The wind was quite moderate; off the coast of Donegal gale force ten winds were not uncommon. But it was gusting enough to make his eyes water, and he had to rely more on hearing. He glanced at his watch; almost four a.m.

He skirted the shipyard, body heat now building up under his clothes. The sea was an eerie mass in front of him, forbiddingly dark like a massive pit with a surface skin split by a wavering moonrake. The sea was running a gentle swell, unseen, but heard softly against the wind and suctioning as it retreated. The boat was where he had hidden it, under the rickety slatted jetty. Half the wood was rotten and he had to tread carefully, feeling the strength of each piece of timber. Finally he lay flat, untied the rope, and pulled the small craft towards him.

Gibbs lowered himself carefully, ever watchful, alert to the slightest sound. The border was too near for comfort, the snow on the low hills a white mist across the estuary. The boat rocked crazily as he misjudged its position when he climbed in. He gripped the jetty to steady himself, then groped for the oars in the padded rowlocks. It would be a long time before he dare use the engine. He closed his mind to the physical and mental tedium of the journey ahead. He was on his way, moonlight tracing an incandescence on his long, fair hair. He could only hope that it would all be worth it.

*   *   *

Paul Craven flew from Washington to London by Concorde simply because it was the quickest way. It was the policy of American Government officials to fly American but patriotism was forced into second place by urgency. He was not in a good mood; he resented having to make the trip, and he could already anticipate the usual obstruction from the British. He was certainly no Anglophile either on or off duty. But "off duty" was merely a term for his subordinates. Craven was unmarried, and considered relaxation as an evening at home reading reports, with a scotch on the rocks at his elbow. Marriage was dedication to his job. He had no hobbies except a psychological analysis of those who worked around him. He knew that he was unpopular – better that than to be unnoticed. He knew, too, that there was constant pressure to get rid of him by weak-kneed senators who believed every sob story that came their way. None of this worried him. He was too good at his job, if into that it was read that his sole purpose in life was to look after the interests of the United States of America in relation to its enemies. No one could argue with that. There were some who were uneasy about the way they *thought* he did it.

Paul Craven sat back in his seat brooding, uninfluenced by the pleasant enquiry of a pretty hostess. He ate as if it were necessary for his energies but gave no sign of enjoyment. He was refuelling. He was also the only person aboard who was armed. This had caused dissent with the Captain. Arms were not permitted on British aircraft, but Craven pulled powerful strings. He was a target, not only for those outside the law, and the weapon was necessary for self protection. Someone in London had decreed it so. For Craven it was a matter of normal routine. That there had been discussion about it at all merely illustrated to him the inherent weakness with which he had to contend outside his own shores – and sometimes within them.

He reflected on Bannerman. His thoughts eroded his natural arrogance. Bannerman was a plum-in-mouth fool, but yet was not always easy to fool. And Bannerman had proved himself to be soft-centred when one of his agents had been killed in the Lebanon; he had dared to blame him, Paul Craven, for that. Hell, those sort of agents were expendable. And the job had gotten done. That was what mattered. How the hell could he be expected to know that Bannerman's agent was his nephew, or cousin, or someone? What did it matter? Emotion was no part of this game: Bannerman could be cold enough when he chose.

When Craven landed at Heathrow his only reaction was one of slight discomfort. The time lag, the loss of sleep, left him untouched. As he went down the steps, his sole baggage in a grip held in one craggy hand, he raised a brief, automatic smile for Ronnie Holder, the British Intelligence man who waited for him on the apron, and inwardly fumed. They had sent a lightweight to meet him.

Craven held his collar up to his throat. Washington was cold but London was damper. The wet chill was his first impression, the one he preferred. Holder held out a perfunctory hand which Craven ignored and he was then taken to the closed car just a few feet away. No Customs. No Immigration. Paul Craven had arrived.

★   ★   ★

There was a growing queue for taxis outside the American Embassy in Grosvenor Square. An old model taxi came round the Square, flag down, one huddled passenger in the back. It ghosted past the queue to pull up on the corner and to pick up a man who had run back from the end of the queue, much to the annoyance of those still waiting.

"I've never known anyone so punctual. How do you do it in the traffic?"

The huddled Bannerman smiled weakly, indicating, with his rolled umbrella, the heavy, bull-necked driver behind the closed glass screen. "Ted. Built in radar. I don't know how he does it either."

The younger man who had just climbed in, rubbed his gloved hands together. "You must know that Paul Craven's in town."

"I've been avoiding him."

"We can't afford him trampling all over things. That guy has feet bigger than his head."

George Bannerman smiled. "That's no way to speak of a superior. His heart's in the right place."

"Sure. For him. Nobody's yet found out where he keeps it."

Bannerman chuckled. "Am I in the middle of a Company war?"

Roxberg grinned, blowing on his gloved hands. "It's cold, though. What's new?"

"Little you don't already know. Do you want a drink, or shall we just drive round?"

Roxberg turned his head, vapoured breath partly hiding the hovering smile. "Both would be nice."

"You've got to know me too well." Bannerman reached forward to the gap between the folded seats behind the cab. He pulled down a narrow flap, produced a bottle of scotch and two glasses from the cavity. There was just enough space for them. "Neat, I'm afraid. No ice," he said as he poured.

"I'll not complain. Cheers." Roxberg raised his glass. "Good stuff. I've always admired your taste."

Bannerman inclined his head, his Homburg shadowing his eyes.

18

Grey tufts of sideburns stuck out beneath the hat, somewhat muting the businessman image. In the shadows of the cab he appeared undernourished, face narrow and drawn, nose and lips thin. At different times Roxberg had seen the grey eyes both cold and passionate with belief.

Belief was something the two men shared. A common denominator that had drawn them and extracted a more than useful combination at certain times. Equally, they were sufficiently strong in their beliefs to operate against each other. Once or twice they had done so, with interesting results.

Roxberg had operated from London for some years. He had done too well, had made too many friends to be moved on lightly. He had a pleasant, open face with eyes that seemed permanently amused. Slightly overweight, he carried a good deal of strength beneath the subcutaneous fat. And yet it was he who felt the cold, shivering slightly as the warmth inside the taxi began to thaw him out. He watched Bannerman sip his drink and waited. His expression didn't change but a different man emerged; as hard and as distant as Bannerman's general image.

"We're dealing with phantoms. Whispers of this, whispers of that; it's rather like a mist changing direction in the wind. Nothing tangible to work on."

"Craven won't go along with you on that."

"It's not Craven's problem. I'll admit he picked up some useful information. But I won't have him telling us how to handle it. We're bound by our own laws."

Roxberg's amusement was back. He gave Bannerman an old-fashioned look. "Of course."

Bannerman did not miss the faint sarcasm. His lips twitched; hands, one on top of the other, firmly clasped the umbrella handle. "Certain laws, nevertheless," he conceded. "What have we? A whisper, so soft as to be overheard rather than reported, of the pack converging. How many? Why? Craven sees it as an opportunity to get the lot. The Government, in common with all other governments, would rather see them disappear again. Arrest inevitably means reprisal of an unpalatably brutal kind."

"Craven sees an opportunity to close the coffin without risk of reprisal back home."

"But whose coffin, Leo? Craven is in a position to stir and to criticise. He runs no risk. He can accuse us of wasting information dangerously achieved."

"And would that be true?"

"The way it was achieved? There's no undangerous way, but I don't think that was your question. Whether we waste it or not will be a matter of opinion. How we handle it is our own affair."

"Are you suggesting that Craven wants you to use methods he couldn't use himself back home?"

"We're very conservative here. Craven would call it soft. We can't use his methods here. The F.B.I. make damned sure he doesn't step on their ground so he rummages elsewhere. If only we knew what is being hatched."

"Which means that you know they are here."

"I believe in the worst possibilities. So do you."

"You're holding out. You have a cuckoo in the nest?"

Bannerman did not deny it. "A vulture's nest. They want to see him react like a vulture."

"In which case he had a hard neck to enter the nest at all."

Bannerman smiled briefly. "How did we get on to birds? But the simile's not far out. It's not quite so simple. The timing was right but he needs help."

"The cuckoo found no eggs?"

"He found the eggs, but he hasn't been accepted in the nest yet. He was depending on something that didn't materialise."

Roxberg was more relaxed as the cold left him. He rubbed the mist from the side window with his gloved hand and peered out. "Would you believe Grosvenor Square?"

"Ted was never a great one for big distances."

Roxberg said bleakly. "Your man sounds in a spot. Can he get out?"

"Only he knows that."

"If he's desperate he may not be able to."

"Quite. One of the more intriguing items from Craven is that Raul Orta is in town."

Roxberg turned so quickly he splashed his drink. He wiped the damp spots away from his coat. "You're not having me on, George?"

Bannerman glanced over laconically. "I knew before Craven that Raul was on his way. With his record it really looks bad. For him to come out of hiding with almost every police force in the world looking for him it's clearly something big."

"You believe he's here?" Roxberg was rejecting it.

"Amongst others. Craven is right, you see. A little slow off the mark, but right."

"But you don't intend to tell him."

"I've never believed in telling him anything that affects these shores. Let him talk. I'm a good listener. Can I rely on you?"

Roxberg gestured. "I owe him no favours."

"You're still American. I may need your help and I may need it in a hurry."

"You've got it. If it doesn't interfere with our own interests."

"That will depend on your viewpoint. I have an idea that will need immense luck. It's rather like waiting for a donor for a heart transplant. It may never happen. And there's quite a severe time limit, a week at the most."

Roxberg was interested – not only in what George Bannerman might have to say, but in the working of the mind behind the well-groomed image. He doubted that he had ever met anyone as devious, or as dependable.

Bannerman said, "We can only arrest them if we find them and that brings with it every fear we know. We can't go out on a locate-and-destroy because no one would stand for it. What we really need is a third arm."

*   *   *

Ross Gibbs could feel Nuzzale looking down at him. The lean Arab was behind the head of the narrow bed. Cheap tobacco smoke drifted down as if Nuzzale was deliberately blowing it his way.

"Do you mind smoking elsewhere? You're clogging my lungs." Gibbs looked upwards and backwards as he lay on the bed, shoes off, tie off. A gas fire was on full blast, making the dingy room too hot and stuffy for Gibbs, not hot enough for Nuzzale who was cocooned in a heavy sweater, his hair bushed out above his narrow face.

Nuzzale drew on the cigarette again, sending another cloud over Gibbs's head. His eyes smouldered like the top of the weedy cigarette. "You expect me to smoke outside?"

"No. Just don't blow it my way. The room is fuggy enough."

"Fuggy? You can't sweat properly?"

"Don't goad me, Mohammed. You've no call."

"Maybe." Nuzzale came round the bed, looked down more openly, smiling lopsidedly. He was holding his cigarette Russian style, the centre almost crushed between the long brown fingers. The heavy sweater was pulled down as far as it would go over the crumpled jeans.

"You don't have to like me. Just believe that I'm useful. That our aims are the same." Gibbs put his hands behind his head, crossed his feet on the bed, remembered: Nuzzale, a humourless hardliner with no interest outside his cause. His emotions had been scrambled when his girlfriend had been shot dead during an aircraft hijack. He had cried for days until the love he had held for her was channelled into intensified hatred he had of his enemies. Planning against them was his life. He barely trusted anyone.

The man stood with a hand on hip in a strangely sensuous posture. "We will see if you are useful. It is your background I don't like."

"The training, or what it stands for?"

"What it stands for. I'm not forgetting the part played by you people in Mogadishu."

"Which shows we know a thing or two. You went to the Patrice Lumumba University in Moscow." As Nuzzale's eyes hardened Gibbs added easily, "You didn't expect me to know? What do you think they taught us? Let me tell you, our training is better than the Lumumba. Like it or not. You'll use me."

"It's not your war."

"Balls." Gibbs swung his legs down, sat on the side of the hard bed. "You've been telling the world it's everybody's war. So why exclude me? You can't have it both ways, Mohammed." Gibbs smiled softly, ruffled hair now darkened. His fair skin was weathered, his gaze easy-going until Nuzzale had annoyed him. His mood was part simulated. He knew what was going through Nuzzale's mind. He was not far from the point of no return; he might have to abort. But it wouldn't be that easy. It was not quite clear who had invited him over. The Provos had merely passed on the message. He had been told where to locate Nuzzale who undoubtedly had expected him; but with resentment. Gibbs knew every technique that could be used against them. Nuzzale saw it as a shortcoming. Gibbs had yet to prove himself. Only then would his undoubted talents be used. But that wasn't all they were waiting for.

Gibbs rose slowly, ran hands through his hair. Standing, he accentuated the wiry thinness of Nuzzale. And he made him look shorter. Gibbs was uneasy. It was a feeling he had suffered often enough before.

He had always been a loner. At school his sports were those of single combat. He had been good at team games but always better on his own. His father had been a Royal Marine Commando during World War II so it had come through the genes, too. Wounded twice, once in the legs by mortar shrapnel and later by sub machine-gun fire, his father had died just over two years ago through smoking too much. That was when Gibbs had given it up. Yet his father had not pushed him, had really not directed him in any way as if he accepted, as he himself had done, that Gibbs would find his own way.

He stood beside the watching Nuzzale. Loner or not, there were times when he felt very lonely, cut off, friendless. At such times he would give anything to be in an office just for a while. To be in comfort, amongst people he did not need to deceive. To have a drink with a real friend, a girl maybe whom he cared for. He put a hand on Nuzzale's bony shoulder. "I understand your feelings; I'd probably feel the same in your place. You don't trust me. Someone does, Mohammed. All that's different is my military background, and that's useful. You wonder why I left? Then think why I planted firebombs. They did one helluva lot of damage."

"Nobody got killed." It came out as both accusation and protest and showed that Nuzzale was aware of the details.

"That's the present policy. I don't make policies."

"Ours are different."

"I expect them to be." Gibbs gave a twisted smile. "Kill me or kiss me but while you've got me use me."

"We shall expect something of you."

"I understand that." He had better make contact.

"A job will be lined up for you."

"Naturally."

"There is someone you must kill."

Gibbs avoided Nuzzale's gaze. Expecting it made it no easier.

"Who?" It was an effort to say it without faltering.

Nuzzale was watching him closely. "You will be told. Not by me."

"When?"

"Any day now."

Bannerman had been right. He always was. "I'll be ready." But he knew that he wouldn't be. Time was evaporating.

The telephone rang on the landing outside. The two men stared questioningly at each other as if the persistent ringing was part of the dialogue. Nuzzale ran to the door leaving it open as he unhooked the receiver.

Gibbs listened through the open doorway but Nuzzale grunted affirmations, nothing more. When the Arab hung up he entered the room smiling, but from satisfaction rather than pleasure. He carefully closed the door. "We have a victim for you," he said.

3

"Good," said Gibbs easily. "Anyone I know?"

"A secretary at the Iraqi Embassy."

"I thought they were on our side."

"A few aren't."

"That's a reason for killing?"

Nuzzale bridled. "Well, isn't it? He's treacherous."

Gibbs started slowly to pace, head down. Watching him Nuzzale added, "Don't worry. He's a soft target."

"That doesn't worry me. I prefer to choose my own victims."

"You're not acting for yourself here. You were summoned."

"Invited."

"Then you accepted."

"To listen. To see what is wanted of me."

"Now you know."

"No. This isn't why I'm wanted. Any fool can kill an unsuspecting victim. This is my entry exam. Something dreamed up by children *for* children. I don't need it."

Nuzzale's mouth tightened. "You will find that we are anything but children. You will do as you're told."

"You giving the orders?"

"Yes."

"No, you're not. You're passing them on. I'm not taking those sort of orders from you, Mohammed. I want them direct from the person who gave them."

"You will meet him after."

"Before, or the job won't be done."

Nuzzale stood with his back to the gas fire, hands on slender hips. He angled his head, dark eyes glaring at Gibbs. "Is that what you want me to report?"

"Precisely."

Nuzzale nodded slightly. "All right. As long as you realise that you could well finish up in the Iraqi's place."

"You'd better think carefully before you make that kind of threat again."

Nuzzale stared, tight-lipped, fingers clenched. Then he turned quickly and went back to the telephone, slamming the door behind him. When he returned he appeared disgruntled. "Put your coat on," he said brusquely, "We're going out."

*　　*　　*

No attempt was made to deceive Gibbs; no sudden change of direction or back-tracking. They were in North Kensington, not far from the Portobello Road. A cosmopolitan area of colour, race and creed. What better? They mounted steps not dissimilar to those leading to their own apartment. Nuzzale had a key to the front door and they climbed dingy stairs leading from a bare, unfriendly hall. They went up one flight and Nuzzale knocked on a door in a special way that Gibbs noted. There was a spyhole and Gibbs could feel the critical observation before the door was opened.

A jolly-faced, medium built man in his early thirties greeted them with a wide smile and brilliant teeth. His complexion was sallow, eyes light brown and humorous. His face had grown plumper since the last photograph Gibbs had seen of him, and he wore a full beard which appeared incongruous with a head now shaven. Big framed spectacles also added distortion to the earlier image. It all made him look older. The patterned waistcoat and flared, pink panelled trousers provided unexpected flamboyance, but the man was the same. Gibbs was only momentarily in doubt. Perhaps he had instinctively known that he would be taken to meet this man. Raul Orta. Probably the most wanted man in the world.

The room was comfortable: bed and easy chairs of good quality; a modern, upright piano stood in one corner. Without asking, Orta poured out a liberal Teacher's for Gibbs and white wine for Nuzzale. It was a deliberate act to show that he already knew what he needed to know about Gibbs down to his preference for drink.

"Cheers, Ross. It's good to have you with us." Orta raised his own scotch high then flopped on to a chair, draping his legs over the arm.

26

Ross made no pretence. It could be folly. As he sat down he said, "I thought it might be you."

Orta laughed, slapping his thigh. "There goes my disguise. Recognised at once."

"The disguise is okay. Few would penetrate it."

"You did. Straight away." A tubby finger unfurled from the glass to point at Gibbs. The smile was still there.

"I've had better opportunity than most to study your pictures, but you're not recognisable from them. It's the aura; perhaps we have a secret affinity."

"I like that, Ross. I really do. Thank God we're on the same side or I'd be blown, eh!" Neither smile nor tone hardened but the threat was there, a soft thread twining through the bonhomie.

Ross smiled, and raised his glass while Nuzzale sat quietly watching them both. "You don't need me to kill an Iraqi. What do you need me for?"

"Direct, too. What a fellow." A vague shift of expression had the effect of making Orta's general trendiness suspect. "You will still have to kill the Iraqi."

"Why?"

"Because I say so." Suddenly the smile was back. *So that we can be sure of you.*"

"I've never known you to be guilty of indiscriminate killing. That's my point."

"Oh, it's not indiscriminate. The man's a traitor. He leaked the contents of a diplomatic bag to Scotland Yard, Special Branch." Orta got up, rummaged in a desk drawer. "That's him."

He handed a photograph to Gibbs. A black-faced Arab stared from the gloss, the only expression where a badly placed arc lamp was reflected in duplicate in the eyes.

Gibbs tapped the photograph against his fingers. "I don't like it. I don't think I need to prove myself."

"You don't, not to yourself. But to us you do. We don't know you, and we're careful. That's why we're still operating. That's reasonable, isn't it?"

They were discussing taking someone's life. It didn't matter either to Orta or Nuzzale: there was no point in Gibbs raising it on that basis. "I've no objection to a traitor being put down. That's sensible. I just resent your attitude to me."

"Come now, Ross. One of us must do it." The smile again, soft, loose lips under the beard. "Don't blow it up out of proportion. We've done all the homework for you."

"I need to think about it." It was a dangerous remark.

"Of course. You're new to us. I expect it."

Gibbs stared across at Orta and the smiling eyes were iron hard. He waited for the punch line.

"You have until two p.m. tomorrow. He must be dead twenty-four hours later."

*　　　*　　　*

Nuzzale was angry. He pulled his coat collar up as they went down the steps. "We've wasted time. Did you think Raul would let you off the hook?"

"No. I just wanted him to know how I felt." Gibbs stopped at the bottom, viewed the street either way. There was little movement. He saw a pub sign on a corner about fifty yards to his right. "I need another drink." He started to walk towards the pub.

Nuzzale caught up. "I only drink occasionally." He caught Gibbs's arm. "We go back home."

"You do what you like. I'm having a drink." It was too much to expect Nuzzale to go back on his own. He neither liked nor trusted Gibbs. Nuzzale showed his anger again then fell in beside Gibbs.

The pub was like a steam bath after the outside cold, and it was crowded. Gibbs elbowed his way to the bar. Nuzzale refused a drink so Gibbs bought him a glass of lemonade and a pint of bitter for himself. He sipped slowly, gazing round the mass of faces. Which of them represented Bannerman's back-up team? Nuzzale got more agitated as Gibbs deliberately took his time. As an aside Gibbs said, "While you're in an English pub you'd better look as if you're enjoying it if you don't want to draw attention to yourself."

Nuzzale cooled down a little but flashes of resentment showed; he would not be bossed by a newcomer, yet he would not leave Gibbs.

After a while Gibbs put his drink down and said, "Keep an eye on that. I'm going to the gents."

He took his time getting through the crowd, squeezing, apologising. Someone was going in ahead of him. As they stood inside the stranger said, "I thought you'd never move. I could see your problem, though." The man was scratching his ear with a thumb.

Gibbs said, "Get a taxi round in exactly fifteen minutes." He dived into one of two cubicles, sat down and wrote quickly in a small loose-leaf notebook. He folded the note as small as he could.

When he went outside Nuzzale was there waiting for him. "We must go now."

"I'm having a short first."

"Are you a drunkard as well as a coward?"

Gibbs held his temper, went back into the lounge bar. His drink had gone. There had been little in it. He called for a scotch and water. Nuzzale came up to tug his arm.

"Look, cocker," murmured Gibbs easily, "if you spill my drink, you'll stand me another."

The threat of further delay quietened Nuzzale again. Gibbs watched the time, finished his drink, and took Nuzzale by the arm. "I'm ready now. Let's go."

Gibbs called the taxi the moment he saw it, flag down, across the street. Nuzzale was somewhat mollified at the thought of a short ride home at Gibbs's expense. When Gibbs paid off the cabbie the note went with the fare. But that was only part of it. Even Bannerman couldn't work miracles to order.

*   *   *

Bannerman faced the problem of creating a miracle in the solitude of his office. He read Gibbs's scribbled note, held it, flashed the intercom then went in to see Sir Henry Winter. With the safety of a field man at stake neither man attempted to bait the other.

"So what went wrong?" queried the admiral.

"Basically Gibbs's own reluctance to shoot a sitting duck regardless of his record."

"Understandable."

"But an out of date concept."

"Obviously he doesn't think so. It's nice to see a young man with old values."

"Not in this game. With respect, Sir Henry. I'm not trying to goad you."

"I know. You're worried. So am I. Why let him get into this situation?"

"Luck ran out. Grant Fabor at the U.S. Embassy was given twenty-four hours to live. That was a week ago. He's still critically ill but now it seems that his state could continue, though he's still on twenty-four hours' notice."

"A cynical view, George."

"He doesn't know. He's in a coma. It's been kept deliberately quiet because the Americans had agreed to let us use him. He's a widower without children. Heaven sent."

"Evidently heaven doesn't adhere to a strict itinerary."

"Certainly no one expected him to hold out this long."

"So if he doesn't oblige us by passing away before midday tomorrow Gibbs is in trouble?"

"We'd have to try to get him out quick. But it will be disastrous all round. They will then know he's a plant, and he'd be hard pushed to start again. We don't know why they're here. Or how many."

"We could round up what we have."

"Not while Gibbs is there. Afterwards it could be too late and at best we'll have grabbed two men. Two particularly red-hot numbers. It's not at all what we want."

"What exactly do we want, George?" The admiral reached for his pipe.

"I don't want any arrests. I want a solution."

"That's what I thought. It might be better if I don't press you further."

"If I don't find one Paul Craven will try. And he'll try it on our soil."

"Don't turn it into a private war with him or the pack will fly out between the pair of you like a lemon pip. He's raging that you're avoiding him. You can't for much longer."

Bannerman edged towards the door, glancing down once more at the message Gibbs had sent. "I'll see him tomorrow night at my place. He can have the pool car I've been using."

The admiral still hadn't lit his pipe. "You'd better get Gibbs out fast. I don't fancy his chances."

"Let him hang on until tomorrow."

The admiral lit a match, tamped down the bowl of his pipe. "I just hope you know what you're doing, George."

Bannerman well knew what he was doing. He went home late that night by train, catching a taxi the other end to his country house. He had a snack meal then went to the big double garage, took off his jacket and tie, put on dungarees and turned to the Jaguar double six. It was up on ramps above an inspection pit. Bannerman put on an old cloth jockey cap and slid beneath the car into the pit.

He worked through most of the night beneath the chassis. He became a different person beneath the car, all fastidiousness gone as oil and grease covered his hands and slid under his fingernails. Because he wasn't a professional mechanic he took a long time over what he was doing. While he worked he convinced himself, with good reason, that Ross Gibbs was dead if something drastic wasn't done. Gibbs was unarmed at the moment in the knowledge that his kit would be searched. The slightest hint of betrayal or of a move towards them and either Orta or Nuzzale or others yet to emerge would kill Gibbs out of hand. Both men had killed to avoid arrest. Orta had shot dead three policemen out of the four who had come to arrest him in Brussels two years ago. It had taken only one shot for each.

While he worked, with all the tools and equipment he needed, Bannerman weighed one life against another and a slow hatred built up. Outwardly he showed nothing but a quiet determination to finish what he was doing. He was aware that he'd let personal feelings enter an area they had no right to be in. It did not matter. He reflected on a stepson who had been needlessly killed in the Lebanon and of the wife who had blamed and ostracised and finally left him as a result. Steve would have been about Ross Gibbs's age. The situation of the two men bore no similarity. Gibbs knew the risks and had accepted them. Steve had been unaware they existed when the bomb blew him to bits. He'd had no reason to believe himself to be in danger at that particular time. It was true that as a result the diversion had enabled two American agents to escape after dealing with a group of terrorists. The sacrifice had been unnecessary, though, the real aims diminished. Bannerman had always seen it as a loud-mouthed betrayal to safeguard others. As the sweat began to runnel through the oil on his face, he could not forget. Nor forgive. It wasn't going to happen again.

When he drove the car back to London the next morning he did so very carefully and at modest speed.

*　　*　　*

Meanwhile, as Gibbs undressed in Nuzzale's apartment after meeting Raul Orta, he noticed the Arab lock the door and hook the key to a chain round his neck. He was sitting on the edge of the bed taking off his socks when he observed, "Locking me in?"

Nuzzale looked innocent. "Locking the enemy out. We don't want to be surprised, do we?"

And that was how it would be. Nuzzale's automatic disappeared under his pillow with a deliberate flourish. Gibbs knew that if Bannerman was foolish enough to raid the apartment Gibbs himself would be the first fatal casualty. He did not think Bannerman would be so foolish.

As if to confirm his thoughts Nuzzale, after swinging his legs between the blankets, said, "We Arabs sleep light. Goodnight, Ross. You'll need your strength for tomorrow."

*　　*　　*

The dangers multiplied with the darkness and failed to disappear with the light. Gibbs washed, shaved, dressed with hardly an exchange with Nuzzale, who was watching him too often for comfort. He made coffee, gave a cup to the Arab and wandered over to the window, drawing back the lace to see across the street.

"I wouldn't do that," said Nuzzale.

"Why not?" It was nine o'clock. Time for a sign. A taxi drew up across the street. A man paid the cabbie and mounted the steps opposite. He gazed up at the door number as if he'd made a mistake about the address. His annoyance was clear. He turned his back on the door, gazed up briefly to where Gibbs was watching, adjusted his hat then ran down the steps and walked briskly away without looking back. Gibbs had stiffened. He hoped Bannerman knew what he was doing. This wasn't going to be easy. He came away from the window sipping his coffee thoughtfully.

"Have you any preference for a gun?"

32

Gibbs had been expecting the question. "A Sterling sub. But I'm not doing that particular job."

Nuzzale stared, unable to believe what he'd heard. "You're committing suicide?"

"I'll do a job all right. I'll do it, as arranged, within the next twenty-four hours. Let's go see Raul."

Nuzzale couldn't wait. He wanted to see Raul's reaction and to see Gibbs squirm. He kept his eye on Gibbs all the way ready to gun him down in the street if necessary.

There was the smell of perfume in Orta's room but if a girl had been there she had since left. The bed hadn't been made and Orta conveyed the same untidiness; he was a man who best came to life the other end of the day. The bonhomie too had gone.

"You needn't have called so early. You have until midday."

"He's not doing it," said Nuzzale vindictively.

"Oh, dear." Orta sank to the arm of a chair while Nuzzale remained behind Gibbs. He rubbed the back of his neck as he eyed Gibbs blearily. "If this is true, Ross, we can't leave you floating."

"It's true. But there's more. I object to a revenge killing just to prove a point that needs no proving. I said so yesterday. However, I do see your position and reluctantly accept it. I'll kill for you, but not a fifth-rate target that will be non-productive. I'll kill in the time you've given me but the choice of target must be mine."

"Who?"

"You'll know after the event. You'll be delighted."

"That's easy to say." The voice came from behind Gibbs.

"Shut up, Nuzzale. You're a pain in the arse. Stop needling me."

The beginning of a smile stirred in the untidy depths of Orta's beard. "Mohammed's right though. It *is* easy to say."

"Not when I have only twenty-six hours to prove my point."

"How can this have arisen since yesterday?"

"It's been on for months. A certain person is in town. I want him. I need freedom from Nuzzale here. And from any loose heads you may have watching me."

"My dear Ross, why should we trust you? We hardly know you. Besides, Mohammed likes your company, don't you, Mohammed? He likes being with you."

"I've always worked alone. That's what I've been trained to do. As for trust, well, that's true. If you think letting me loose for a few

33

hours is risky then go to ground until I've done the job. I shall still stay with Nuzzale. I simply want breathing space without distraction."

"Don't trust him, Raul."

Orta glanced over Gibbs's shoulder. He was shaking his head slowly, unconvinced.

"I'm asking you," said Gibbs patiently. "I didn't need to. I could have taken this goon behind me any time. I could have presented you with a *fait accompli* by midday tomorrow. Or I could have betrayed you the moment I lost Nuzzale. I'm trying to do it right. I'm not fool enough to think you want me just for one job. There'll be others. By tomorrow I'll be qualified by your own standards. Disappear while I work."

"And you think I'll be delighted?"

Gibbs smiled. "Over the moon."

Orta smiled back, impatiently waving aside Nuzzale's protests.

Gibbs wasn't sure what Orta was really thinking. He was left with the impression that he was being given enough rope to hang himself.

4

PAUL CRAVEN WAS quietly seething. He had been received graciously, had been cosseted and introduced around. He didn't need introductions; he needed one set of authoritative ears that would listen and one voice that would demand action. He had seen Sir Henry Winter but it was George Bannerman who did the real work and he, apparently, was "out of town".

Craven felt that he had been received like a social caller instead of someone bearing top information. He'd been listened to as if he'd been giving a weather report. Smiles and nods and that infuriating air of superiority carried by some of the British. As if they could afford to act this way. He'd been against information-sharing with the British for a very long time. They had been warned before without actioning it, hiding behind their old school ties as if they were symbols of integrity. They had been shown that they were not – had almost been strangled by them.

Now he had to meet Bannerman at some damned country house some thirty miles outside London. Bannerman, for some reason he had better goddam explain, couldn't come in to meet him. It couldn't be the old grudge, that was ridiculous. They had all been terribly nice, of course, all charm and bullshit, and had offered a chauffeur-driven car which would bring him back to London; but Bannerman had offered a bed at his own place. Craven detested the velvet glove treatment. He hadn't objected to the car from London Airport because he had been able to talk to Ronnie Holder, on the way in. But there was nothing more to discuss until he met Bannerman. He did not want company, he wanted action. They did not seem surprised when he accepted the car but refused the chauffeur. They would know his background. It satisfied him that they should.

He had started his working life as a New York City traffic cop. He was still a brilliant driver. So when a smart, scrubbed young man with a civil service image had produced the car and chauffeur,

Craven reacted in typical fashion. He was given a route map, but the gesture was spoiled by the warning that the roads were dangerous and icy and he was driving at night. It took him all his time to make no retort. Did they think he hadn't driven on ice before? Did they imagine he would get lost?

They gave him a Jaguar double six. It was a bit cramped for his size and his thick hair brushed the roof, but it could move. They hadn't managed a left-hand drive but that didn't really matter. He started out from the Grosvenor Hotel just after the rush hour. He had been asked to be there by eight. Well, he would be; let them try giving him a speeding ticket. He eased the car through the traffic with extreme skill, thinking as he went that something should be done about the traffic system. A few hundred gallons of white paint could work wonders on some of the unmarked roads. Most of his thoughts were bitter or critical.

Back in Washington there were colleagues who had found the necessity of his trip to London suspect. Craven could handle them. Telexed messages would have been considered quite adequate in some quarters. Two convictions had made him travel. Messages passed through too many hands in his view. And he could not contain the forceful opinions he had brought with him based on the hard and dangerous work of his field men. His views hadn't got him anywhere. Not yet. Bannerman would have to be convinced. He was a smooth, crafty devil but the sort who could get things moving if he chose.

He was ten miles out before he was convinced he had a tail. In a thin traffic stream moving at roughly the same pace it was difficult to tell. It was dark and murky once out of town. Street lights were well spaced; it wasn't always easy to pick up the exact shape of a car in his mirror. But they had been too clever, occasionally changing from dipped headlights to fog lights to give an impression that it was another car. They had to be learners to try a wheeze like that on *him*. He felt insulted. He checked his dials then started to drive.

Behind him in the following Ford, Ronnie Holder smiled to himself. He released the special aerial and groped for the hidden microphone. "Lone wanderer to base. Have been seen as expected. Will follow through. Out."

They were already in the fast lane but Holder knew that the real speed couldn't start for another five miles or so. There was still traffic and too many lights and roundabouts. He chased Craven hard and had no illusions about the problems of keeping him in sight. When they had to slow down for traffic lights he drew closer and gave Craven a friendly flash of his full beams to show that he was in touch.

Craven received the message. At no time had he believed his follower to be hostile. Wet nursing did not appeal to him particularly when he was armed and at the wheel of a car. And more particularly when he had not been advised that he would have an escort. He accepted the friendliness of the flash while resenting it. It would be interesting to see just how good a driver his escort was.

*   *   *

The last of the street lamps had disappeared with most of the traffic. Over twenty miles out, on this particular road, there was little competition. It was incredibly dark, clear sky but no moon. The frost was an unwinding carpet of diamonds he could hear crackling under the tyres and see sparkling in his headlamps. His steering was beautifully controlled, his mood easing with the poetry of being one with good machinery. The car held and moved like a dream, the extra wide tyres gripping well. Craven had good night vision and most of the time now he was on full beam. He was well above the speed limit, but by his standards was in no way driving dangerously.

In icy conditions he did not like power steering, sensing at times that he had lost touch with the road. These moments were fractional; he was content.

Occasionally he caught a glimpse of Holder's beams as he crested an undulation but they were way back. During brief periods of malicious humour Craven would let him get close enough to sight his tail lights and then pull away again. That would teach them to dump an unwanted escort on him. It did not occur to him that he might be placing the other driver in danger. Craven was a realist. If the other guy couldn't cope with the conditions, he shouldn't be allowed out in them. He had not been quite forthcoming about some of the reports that had come his way. After London, where next? He thought he knew. He watched the road, never taking his eyes from it, slowly chewing gum. The route was like a well-learned poem in his head, his visual memory projecting it just above the windscreen.

It was open country now. Trees and ditches and ethereal whiteness with a frosted, wire-meshed strip on a winding narrow island separating the two sets of treble lanes. Woodland increased as the road began to snake more. Headlamps swept up the pale beauty of the ice-cold night. The car heater gave him just sufficient warmth and he had one louvre open just a fraction; it made wind noise and stopped him from drowsing. By this time, no more than five miles from his destination, a good deal of his bitterness had gone but his aim was still clear-cut in his mind. He negotiated a series of bends, easing on the accelerator but not using his brake. The next moment he was airborne.

Fear gushed through him as he lost control. He did all the right things in a mechanical, highly competent way but the steering did not respond. The car sped off the road, hurtled into a wide ditch, buried her nose and crashed over backwards, and then slid sideways, back into the ditch. The sound of smashed glass, aimlessly revolving wheels, of steam hissing from a broken radiator, startled a colony of rooks bedded down in the stark winter trees. They rose as a huge black cloud, screeching fiercely.

In the second or two it took to happen, Craven had an all too brief terrifying insight into what had gone wrong and in a last, split-second action of superb professionalism he switched off the engine while the car was falling on its spine. He was aware of excruciating pain in both legs and that was his last recollection. The rooks wheeled above him in haphazard formation, cutting off the stars, deepening the darkness. They responded with glee when the headlamps were crushed and the beams cut out. The light, above all, had disturbed them. The angled tail lights were all that was left, like suspended danger lamps well off the road.

Ronnie Holder had been conscious of the odd tail switch on the ice. His car hadn't the wheel base of Craven's nor such a low centre of gravity. Nor were his tyres as wide. Prudently, he drove within his limits. If Craven wanted to play games that was his affair. For himself, he had done what he had been told but he wasn't going to break his bloody neck to try to prove a point he knew to be beyond him. Craven was a better driver and had a better car. From time to time he saw the forward flash of headlamps. He lost them as the road dipped then picked them up again as he crested a rise. Then suddenly the moving glow went crazy. The headlights swept at right angles to the motorway, then upwards like searchlights pathetically scanning the sky before plunging and disappearing completely.

Holder was shaken. He put his foot down hard on the accelerator, uncomfortable at pushing his luck, sick at heart about what might have happened. He almost missed the tail lights. What caught his attention were a few low-flying rooks on the upper fringes of his beams. Rooks at this time of night? By the time he had pulled on to the hard shoulder and climbed out, the wheels of Craven's car had stopped spinning. Holder ran down the slope, twice slipping and falling, thinking that at least the car had not caught fire. The frost had melted from around the burst radiator but the escaping water would soon freeze. The car was wedged partly on its spine, partly on its side. The driver's door was impossibly placed and when he tried to open the nearside doors they were locked from the inside. He shone a torch through. Craven's head was visible over the collapsed steering wheel. The specially strengthened windscreen was bulging inwards, held together by a web of cracks.

Dashing back to his own car Holder produced a tyre lever and smashed in the glass of a rear door so that none would fall on Craven. He opened the forward door from inside, leaned awkwardly over the angled seat and groped. He drew back, his breath joining the slow hiss of steam. Craven was dead. Jesus.

He scrambled back to his car again, raised the aerial, reached in for the mike, leaned against the body, dazed beyond belief. The words came out awkwardly, "Lone wanderer to base. Lone wanderer to base." Even while he related to Bannerman what had happened he was thinking of the repercussions. Craven wasn't small fry.

After the first expression of incredulity, Bannerman took it coolly. Bannerman always did. Holder was saying, "I'd better raise the police and an ambulance," and Bannerman after only the slightest pause, "No. Don't do that, Ronnie."

"Christ, I can't leave him here."

"Are you certain he's dead?"

Holder held his temper. His hand was beginning to freeze to the mike. Before he could answer Bannerman said, "All right, I just had to be sure. Can you get him out without help?"

"I suppose so. I hadn't considered it."

"*Can you?*"

"Yes."

"Hold on a minute."

It was much longer than a minute, and cold and reaction were setting in on Holder before Bannerman came back. "Ronnie, where exactly are you?"

Holder leaned in, read his trip meter. "About four and a half miles out from your place. It's a big copse. Regimented trees. Forestry Commission by the look of them."

"I know. Is Craven's car towable?"

"I'll have to go look to make sure."

"I'll hold."

Holder eased his way down the ditch again. Used his flashlight. What the hell was Bannerman playing at? Whatever they thought of Craven, the poor sod was dead and far from home. He weighed the position. The wheels and chassis were all right. As far as he could see the roof was crushed in on Craven's side and probably the door. Radiator stove in but, hooked, it would carry. He climbed back up. The odd car went past but his own car was blocking the scene from the shoulder and Craven's wreck was in darkness and well back from the road. He seized the mike, barely able to feel it by now. "It can be towed by a breakdown truck. It needs pulling over, but then it would be fairly straightforward."

"Good. I'll get a breakdown truck out straight away. Now this is what you do. Get Craven out. Work as fast as you can because I want him out before the truck arrives. Be as careful as you can. I don't know what state he's in but don't add to his damage if you can possibly avoid it. Then bring him here."

Holder looked at the mike as if it had gone mad. Then quite lifelessly he said, "Roger and out." No one ever knew how Bannerman's mind worked. Not even Bannerman. With this sceptical thought Holder returned to Craven. Without help it would not be easy, but already it was clear that Bannerman wanted no other eyes. A cold-blooded bastard if ever there was one.

Craven was a weight and it was difficult to get at him. Holder felt the car moving as he climbed in. He switched off the tail lights. So far as he could judge there was no blood, yet Craven must have injuries. He was sweating profusely by the time Craven was hanging out from the door. "Don't damage him": Bannerman's instruction came back as Holder pulled on the arms. There was nothing else he could do. It was difficult enough to keep his feet.

Craven fell like a shot bullock. Holder panted over him for a while before slowly dragging him up the ditch. By the way the lower legs flopped in all directions it was clear that they were smashed. But that would have happened on impact. Leaving Craven stretched out, Holder went back to his own car and edged it as near as he dared to the lip of the ditch. The ground was frozen hard which helped. He opened the passenger door. Somehow he got Craven on to the seat then held him there by using the safety belt. He made sure the road was empty before he pulled out.

There was no speeding now. Craven was flopping around as if he had been filleted, in spite of the strap. In a grim mood and highly dissatisfied with the instructions he'd received, Holder reflected that all that was now needed was for him to be stopped by a police patrol car. The shortest part of the journey now seemed the longest. Another mile on and he left the motorway.

Bannerman lived in isolation on the fringe of an Oxfordshire village. High walls surrounded a precise acre. Water was pumped up from a nearby river to form pools and small waterfalls in the grounds. Holder often wondered where the money came from. Establishment money would not provide this luxury. He knew Bannerman had a wife somewhere. They had lived apart for a couple of years. Nobody quite knew where she was and ghoulish jokes floated round the department. These irrelevancies filled Holder's mind as he approached the gates of the house. Anything to take his mind off his passenger and the inevitable repercussions that would follow.

He was near the gates when headlights spilled from them. He braked, waiting for the other car to pull out, wondering who it might be. His dipped lamps were sufficient to pick out the other driver who looked straight ahead as he drove past. Leo Roxberg. Here? He had been wearing a hat pulled down, but Holder knew him too well not to recognise him. It was difficult to envisage an amicable meeting between Roxberg and Craven. Craven had been very near the top of the tree. Two Company men at Bannerman's? But those two in particular? Collections came no stranger. He drove in, the gravel hard and welded by the heavy frost. Bannerman already had the front door open as he heard the car approach. Another car was collecting ice outside the garage.

They carried Craven in without greeting or a word passing between them. The first essential was to get the corpse out of sight.

In the drawing room, the heavy body still between them, Bannerman said, "Over here by the fire," as if the warmth would restore Craven to life. "Help yourself to a brandy. On the sideboard." Bannerman knelt beside Craven as Holder poured himself a liberal drink.

"Few signs on him. Broken legs. One would expect that. A damned big bruise on his forehead and a broken nose. Bring a wet flannel from the bathroom. I'll wipe this blood away from his nose and mouth. No teeth missing. Good."

Drink in hand, Holder stared at the kneeling Bannerman. No remorse. No regret of any kind. Just a clinical analysis of the damage and that as an appraisal. Holder stared for too long. Bannerman looked up sharply and snapped, "The flannel, dear boy."

When Holder returned Bannerman had eased Craven out of his topcoat and was looking down thoughtfully, one arm on a raised, bony knee. He took the wet flannel abstractedly and cleaned up Craven's face. "I can't see what killed him. Where's Barnard?"

From which Holder gathered that Bannerman must already have telephoned for the doctor. Barnard was one of two they sometimes used and lived about ten miles away. It was another hour before he arrived by which time Bannerman had joined Holder in having a drink.

Barnard cut Bannerman's protest short at root. "I had another call." As he stripped off his coat and dropped it over a chair he stared down at Craven critically. "And anyway I'd guess there's little I can do for *him*."

Holder backed to the sideboard and reached for the decanter. All he now needed to complete a bizarre evening was to listen to Barnard and Bannerman needling each other. Bannerman did not bite. "I'm sorry, Tony. We know he's dead but we don't know how."

Barnard stroked his moustache irritably. "Why didn't you get him to hospital? There's nothing I can do." He produced his stethoscope as a routine measure.

"You can tell us how he died."

"I can't conduct a post-mortem here. I'm not equipped." Barnard was unbuttoning Craven's shirt, kneeling, taking over from Bannerman.

"You might find the cause of death quite obvious. If it's internal then, I agree, this is not the place."

Barnard grunted. "How did it happen? How did he get here?"

"Car crash. Ronnie brought him in."

Barnard glanced up. "That would explain the legs. All right. Help me get him undressed."

"One other thing," said Bannerman quietly. "Is it possible to stave off rigor mortis?"

Barnard removed his stethoscope, shoved it in a pocket. He rose wearily, looking at Bannerman with distaste. "Is that why you have him by the fire? You want to confuse the time of death?"

Holder, who had put down his drink to help, hesitated as he crossed the room. He felt the cold again, suddenly in this very warm room. How could Bannerman think so rationally in the face of tragedy? The man had only been dead a couple of hours.

"It might be useful," said Bannerman coolly.

"I can advise you. Don't expect me to be part of it."

The cause of death was quickly found. Barnard's fingers were exploring the base of Craven's skull. "A broken neck. Not immediately obvious as the vertebrae have almost relodged. That's my guess."

"Guess?"

"You want him dressed again? I thought you might. Guess it remains. It needs a more thorough examination than mine to be absolutely sure."

"But a qualified guess?"

"I would expect to be right." Barnard was putting his topcoat on, closing his bag. "You don't want me any more?"

"Nor for this to be placed on record."

Barnard turned to the door. "One of these days you'll get me struck off."

"You joined of your own free will."

"Yes. Well, keep him by the fire. Precise timing of a death is an overrated pastime. It can be quite difficult. That should help you."

43

When Barnard had gone Bannerman turned to Holder. "Help me fill some hot water bottles. We must get back to London."

Holder faltered. "Weren't you arranging a dinner? I mean . . ."

"When you radio'd that Craven was dead I sent the cook home at once. You'll have to miss a meal, Ronnie. Your weight can stand it."

★   ★   ★

Gibbs wasn't sure whether Nuzzale was acting on instructions or personal suspicion but he seemed tuned in on Gibbs's present discomfort. Gibbs knew that Nuzzale was waiting for something, as he himself was. There were others nearby, he was sure of it. The pack was gathering. Once they had cooked their breakfast on the tiny, two-ringed gas stove, they washed up. The room was at times untidy but both men kept it clean. Cleaning was almost the only relief.

Gibbs said, "I've got to make a phone call."

"You have contacts we don't know about?"

"I've *one* contact you don't know about. You got contacts *I* don't know about?"

The deliberate jibe irritated Nuzzale. They went out on to the landing to the call-box. Nuzzale was trying to look over Gibbs's shoulder as he was about to dial. Gibbs turned brusquely: "Push off. Raul agreed. Period."

Nuzzale drew back leaned languidly against the wall as Gibbs dialled. It was now that Gibbs felt the isolation. If this went wrong he would have to get out fast. The receiver clicked; no voice the other end but someone was listening.

"Ross Gibbs." The open admission contained a message. They would now know that he had company that he could not safely shake off. Whatever they had for him would come over the telephone and he would have to memorise. The voice spoke as if reading news for the deaf. Near him Nuzzale was trying to listen, but Gibbs had the phone too close to his ear and the speaker was keeping his voice low. The information he received consoled and surprised him.

Nuzzale was satisfied at least that Gibbs was not passing information. He had said nothing since announcing himself. Then he said wearily, "Repeat," and half turned to face Nuzzale while the message came over again. Nuzzale, while he watched Gibbs's face, had to admit to himself that, whatever the outcome, the Englishman was a cool one. They all were. Cool or cold-blooded. It made no difference which, as long as the broad revolutionary conviction was the same. They had discussed it many times during their short acquaintance. He couldn't fault Gibbs on it, nor on his spasmodic fervour. But he did not trust him, and if he had one real concrete suspicion he would kill him and move on.

Gibbs hung up the receiver slowly and leaned against the wall as Nuzzale still did. While he looked into the questioning brown eyes he was thinking, memorising. "I'll need a S.M.G. A Sterling preferably. Full magazine. By early afternoon."

"I thought you people used Ingrams."

"A Sterling will do fine."

Nuzzale did not move. "We still don't know your target."

"Read about it. It should make the late editions."

"Who?"

"I said read about it. I've got to move." Gibbs went back into the room saying over his shoulder, "Tell Raul to stretch the deadline by a couple of hours." He heard Nuzzale stop but did not turn to meet the suspicious gaze.

5

GIBBS HAD BEEN through the whole routine of tail shaking and he was still not entirely satisfied. It was midday when he set out with the grip containing the sub-machine gun. After taking a series of tube trains, buses, diving into stores, he was now walking fast along the Strand from Fleet Street. His head was down against an icy wind, while he had one hand up to hold on to the old floppy hat. He was moving amongst strangers, the bad weather isolating each one to a silent hurrying column. Only the traffic made noise, and even that seemed subdued.

At Charing Cross Station he went under the arch on to the concourse, going directly to the left luggage. He reserved a box at the counter. A man came up to stand beside him while he was waiting for his key. A gloved hand touched the counter and was taken away again. Gibbs put his own hand over the key that was revealed. The man was still there, face behind the folds of a scarf, as Gibbs left for the lockers. He checked the number of the key the man had left and opened the locker. One small, long, brown-paper-covered parcel. Heavy. He took the parcel out, unzipped a portion of his grip and pushed the parcel into it, re-zipped and went to the locker he had just reserved where he put away the grip. Standing by the bookstall he made a re-appraisal of the concourse, of cold waiting figures, of those on the move, then slipped the stranger's key back on to the counter as he passed the locker reservations. The man had gone.

★　　★　　★

Bannerman had not gone to bed that night. At one a.m., back in London, he had sent a puzzled and rather disquieted Ronnie Holder home, having left himself a great deal to do. There had been standby plans for over a year. He had a whole series of them for possible events. If ten per cent of them came to fruition he would be a very satisfied man. If only one per cent was realised then he had not wasted his time. And if that turned out to be of sufficient magnitude then it was all more than worthwhile. Bannerman had always planned ahead. He had a completely shifting system of anticipation, of re-planning, altering a little here and there, adjusting as personnel came or left his jurisdiction. It was little use having ideas if there was no one to follow them through.

The planning itself was an isolated dedication. He had learned long ago to hide the many frustrations he suffered at the way he was hog tied. Everything these days had to be done within the rules. Whose rules? It was all right for a man to go out to maim, injure, torture and kill totally innocent people, to spatter them about the place or leave them without sight, legs or arms but to lay one finger on him in an effort to save others could not be done within the rules. They were the new breed of the great untouchables; the new jokers in the pack.

He worked through the night. He roused people from deep sleep by constant use of the telephone, and he made sure that they were completely awake before he gave precise instructions. He then made them repeat them. And again. At four a.m. he took to the road and checked streets and certain premises. He did not notice the cold nor the bleak emptiness of London in the dead of night. The stark loneliness suited him. His only interest was in those things which played a part in his scheme. The rest were unnecessary props.

After his night excursion he returned to his office off St. Martin's Lane, took off his wrist watch and laid it on the desk in front of him. He could not meet Gibbs's deadline but he could get within a couple of hours of it. It was up to Gibbs to win the extra time. He put pen to paper, worked out his calculations yet once again and then re-checked.

*   *   *

In Charles II Street off Lower Regent Street, two men waited in an empty room one floor above street level. It was a small, street-facing office, part of a suite of three, the other two of which were inner rooms. The floors were bare. There was no power. And it was freezing cold.

The men complained bitterly about the absence of heat as they knelt on the boards to open their cases. They occasionally rubbed

47

their hands as they assembled rifles and carefully added telescopic sights. Godbear, the short, thickset man was saying. "How can this job be done with frozen fingers? It's mad." And yet, for a clumsy-looking man his fingers worked extremely delicately and with the speed of an expert.

"Wait till we open the window. It'll cut us in half." It was Jones's version of a joke. His finger-tips were blue, yet when it came to squeezing the trigger he would forget the cold, everything but the target. Lean-bodied, of the two he appeared the more likely to be affected by the temperature, yet was the less complaining.

By London standards, Charles II Street is not very busy. Leading to St. James's Square it is short and overshadowed by Pall Mall to the south and Jermyn Street to the north. For some time the two men, rifles ready and leaning against a wall, stood back from the window, gauging the flow of pedestrians. They were high enough to see over the traffic to a point two or three feet above the opposite street level.

Once the guns were assembled they had nothing to do but wait and keep away from the windows. They tested the sights for light pick-up and were satisfied. It was a period between the end of late lunches and early home-going. The bad weather had affected transport and commuters were leaving early. It would not help them. It was already murky – it had been all day – but snow clouds were building up, darkening the sky and the streets.

"That's all we need," said Godbear bitterly. "Snow." Flakes fluttered down as he spoke. Even the more optimistic Jones was depressed by it. He was tempted to go closer to the window but held back and watched the snow begin to bury the V-shaped "For Rental" sign that pointed out above the window. He looked at his watch again.

*   *   *

Gibbs looked at his watch. He left the small cinema where he had contacted Bannerman and walked back to Charing Cross Station. He knew of Craven but had never met him. It was a fortunate death for him but bad luck on the American. From what he'd heard, some of Craven's colleagues might not think so. It had started to snow and fear pangs cramped his stomach. It couldn't be done in snow. It was already prematurely dark and the street lights were on, traffic with head and sidelights. Jesus. Outside the station was a long taxi queue snaking round trying unsuccessfully to keep dry under the lengthy overhang. It wasn't going to work. Yet Gibbs still went to the locker, still took out the grip. And again checked the time.

Wandering over to the book stall he bought a copy of the *Evening News*. He was a little ahead of time and it was at least dry inside the station, but the arctic wind fanned through the approaches.

*   *   *

Ginger Adams checked the time. His nickname was a long-lost legacy dating back to the days before he'd lost a bush of hair and the colour had drained from the remnants. He was about the same age as Paul Craven, roughly the same build. With Craven's hat pulled well down, in bad light and without too critical a scrutiny he almost looked like him. What projected the deception from the shaky to the probable was the fact that he was wearing Craven's clothes. He had no hang-ups about it; he found the topcoat fitted nicely and was warm. The suit jacket had been tailored to take a shoulder holster which Adams was wearing, too. Complete with Craven's .38. He glanced across the room to Bunton who was also looking at his watch.

*   *   *

Ross Gibbs crammed the news-sheet into a litter bin and walked down towards the Strand. The taxi queue had grown longer. He walked towards Trafalgar Square, travelling slowly in spite of the weather, constantly looking back towards Fleet Street. Cabs were either turning into the inverted U of the station forecourt or continuing along the Strand. It was a bad time to seek a cab. In this weather it was always a bad time.

A cab came coasting along, flag down. Gibbs glanced back to see the driver give a brief sign. Gibbs acknowledged; the cab pulled in. Gibbs gave no destination. If the driver did not know then by an unlikely coincidence he had chosen the wrong one.

Gibbs sat in the back. The rear window was darkened. He unzipped the grip, pulled out the Sterling Nuzzale had provided, removed the magazine, cocked the gun to remove the possibility of a breach round, then released the trigger. He laid the gun on the seat, undid the brown paper parcel and produced a magazine of

49

blanks which he loaded into the sub-machine gun. He cocked again. When he looked out of the side window the snow was easing but one flurry could destroy everything. All he could do was to sit there willing the snow to stop. The driver must have been thinking the same. Neither man had spoken a word. Still without comment Gibbs tapped on the driver's glass and passed the live magazine through.

*　　*　　*

Godbear said, "Time to fix the silencers. I hate the damned things, they spoil the aim."

Jones agreed. "The traffic noise will cover the shots. But we must reduce the flashes. It's dark enough to notice."

Godbear nodded. "The snow's easing. Still too bad to chance it, though."

Standing well back Jones observed, "It's stopped. These are small flurries being carried by the wind. Bannerman must have a direct line to God up there."

"His friend down below, more likely. We've done some strange ones, Jonesey, but this takes the biscuit."

"We'd better be on target. Let's ease that window up."

They stood either side of the old-fashioned window. Jones, with the longer reach, undid the catch, and then, both keeping close to the wall, eased up the lower window about four inches. The air cut through around their thighs. They knelt down, one each end, verbally rehearsed in what they had to do. Their position was not comfortable. Aiming down always induced the risk of aiming too low. And they could not stick their barrels through the gap. The best they could allow themselves was to have the silencers just supported on the frame so long as they did not protrude outside.

The wind was now exploiting the narrow gap. Both men had difficulty in seeing as the cold air whipped into their eyes. Jones pulled out a pair of spectacles. He hated shooting with glasses on but they blocked the air blast. At the other end of the window Godbear wiped his eyes with the side of his hand and started a long stream of invective. The swearing, the complaining, was a safety valve for him. He was always the same before a job. He would change completely during the actual work and yet again after it when he would be quite jovial.

Two minutes to go. Rifles ready, cocked and resting lightly on the sill; people, heads down, passed across their sights. They needed good peripheral vision but if the job were done properly there should be no problems from passers by.

"Here he comes." Jones did not turn his head but tightened his grip on the rifle, pulled it well in to his shoulder. Godbear did not reply. Without shifting aim he was watching the approaching figure from the corner of his eye. The man slowed, finally hesitating against a wide wall space between two shop windows. Fingers on the triggers took up first pressure. They waited, cold discomfort forgotten. The taxi crawled along, wipers removing the last trace of snow, smearing the windscreen. It stopped suddenly.

Inside the cab Gibbs already had the window down, suffering much the same as the two gunmen. He waited a second to be sure that no one was in danger then levelled his Sterling and fired until the magazine was almost empty. A fraction before Gibbs squeezed the trigger Ginger Adams saw him, had his gun half out of his holster before he hurtled back against the wall, reeled sideways against it, then buckled. While the machine gun exploded in the quiet street. Godbear and Jones fired two precisely aimed shots each and immediately withdrew. Before they closed the window they heard the first of the screams. They dismantled their guns without comment.

In the street the taxi drew away at speed while Gibbs raised the window quickly. He then packed the gun in the grip, sat back, nerves on edge. Behind him another cabbie who had been closing in decided that he was not taking on a machine-gunner, but did make a note of the number soon after pulling in. Both he and his two passengers ran back to where the man lay huddled on the pavement. Already a small group was forming round him.

Bunton was also on time. He reached Adams before anyone, and was already kneeling beside him when the first horrified onlooker arrived. Bunton took off his topcoat and laid it quickly over Adams and then kept the growing crowd back by announcing that he was a doctor. Relief came in the form of a policeman. Bunton produced an identity card and thereby took control. He pulled the topcoat back briefly to show Adams's side-turned face. "He's dead," said Bunton. "He must have taken the lot."

The policeman looked quickly around, saw the deep pock marks on the wall where bullets had chipped the outer skin of plaster. "Not quite, sir. I'll get an ambulance up."

"No." Bunton was keeping his voice low and his back to the crowd. "This man is an important American security expert. Did you look closely at my identity?"

"Closely enough, sir."

"I was supposed to keep an eye on him. I want him taken to the Julian Clinic. It's near here. You probably know of it. Get a police car."

The police officer was already on his radio. Within seconds the siren could be heard. Bunton was wiping his face. He reached under the topcoat and gently removed the gun, his gloved hand smoothing away the prints. "His reflexes were a damn sight better than mine but he didn't get one off. Do you want this?" He handed Craven's gun over.

Behind them the cab driver witness called, "I got his number." Bunton wasn't disturbed. The police officer made a note of it, radio'd again, and then started to seek witnesses as the police car pulled in. There was a tricky moment getting Adams on to the back seat without dislodging the topcoat but Bunton climbed in with him, nursing his head on his lap. They left behind a startled crowd, the bullet-marked walls and two red stains on the pavement from capsules Adams had released. Bunton filled the policeman in during the short journey, again showing his identity card. He did not himself feel shock until after Adams had been stretchered from the car and taken to the prepared room. It was often the same with Bannerman's schemes. They seemed logical enough, always well planned and well explained. It was only afterwards that the sweat of uncertainty flowed, but by then there had invariably been a perfect operation. Yet this was the most bizarre in Bunton's experience.

The cab driver who had carried Gibbs reported in at Saville Row police station in a highly agitated state. He was a driver of some experience, had picked up his fare near Charing Cross and the next thing he knew was a gun in his neck followed by the most horrific experience of his life. He did not know where the gunman had gone. He had got out in Swallow Street and run off. He wasn't going to chase a fanatical gunman. Yes, he could identify him; gave a description but he still felt shaken up. He was given tea and was treated for shock.

Gibbs was wrong about making the late edition of the evening papers. But the event did make the next radio news bulletin. It was the lead story. A highly placed American Government official on a visit mown down by machine-gun fire on a London street. Nuzzale's suspicion disappeared as he listened. His face broke into a smile of satisfaction as if he had just won a fortune instead of listening to a report of a gruesome death. He threw his hands up in joy and clasped Gibbs firmly, repeatedly patting his back. All animosity had gone. It had been much better than he had hoped. The name had been withheld but Gibbs had by now told him. They all knew about Craven.

Gibbs responded with difficulty. He could still see Adams falling and worse, the wall chipping beside him. That worried him sick. The only other incident that stayed in his mind was when the driver was tying the traffic up in knots during the hectic escape and Gibbs had suddenly shouted, "Mind that dog," as a stray mongrel had scuttled across the road. The braking had almost caused a crash. But the most ludicrous thing about it was the extent of Nuzzale's unhealthy jubilation. Gibbs felt sick.

*   *   *

Bannerman received the news but could do nothing until Craven's clothes were returned to him. He was pacing the basement range, the dead and naked Craven on a raised stretcher at the target end. At the firing end a Sterling S.M.G. was gripped firmly in a vice. The long, narrow, soundproofed room was darkened, most of the lights switched off. This part of it Bannerman could handle without the armourer.

When Adams and Bunton arrived, all three gave a hand in dressing Craven, complete with holster and topcoat. It was not easy nor pleasant. They strapped him to the stretcher, head, shoulders, upper thighs and feet. With difficulty they removed the stretcher from the trolley and erected it against the wall in front of the lowered targets.

"Raise him a little or we won't see his lower legs." Bannerman as matter-of-fact and as cold-blooded as ever. Adams had to go off for blocks to place under the stretcher staves.

Bannerman observed the result critically. "The angle may be wrong."

Bunton thought not. It was too minimal to consider. But there was another consideration. "He'll fall forward."

"Someone will have to hold the top stave of the stretcher."

Bunton was staggered. "Not me."

"No. You'll be firing the gun."

This brought Bunton back to reality. He stared at Bannerman incredulously. "I'm not doing that either."

Bannerman, who was still eyeing Craven critically suddenly looked across. "Why on earth not?"

It was difficult to give an answer. They had gone so far. And successfully. Yet this he could not do. "The gun stays in the vice?"

"Of course."

"Then I'll hold the stave," said Bunton. "Ginger can hold the other side."

The protection for Adams was not missed by Bannerman. "You'd rather I did the actual act?"

"I'd rather I did *not* do it."

"All right. A strange squeamishness. I'm surprised you didn't raise it before."

Bunton managed a smile. "Perhaps because you were so convincing."

"I'm also right. Here are the blocks."

With Adams's help they raised the stretcher. Bannerman went behind the gun. They all wore ear muffs. Bunton and Adams stood on the frame behind which the targets could rise and as far to each side of the stretcher as they could while holding an upright each.

In such a macabre scene one oddity stood out more than the strapped corpse waiting to be mutilated. Bannerman, in his black jacket and pin-striped trousers, his tall frame stooped behind the gun, his attitude as concentrated as any banker's during a deal, his head crowned by ear muffs, supplied an almost tragi-comic air. But Bannerman was not dealing in money; his commodities were flesh and blood – and this was only the beginning. He adjusted the gun, tightened the vice, checked his sighting, fired a very short burst, made an adjustment then fired another. Bunton and Adams hung on grimly, glad they were wearing the muffs. Poor, dead Craven.

Bannerman looked through the fixed telescope. "That takes care of the broken legs. I must get a couple of rounds through the neck to answer for the breakage there." Neither Bunton nor Adams found they could look. They hadn't actually heard Bannerman's words. They had no need. The lack of feeling, the intense sense of purpose was all in the pinched features, the silent dialogue self-explanatory in the restricted movement of the thin lips. Bannerman was getting it right as he always did. When he finally put a good burst into the lifeless body, having eased the vice slightly and being careful to avoid the straps, he signalled for the corpse to be put back on the trolley.

They took off the ear muffs and the range was silent. Bunton and Adams were in no mood for comment.

Bannerman asked, "Van outside?" Adams nodded.

"What time does Thurston get back to the clinic?"

"Seven o'clock."

Bannerman smiled. It was the first time he showed any form of relief. "Splendid. Policeman guarding outside the door, you say? Doesn't know there's an intercommunicating door?"

"If he does it doesn't matter. The other room is round the corner. We were lucky Thurston was away."

Bannerman's smile subtly changed to one of self-satisfaction. "Luck doesn't come into it, dear boy; I made damned certain that he was away."

"The Yard might have insisted on a police doctor. A rather special one, I'll admit. Anyway at the moment it's all in the hands of Special Branch and they are doing what we tell them."

"They don't know?"

"How can they? You'd better get Craven to the clinic. When Thurston gets back the whole thing will open up. Don't slip up now whatever you do."

*   *   *

Against his religious beliefs, Nuzzale was drinking white wine. But religion had become a little confused during his activities over the past few years. Gibbs joined him with the wine. The change in Nuzzale was quite extraordinary: he had become ebullient, but through it escaped his undoubted fanaticism. Like this Gibbs felt him to be actually more dangerous than before – his instability had taken a strange course. His dedication, however, was undoubted. He was concerned. "They will be looking for you. The taxi driver, others, will have given a description. Perhaps you should have killed the driver."

"It would have been non-productive. A further risk."

"Will they now tie it to the S.A.S. officer who deserted?"

"I don't know. Possibly. It doesn't matter. For the movement it would be better if they do. Shake them. Hurt them."

"Yes. We must celebrate. I'll bring something in. Then we'll see Raul."

Gibbs was left alone, not sure of his feelings. The crazy thing about it all was that the only image in his mind was that of the wet, bedraggled dog scurrying for its life. He wondered what had happened to it. He was on his own. Severed. He would have to rely on the news media to judge how well things had gone. Safety would depend on keeping eyes and ears open.

He looked round the room: big, Edwardian, adequate. Three beds, a huge wardrobe, tiny kitchen recess, washbasin. A well-worn carpet covered most of the floor, the boards beyond its fringes dark stained. In the far corner behind Nuzzale's bedhead the floorboards were loose. In the space beneath Nuzzale kept his weapons. How much time had he?

Gibbs prised a board up with a knife. Once lifted it came easily. He removed two more, laid them carefully down while he knelt beside the cavity, ears attuned to beyond the door. The Sterling was down there. Two magazines, one of which he had returned empty. Grenades, Russian, British and American. And there were plastic explosives, detonators and fuse wire. There were also two automatic pistols. Gibbs did not touch any of it. He lay flat so that he could see further under the boards between the beams. A long wooden box probably contained ammunition and some small cardboard boxes would be for the pistols. Nuzzale could not have brought these up in one load. But then Nuzzale may not have worked alone. Gibbs put the boards back carefully. Residue, tell-tale dust he hand brushed and rubbed into cracks between the floorboards under the carpet. When Nuzzale returned with the smell of cheap curry, Gibbs was listening to the radio.

They left about half-past eight, with the warm comfort of the over-paprika'd meal in their stomachs. It was still bitingly cold and Gibbs almost felt sorry for the shivering Nuzzale, huddled in inadequate clothing for someone born to a blazing sun.

6

THE SURGICAL MASK drooped round Thurston's neck, the grey eyes above it angry. He whipped off his white cap and screwed it in his hand. He closed the door with a rubber clad foot. In spite of his obvious anger he spoke very quietly. "What are you trying to pull, George?"

Bannerman was sitting on a hardback chair by the side of the bed from which Craven had been removed. He was quite relaxed, legs crossed, arms folded. "I really don't know what you mean."

Thurston threw the cap on to the bed. "An air of innocence hardly suits you. That man was dead before a bullet touched him."

"Of course. Do you imagine I thought I could deceive you about that?"

Thurston suffered the exasperation that most people eventually did when dealing with Bannerman, but he had no intention of being misled. "Perhaps hope springs eternal in you. I've heard the bulletins; Craven was in no way killed as the media have announced. Did they get it from you?"

"Certainly not." Which was true.

Thurston pointed to the curtained window. "People out there believe that Craven was gunned down in the street. If he was, he was a walking miracle. He was already dead. How did you do it?"

"That's hardly your affair, John."

"What is my affair is to ascertain the cause of death. A good deal of damage has been done to earlier fractures. The tibiae are smashed. So is the vertebrae extending from the skull. You must have been mad to think that I'd be fooled."

"I repeat: I did not." Bannerman was deliberately unhelpful. He wanted Thurston to work it out for himself.

"How was he killed? The area of the leg wounds could suggest a car crash. There is a deep bruise on his forehead which could have come from striking a dashboard." Thurston gesticulated when Bannerman made no reply. "*Well?*"

"Well what? What do you want from me?"

57

"I want the bloody truth, George. I've no intention of perjuring myself on a death certificate."

"Surely there's absolutely no need."

Thurston was perplexed. "I'm reporting this to Sir Henry."

Bannerman uncrossed his legs, rose, took Thurston lightly by the elbow and moved to the window. "I can't stop you, John, but I'd rather you didn't."

"There's nothing else I can do. I won't issue a false certificate unless directed by him."

"I think you're taking this all far too seriously. The Americans know about this. It was their original idea. No one is asking you to perjure yourself. Certainly not I. There are, however, concessions you should be willing to make without risk to yourself."

"I can't say he was killed by shooting. Nor will I."

"Did he die of a broken neck?"

"Possibly."

"Couldn't you simply give that as the cause of death in your opinion?"

"I can't ignore the bullet wounds inflicted after death."

"Surely you need only report that the wounds are there. No one is going to ask whether they were inflicted after. It will be *assumed* that was how he died."

"It's still a lie by omission."

"But never provable, surely? Tomorrow he's being flown back in a sealed coffin for cremation. Either way it will be over."

"I have to state the probable cause of the broken neck."

"Could you ever be sure of the correct answer?"

"You've made damned sure of that. We could go further with the examination."

"His relatives may object to that if it slows down his removal. It would be better all round if it was believed that he died bravely in the line of duty. Somehow the television newscaster has got hold of the story that his reflexes were so fine that his own gun was half out of its holster before he was shot. That's how a man like that should die. Not on an icy road as a very expert driver who should have been old enough to know better than to indulge in over-confidence."

Thurston glanced at Bannerman. He did not know why they were standing in front of the window; neither could see out.

"So I was right," he said softly. It had a calming effect on him.

"You were bound to be. You are too thorough."

"Don't soft-soap me, George."

"Look, John, that's how it happened. A few miles from my home. Leo Roxberg was with me. Craven was to join us. It was tragic but, once it happened, God sent. The decision, right or wrong, had to be instant. When we got Craven to my place Tony Barnard was already on his way. He will tell you exactly what happened."

"So you've involved him, too?"

"We're all involved, for God's sake. What the blazes do you expect? It's what we're here for."

"It's a nasty one, though. Very nasty."

"Some of them are. It's nothing to what 'our friends' get up to."

"You say Leo Roxberg knows?"

"Leo may not have liked Craven, but you're really stretching it too far if you're suggesting that he would be vindictive after his death." And then: "I really don't understand you. You hope people will bequeath their bodies to research after death. Paul Craven would have bequeathed his for saving lives in a different way. A go-getting bulldog like him. Anyway, there are precedents for it."

"This is not wartime."

"Then you're living under a delusion."

Thurston was thoughtful. He turned away from the window and faced the empty bed. "There are ethics involved. And Sir Henry should know."

Bannerman walked back into the room, turned and faced Thurston across the bed. He appeared vaguely disgusted. "What on earth have we got you for? It's politic to keep the head away from the detail. It gives him leeway when confronted with the Minister. It enables him to make honest answers. To bring ethics into this game really is an off-beat thought. None of us is devoid of scruples. Because of the nature of our work some decisions are often hasty and not always sound. This one *is* sound. Yet there's another reason. A few good men have been involved in this. Unless this goes through one young man in particular, a very brave young man, is going to die rather unpleasantly. How does that meet your ethics?"

Thurston thought it through. He did not take long to arrive at the purpose. He had, in any event, been wavering, not because of

59

Bannerman's pressure – that left him cold – but because he could see the other implications. Had he not been a doctor he might well have gone along with it at the outset. He nodded slowly. "You win. You invariably do. I just hope your young man is able to survive what you've planned for *him*. Poor sod. I'll make out the report."

*　　*　　*

Raul Orta raised his glass of whisky. He was a man who did not want for anything.

"I've already seen it but it's worth a second look. It will be on the ten o'clock news." He indicated the huge television set in the corner.

As Gibbs raised his glass it was very difficult to accept that this soft-eyed, jovial man was a multi-killer. He had even killed a man in his own organisation: the victim had disagreed on a fundamental issue. No more than that.

Orta was lounging back, one leg over the arm of his chair. He wagged a slightly admonishing finger at Gibbs. "You should have made a claim for that death. We could have cashed in on it."

Gibbs, forming the apex of the triangle between the three men and furthest from the door, shook his head. "On whose behalf? Surely you don't want publicity at this moment? The death of Craven will puzzle them. They'll be wondering who gains most, and with the pies Craven had fingers in, that's a very broad issue. He enabled me to prove a point, that's all." He was deliberately callous and sipped his drink.

Orta smiled at Nuzzale. "Hear that, Mohammed? He can think too." He turned back to Gibbs. "I agree with you."

Gibbs smiled without rancour. "When do you chaps stop sounding me out?"

Orta laughed, throwing his head back and brandishing his drink. "*Olé!*" A warm personality emerged while he was like this. The conceit was always there but he did not forget the rules of the game. He had, after all, the greatest reputation of them all. The most wanted man on earth. And yet no one *really* wanted him. After the Belgium murders he had disappeared. Libya, of course, was rumoured, and the Lebanon. Even Algeria and Syria would not take him. Yet he was known to have organised and participated in two major acts of terrorism in Europe since then. Dangerous

60

prisoners had been released, huge sums of money paid. He – as most of them did – had a whole series of safe houses throughout Europe and almost as many different passports. His father, a wealthy industrialist, doted on him, openly bragged of his son's firmly held beliefs and prodigious acts of terror. He boasted that Raul Orta had made his reputation on his own, without his assistance. That was not true. During his early training in Moscow, Orta's affluence had been a great source of embarrassment to the Russians who bore it only because they recognised his potential. He was also a womaniser. Looking at him now Gibbs could well understand young girls falling for his easy charm. His accent was pleasant, his English excellent, his looks sometimes compelling in spite of his shaved head.

Orta was still chuckling. "Relax, Ross. Your background is different. We were bound to show an interest in you."

"My background?" He reflected that Orta fitted in with other international terrorists in one main respect; they nearly all came from middle class families. They had no problems of poverty though they claimed to support those who had.

"Training, my friend. Moscow and Hereford. One day we must compare notes."

"Perhaps the comparison will come out during the real thing."

Nuzzale enjoyed that reply as much as Orta. The mood in the room was good.

"So what's going on?" asked Gibbs.

And that was where the mood changed.

Orta stood up. He finished his whisky, placed the glass carelessly on the wide mantelpiece, part of the base overhanging. He inclined his head thoughtfully. "What you call here, a good point." He walked across the room to the small, electric piano pushed flush with the wall. He sat on the chrome stool and fingered his beard as he looked at Gibbs thoughtfully. "It's best you don't know until necessary. I know what I want to do. When I have one more piece of information I will even know when."

"Isn't it dangerous hanging around meanwhile? Supposing it's some time before you – strike?"

"It's a situation we are used to, Ross." Orta was totally serious now, a different person, and it suddenly made his clothes appear ludicrous. His emerging thoughts weren't flamboyant, they were rational. "It's important to absorb ourselves in the scene. Certain observations can only be made from here. The actual notice could be short – too short to get colleagues into the country quickly."

"So you're all here?"

Orta looked quizzically at Gibbs. "You are not pumping one of the boys in a Derry bar now, Ross. You are among experts. Your S.A.S. training is showing."

"I'm not apologising for it. I'd like to know."

Orta conceded with a slight nod of his head and an amused glance. "We've a lot to learn about you but I like your style. I'm not singling you out. Mohammed knows no more. It's the only way if one of us is picked up. Right now you are very hot property."

"What do I do meanwhile?"

"Mainly stay out of sight. They will be looking for you. And I think you should now split with Mohammed. It is better that we are scattered."

"Okay. I'll look for a place."

"We don't want you knocking up landladies. I can give you a safe address, not far from here."

Gibbs rose and paced the room, aware they were watching him. If they could get inside his head they would. He still held his drink, had hardly touched it. Now he sipped it.

"They may think I've fled the country. We'll know better when we see tomorrow's papers. But I'd still like something for morale. Some idea of how long I must wait. Sitting on the sort of energy I have is not easy. Days? Weeks? Months?"

Orta had straddled his legs, was gripping the stool between them. "We've all suffered it. Weeks. Adapt your system to that."

Gibbs looked relieved. "Well, at least I've some idea."

Orta switched on the television. "Two minutes," he said. "Let's see what else they've got."

The affair was the lead item. Television cameras had been rushed to the scene. Interviewers had even managed to get hold of a witness. A young girl, by now over the shock, related fairly accurately what had happened and embroidered a little under pressure. The snow had held off but the obvious cold came through, the arc lamps showing the freezing onlookers as the camera panned, bated breath rising like steam. Then came shots of a roped-off area, of the pock-marked wall, the two stains on the sidewalk. Afterwards, a high-ranking police officer gave a description of the wanted man which bore little resemblance to Gibbs.

Orta switched off when the news changed. Both he and Nuzzale displayed a sort of pride, a bond with Gibbs. It was difficult to understand their relaxed and obvious pleasure at someone being gunned down so brutally.

Orta said, "One for the road." And then to show that he really missed nothing. "You went a little high with some of those shots. Not bad though."

"It's not that easy from a taxi."

"No. But you shouldn't complain. A good job, Ross. One more pig out of the way."

"An important one," said Nuzzale. "The Americans will be mad."

Orta handed the drinks round, white wine to Nuzzale. He took his own drink to the piano, placed it on top. He started to play a soft Spanish tune, beautiful under his touch. As Gibbs watched and listened it was clear that Orta possessed far more feeling for music than for people. He would never have that deep inward look in his eyes if he saw a body fall mortally wounded. When he had finished he swung round on the stool to face Gibbs. "You like music?"

"When it's played like that."

"What arms have you?"

"I can lay my hands on a Browning. Army issue."

Orta chuckled. "Can you use it as effectively as you do an S.M.G? You will need to."

*　　　*　　　*

Roxberg climbed into the cab and took up his position beside Bannerman. After a nod to his silent enquiry he helped himself to a drink from the recess. "Cheers. I like your mobile board-room."

Bannerman had changed into well-cut tweeds; they did not suit him. He had left his umbrella behind on the correct assumption that it was useless against fierce snow flurries, but was now in difficulties as he did not know what to do with his gloved hands. He held on to the side strap with one. "It's better that we keep it between ourselves."

"And you don't like my office?" Roxberg tried to knock some life into the meeting.

"That too. How did they take it?"

Roxberg sat back, blew out his cheeks. "They're deeply shocked, of course. Regret is another matter. They're all going round with long faces making the right noises. Even those who openly disliked the guy. He brushed a lot of people up the wrong way." He raised his glass. "God rest his soul." He drank half his drink at a gulp and Bannerman realised that beneath the bravado he was disturbed.

"You didn't think we'd get away with it?"

"It sounded fine at the time. When I saw it on vision it was scarey."

Bannerman turned his head in surprise. "But that was after the event?"

"Yeah. It made me realise just how much we'd chanced our arm."

"It went splendidly."

"It certainly did. You did a great job, George. But there are going to be a lot of ripples across the pond. Washington is going to scream action. Already is. The Ambassador is in a difficult position trying to preserve the Anglo-American détente while under pressure to demand why no arrest has been made."

"The descriptions were vague and contradictory. We've got the Yard to do an identikit based on eye-witnesses."

"You mean it looks nothing like the guy?"

"I understand the taxi driver, who was best suited to give a description, disagreed with some others who in turn could not agree amongst themselves."

They were silent for a while. Roxberg was looking straight ahead, mulling something over, the glass tilted in his hands. "I don't want you to use my name in this, George."

"Of course not. There is absolutely no need."

"I mean it was your man you wanted to plant. Your show."

Bannerman briefly patted Roxberg's knee. "Don't worry. It would not occur to me to use your name. I was grateful for your consent."

"Yes, well. You're a pretty persuasive guy."

"Don't you think I was right?"

"Oh, sure. Craven would have insisted on it. Meanwhile I have to live with the hustle in the Embassy. I don't want it worse than it is."

"Have no fear."

But Roxberg had not reached his point. "It was a pretty convenient accident, though, wasn't it? I was thinking after –"

"Very. Then Craven was showing off. He disliked an escort. He was a marvellous driver and was determined to show poor Ronnie Holder just how marvellous."

"He wasn't good enough to pull out of it, though, was he?"

"Its happened to even better drivers than Craven. English country roads are treacherous in icy conditions."

"You didn't by any chance send Holder, knowing that Craven would try to shake him?"

"That worries you? My dear Leo, I would have sent an escort in any event. Craven's feelings didn't come into it one way or the other. I had my job to do. I would hardly expect him to react like a schoolboy."

"That's just it. A bull maybe. But never a schoolboy. I just can't see Craven over-reacting to a point of recklessness. Not behind the wheel of a car."

"You're probably right. Then the conditions must have beaten him. Anyway, it's over. Put it out of your mind."

*   *   *

It was difficult to imagine that he had been an Olympic silver medallist for pistol shooting. He was tall and thin, so that even the lean Bannerman seemed more substantial in his company. The suite was in London's Savoy hotel.

Ernst Vogel looked a good ten years older than thirty and with it he appeared unhealthy, even emaciated. It could be argued that he had taken the brutal murder of his father unusually badly. The vast difference between a natural death and one that had been anticipated and headlined by the German and European press for several weeks before the final, callous act of shooting Kurt Vogel three times through the back of the head, had affected Ernst very considerably. Had the men, who had kidnapped Kurt Vogel for the usual demands of money and the release from prison of colleagues, set out to destroy a close-knit family in addition to shocking humanity, they could not have chosen better. The fact that they achieved this was coincidental.

Kurt Vogel had been powerful at all levels. His industrial empire bore a name that was itself a password from Frankfurt to Washington to Peking. He had been politically outspoken, voicing what he believed; and although with his own family he had been anything but a despot, from those around him he insisted on the highest degree of honour and integrity. Honour had probably sentenced him to death. He would not plead for mercy nor condone a ransom for him. The whole episode had been harrowing enough for the family of mother, two married daughters and Ernst, but what made it unbearable was the fact that Kurt Vogel had been unbelievably tortured before his death. That had only become known when the ravaged and shattered body had slumped from a telephone kiosk some two hours after the last frenzied ultimatum had been issued.

Frau Vogel, after a month of sedative-cloaked anguish, sprung a mental defence mechanism that shut off the gruesome, repugnant period of her dear husband's suffering for ever. She could not recall it these last six months, nor even her husband's name. In very little time she could not recognise her own family. The family disintegrated, kept away from each other in the knowledge of how the conversation would inevitably turn. And young Ernst Vogel, who had always had the best of things, found himself alone. He kept away from his friends, wary of their sympathy, afraid to be reminded of the destruction of his parents. He slowly developed his own kind of fanaticism. During this tragic period he lost three stone in weight. From a well-built young man he shrunk to near skeletal size. His long fingers shook if they were not occupied. They were shaking now as he faced Bannerman.

Ernst Vogel used his father's considerable chain of political contacts to find employment in intelligence circles. He had much to offer and he had no need of salary. He did not want to find terrorists: he wanted to kill them – as many as he could. Authority wisely held him at bay: revenge was no condition for intelligence work.

In Germany, officialdom would not touch him. They had known his father and well recognised the dangers of using his son. Bannerman too, had known the father. Both Kurt and Ernst Vogel had visited London regularly, while Bannerman often needed to

66

visit West Germany. In Bonn, he had listened to young Ernst's protestations of his services to his country being rejected, no matter how velvet gloved the rejection had been. Bannerman sympathised. His scruples need not be so refined when dealing with a cry from the heart of a foreign national. He knew a man in London, he explained, who might possibly be able to help. Given time. Be patient, young Ernst. Perhaps I can do something for you. I'll try, but only if you're sure you want me to. Might be able to contact one of these underground chappies; or whatever they're called.

It was the only carrot Ernst received. He had never met Craven, and by the time the American caught the whispers Bannerman had Ernst sewn up. Ernst Vogel was in London on business. There was nothing unusual in that. Bannerman, watching the hollow eyes, the fever still evident, had an unusual twinge of conscience. Ernst really wasn't stable. And yet the exercise he was planning might well be the right mental therapy. The question was, could he still shoot straight?

"You sure you want to go through with it?" Bannerman asked.

The hands stopped shaking. "Of course. I've waited so long."

"We can't protect you. You realise that?"

Ernst shrugged. "I realise I'm a foreigner here. Your police are bound to make enquiries."

"They may have heard of your – wishes. It could be awkward for you."

"But if I'm caught they won't hang me?"

"No. No capital punishment here. Prison could be unbearable for a man like you. Think carefully, for once you commit yourself I must rely on you, or others will die as your father did."

Ernst's eyes flickered. "I understand why you said that. I hold no rancour." With a slow, deliberate movement he pulled out a wallet from inside his jacket. He opened it carefully and removed some half dozen photographs. Without change of expression he looked at each one in turn then handed them to Bannerman.

Bannerman winced when he saw the first one. He barely glanced at the others. "These are copies of the police photographs?"

"Yes."

"You carry them with you all the time?"

"All the time."

"You want to be constantly reminded?"

"I don't need reminding. When I'm satisfied that justice has been done I will stop carrying them."

"You're torturing yourself unnecessarily."

"I'm no masochist. But I don't *want* to forget, ever."

Bannerman could make no further comment. He knew what he should say. Ernst was twisting his mind into an impossible knot.

Ernst said. "If you can't protect me you will at least not give me up?"

"I can't protect you in a court of law. I'll hardly send the police after you. In that sense I can possibly help you. I'll supply an unmarked gun. I'll cover you wherever I can. Is your aim still good?"

Ernst smiled quietly. For a moment his youth reappeared. "Don't worry about my aim. In Germany I practise almost daily." He held out his hands. "Watch." The splayed fingers trembled then gradually quietened until they were completely steady. It was a superb effort of will. The fingers suddenly clenched into balls. "They know what is expected of them."

*   *   *

The room was not bad. It was not as big as Orta's or Nuzzale's but was similar in many ways. A high ceiling, and a huge pine door whose lintel he couldn't reach. Two-old-fashioned but serviceable single beds, a wardrobe and the inevitable washbasin. Two arm-chairs, a wooden straightback at a fold-down table. Shabby carpet. Gas fire. The usual recess for limited cooking.

Before he unpacked his grip, clothes he had bought since arriving in London, Ross examined the room thoroughly. He went quickly through the more obvious places, more slowly over the less obvious. Unless there were bugs in the wall the room was clean.

He unpacked, then taped his gun to the underside of the dropleaf table so that it remained hidden when the leaf was raised. When he had washed and settled in he went out, cocooned in his topcoat and with a Donegal tweed hat low on his head.

The streets were wet after the snow, with frozen slush piled into the gutters. He had already seen the morning papers. As he did not believe that Bannerman's strings would extend to every editor, or that he would try pulling them, even if they did, on a matter so delicate, the journalists would seem to have been kind to him. Most thought he had already fled the country, which was helpful. Even so, all ports, airports and stations were being watched. The descriptions of him could fit so many. The identikit photos all newspapers carried left him relieved – relieved enough at any rate to find a Pakistani restaurant nearby and to enjoy a good curry lunch after the mock-up of the previous evening.

It was not Gibbs's only reason for going out. Suspicion was with him all the way. He would not really believe that he had been accepted until it was all over. If Raul Orta was lonely, so was he. So far he had no part except to be available, and meetings between them were going to be strictly limited. Raul Orta had assured him that the notice would be adequate. Orta had also been generous and had funded Gibbs sufficiently to buy, after lunch, a black and white portable television set.

Satisfied that he was, for the moment, free of scrutiny, Gibbs made a telephone call from a call-box. While he gave his instructions he watched the street and everyone in it. In this weather, in this part of back-street Kensington, there were not many people about. He hoped that what he wanted would be on standby, for he must have it within hours.

His back-up was sound, his only complaint being that this time the collection point was Victoria Station, a good deal further than he wanted to travel. The pick-up did not worry him. What did was the number of parcels he had to get back into his room without being seen should Orta have a watch on the house. Partly to disguise his load, he also brought back groceries. Ross Gibbs was settling in.

At eight he left the apartment, standing on the steps for a while, feeling the wind penetrate his topcoat as if it were made of paper, and icy fingers of sleet sting his face. With hands in pockets he went slowly down to street level, pulled his hat down harder as the wind nearly removed it, and walked off, body bent into the wind. He did not hurry because he could not with the equipment fastened to his body and in his topcoat pockets.

The sleet gradually turned to snow as the temperature dropped. The snow was at least an effective screen. It was some time before he approached Orta's apartment. He made a detour and came

69

towards it from the far end of the street. Window lights taunted him with their suggestion of warmth, and he shivered.

Without hesitating, Gibbs went down the basement steps of the house opposite Orta's. He gripped the railings, in danger of slipping on the snow-covered stone steps. He reached the basement as the door opened and he was flooded by light.

7

THE FIGURE WAS as huddled as he, a fur hood covering head and ears. Her face was shadowed, the light behind her, and he realised that he was much more on view. Gibbs shrank back inside the raised collar of his coat.

"Yes?" She was peering at him, eyes screwed against the sharp little gusts of wind. A pleasant voice, with a touch of surprise.

He huddled in front of her while she tried partly to close the door to keep the weather out. "Mrs. Mayhew?"

"No. You must have the wrong address."

"That's not difficult in this weather." He had one hand at his collar, head bent down to make it difficult for her to see him. "Do you know where she lives?"

"I don't know a Mrs. Mayhew. Look, I'm awfully sorry but I'm on my way out, and I'm frozen standing here."

"I'm sorry, too." He moved back towards the steps. "This *is* Darcy Place?"

"Turn left and the second left."

"I'm so sorry. And thanks." He went up the steps. He did not peer back until her footsteps faded up the street. He risked a look, stepped back against the railings. For how long would she be gone?

It might be too risky to return to the same basement but he could not operate in the open street. He waited until she disappeared then went back, taking the basement next door. Hiding under the arch of the steps he produced his equipment. It was not easy. The snow had been cleared from the front door of the basement apartment with a narrow, now frozen path to the steps. Which meant that he had to stand in the heaped up snow in order to keep cover and to be able to shrink back among the dustbins in an emergency. His trousers were already wet, the damp creeping up his legs.

To facilitate working he wore mitts, leaving his fingers free. It was not long before they lost feeling. As he extended the telescopic rod he recalled Bannerman's words.

"It's not as good as the galium arsenide laser with opto-electrical linkage you used in Ulster. It can't possibly be. It won't pick up vibrations from closed window panes. The boffs have done a wonderful job, though. They had to develop a very high power portable battery and a directional microphone that would adequately amplify. It's not perfect and will be reasonably effective only over very short distances. You'll need to get as near as you can. But one man can carry the lot, and that was the criterion."

Gibbs inserted the miniaturised earphones. The bloody battery, though fairly small, weighed a ton. If the equipment was Banner-man's idea of unobtrusive portability, it was not his. He fixed the rod to reach just above the top of the railings. With a few adjustments he could barely pick up the conversation in Orta's apartment. After a while he was sorry that he had.

A girl was there. Orta had a good approach but it was clear that they already knew each other well. Before the direction of events changed there was an intelligent dialogue between them and it seemed that the girl Orta called Denise was at the London School of Economics and that she knew Raul as Anton. They touched on politics here and there and Orta was so rational in his views that it was impossible to equate him with a mass murderer. At times their voices faded out, subdued though their conversation was, he got the gist.

Gibbs huddled down, legs wet and numb, fingers like clutching icicles on the rod. He breathed down into the collar of his topcoat to prevent his vaporised breath from rising and to keep his nose warm. Sitting behind hedges or in ditches listening to conversations in lonely farmhouses had left him almost immune to conditions that would rapidly defeat most others.

When Orta decided they had talked seriously long enough he played some Spanish music. When the music stopped and Orta's voice became a coaxing whisper there was no objection from Denise. After a while Gibbs felt as if he was peeping through a keyhole.

It had been clear, as he listened, that Denise had absolutely no knowledge of Orta's identity. He told her he had come over to Britain as an interpreter, and they had briefly spoken in French. It was abundantly clear that tonight Orta was expecting nobody but Denise, and was in no hurry to see her go.

With the uncomplaining resignation of the professional Gibbs waited. Wasted time was nothing new. The light in Orta's window had been dimmed. Poor Denise, he reflected. Her affection for Orta had come over as distressingly real.

Midnight passed and the girl next door returned. Gibbs pushed himself deep into the shadows as he heard her pick out her footholds down the icy steps to her basement apartment. The key, the door; he breathed again. Dialogue picked up across the street after a long session of silence and passion, and he increased the volume. Denise was getting ready to leave. He stowed away his gear, tried to get life back into feet and legs but dare not stamp them. When the door across the street opened he was ready to move.

The road was otherwise dead at the moment, the only sounds from distant passing cars. Denise shouldn't be too difficult to follow, but he hadn't expected Orta to escort her. For a moment he thought they were about to use a car and was relieved when they didn't. He followed at some distance and on the opposite side of the street. The girl was muffled up in coat and scarf. They were not hurrying, walking as lovers do, arms round waists. Still, Orta would have ears other than for the girl. Gibbs lengthened the gap and kept as near to the railings as the banks of frozen snow would let him.

Orta and Denise did not go far. Two blocks away Orta cuddled Denise in a doorway and after some minutes left alone, retracing his route. Gibbs was already crouched behind a post box, shifting position as Orta drew nearer. Once Orta had turned the corner Gibbs listened to his footsteps then hurried towards Denise's apartment. He couldn't be precisely sure which door it was. There were still a few lights on.

Something touched his leg as he moved. A violently shivering kitten was crouched against the railings. People were bastards. He only came up against the bastards. They formed a great part of his life. Perhaps he was one himself. He scooped up the juddering fur ball which hadn't the strength or desire to resist. The outer fur was frozen into icy spikes. He tucked the kitten into the top of his coat and held it there. There was little of his own body warmth left to get through. He did his routine check once more and set off.

After he arrived back at his room he turned the fire up and placed the kitten in front of it. He warmed some milk, then opened a can of stew. It was some time before the shivering stopped. A while later before the tiger-striped bundle moved cautiously to the saucer and the little pink tongue came out, Gibbs heard what he had been yearning to hear, a faint purr. He stroked the cat as she ate. "It's all right, puss. You're the only friend I've got, too."

Gibbs made himself some hot cocoa and, with the kitten on his lap, listened about himself on the late news. Before he could sleep there was still work to do. The door was already locked. He set to work on suitable hiding places for his gear. It took him some time, after which he made a small dirt box for the kitten and a bed from a blanket.

He was up by seven thirty and was on long distance vigil of Orta's place before nine. The snow had stopped completely and high pressure had opened a sky of the palest blue which let in intense cold. Gibbs could not take the slightest risk and was forced to watch from a corner a good way up the street. Late office workers hurried past him without a glance. Cars, parked like ice chunks, rasped into slow starts and gradually left gaps in the long jawbone of the street.

Orta came down the steps alone at ten thirty carrying a grip in each hand. Head down, he came towards Gibbs and then walked to the next junction. Gibbs rolled round the corner: he was now playing a game that Orta knew well. The question was, was Orta at the moment playing the same game?

Gibbs increased his pace in order to reach the next corner before Orta reached the last one. He turned round it and stopped, listening. He continued down, back-tracking but a block further on. Making use of car wing mirrors, windows, anything that had lost sufficient snow to reflect, he ground to a halt when he realised that Orta had not come his way. He waited a little while then risked sprinting back the way he had come.

Slowing at the corner, rounding it at a walk, breaking into another run as Orta failed to appear, Gibbs realised that he must have continued straight on. He reached the next corner, used the same careful procedure, and once round saw Orta climbing into a cab at the far end of the street T-junctioned by a main road. Gibbs ran to the main road, could see the cab held up at distant lights but there wasn't another in sight. There was no way he could follow, and it looked as if Orta had moved out.

He walked back slowly towards Orta's apartment block. When he reached it he went past giving a quick inspection to the basement across the street. Making up his mind he turned round and mounted the steps. He stood back in the portico still watching the opposite side of the street. Then he turned and tackled the lock.

Entering was no problem, and he climbed up one flight. The house was soundless, as though listening to him. It took time to open Orta's lock. It was a heavy, old-fashioned mortice. When he finally sprung it he had little difficulty releasing the spring lock above it. Plastic calendars were ideal for the job and an alibi in themselves. He went in, closing the door behind him.

A quick search suggested that Orta had decided to move out for some time. There were no clothes in the room. A door led to a bathroom. The bath had been used. The medicine chest over a washbasin was empty but for half a bottle of mouth gargle and some indigestion tablets. Back in the main room the bedclothes had been pulled up roughly. The piano was still there, unplugged.

Gibbs roamed the room, examining the floorboards and pulling back the carpet where he was able. The most likely place seemed to be under the piano. He moved it quite easily, then knelt down and prised up the floorboards. One Sterling sub-machine gun. A Colt automatic pistol. Plastic explosive. A small clock. Some ammunition. A time bomb could be made from what was there. It was the usual collection.

Gibbs put the boards back. Orta clearly worked on the basis of keeping on the move as being his best safety valve. But the arms had been left here for someone else. Gibbs pulled the piano back into place. He was checking its position when something alerted him. He stood still, listening, hearing nothing, but uneasy. It was time to go. He moved towards the door. The key turned as he dived behind the settee. He had heard no one approach. He only knew that the door had been opened, by the faintest of cold draughts. Whoever was there must have been puzzled; the door hadn't been locked.

Badly placed, Gibbs could only listen. The door closed softly: someone was in the room. Gibbs could hear nothing. Cautiously, he pulled out the Browning, eased the safety catch off and, on hands and knees, ventured to the end of the settee. Something was dropped on to the seat. Too light for a body, perhaps a bag. Then he heard the springs of the bed go. Risking a look round the back of the settee he at first saw one very small foot. A woman's foot in flat-heeled shoes of child size. Above, a few inches of dark tights and above them, blue jeans with ragged edges.

He drew back. A woman was evidently sitting cross-legged on the bed, her body leaning away from him so that he had only seen the one supported leg. Whoever it was would seem to be small and slight and incredibly light of foot. He did hear her as she rose from the bed. Her tread as she crossed the room was barely noticeable but enough for him to trace direction. She was moving less cautiously, as if making up her mind that there was no further need for it.

She was roaming the room as if familiarising herself with it. Gibbs changed position according to his interpretation of her faint movements. The bathroom door was opened and he heard running water but before he could move, the tap was turned off again. She lit the fire, the noise of the gas and the small explosion of ignition reaching him quite clearly. He was beginning to feel the discomfort of his position.

The settee moved slightly against him and he guessed that she had sat down again. As he considered what to do he recalled that there was a copper-framed hanging mirror on the opposite wall. He came to the end of the settee and peeped round it. He had to raise his head dangerously high to catch sight of the mirror and when he did he was disappointed to find that its angle was wrong. All he could see was the wall behind him reflected back.

She rose just as he was about to withdraw. He held still. By good fortune she was looking down, and away from him at something on the settee. She was undoing her case, laying clothes down on the seat. He drew his head back carefully, kept close to the back of the settee. As he did this he could now see her profile in the mirror. It was enough to freeze him.

And then she did what all women do with a mirror available. She dropped whatever she was holding and turned to examine herself. She took the few paces necessary to bring her close to the glass and the heat of the gas fire. Beautiful, small boned fingers came up behind her head to pat the cropped, glossy black hair, and Gibbs could see her full face. She must have seen him too but for her preoccupation with herself. Small and slim, she had the narrow, high-cheek-boned features of her race. By no means pretty her features were, nevertheless, finely drawn. Her mouth was grim, her liquid brown eyes with too harsh a sheen, a depth in them that was immediately disturbing. Gibbs drew back with painful slowness, holding his breath, until out of sight. He sank down as if in prayer, head bowed, hands clasped.

Yukari Kumira. There was no doubt. He had studied too many photographs, too many descriptions. She was believed to have died during the Red Army hijack of the plane that had crashed in Malaysia on its approach to Singapore. Everyone on that plane had been killed. No one had discovered the cause of the crash.

Yukari Kumira. She had operated out of Paris once contact had been made with the European groups, but after the Carlos operations there the student areas, once a haven, had become a trap for all terrorists. The Japanese, for ethnic and other reasons, had been forced back into their own hemisphere to operate from there.

So she had not been on the plane. She had a record that equalled Orta's and in many ways – violent, sadistic ways – surpassed it. Another aspect came to mind, a sad, tragic occurrence that had apparently left Kumira unmoved. She came from a cultured family, her father a designer of the finest silks, her mother, always dressed in the old tradition, a beautiful, diminutive and graciously-clad tribute to his skills. After the first sadistic murders perpetrated by Kumira, her father had taken his life after leaving a carefully typed letter to explain to all concerned that he had done so in an attempt to exorcise the shame and the evil she had brought upon his family. He died a brave and honourable man but had left the burden for his wife to carry. She was alive still, now round-shouldered and prematurely aged, her gaze almost always cast down, her ventures beyond the walls of her splendid villa increasingly rare.

At no time had Kumira expressed regret, not even for her mother. Yet both parents had been fundamentally gentle. The only comment to reach the press had come in the form of a sneer. Why was it that so often this small group of ill-balanced violent people so despised the success of their forebears?

Orta, Kumira, Nuzzale: Spaniard, Japanese, Palestinian. All here. For what? And how many others? Widespread contacts like these took time.

He waited because he could do nothing else. He could not be sure that he hadn't been seen and that she was biding her time, lulling him. She was deadly enough. Cramp was creeping along one leg. He tried to stretch it, to press his toes against the floor.

He had to sweat out her unpacking. Fortunately all her breed travelled light. Finally she went where he had been willing her to go, back to the bathroom. He could hear her rustling and he peered quickly round the settee. The bathroom door was ajar and he could see her through the gap, stripped to the waist.

He rose; gun aiming at her rippling back he backed towards the main door. He used peripheral vision to avoid knocking into furniture. His gaze stayed steadily where she must appear on re-entry. Even when he softly turned the handle of the door he did not remove his gaze. He knew about Kumira's snake-like reflexes. He squeezed backwards through the gap he had opened and stepped swiftly through. He was not careless in closing the door behind him. Placing his head against the wall he let his breath escape slowly. His nerves were strung tight.

Gibbs moved for the stairhead as he heard the main door close downstairs. Running footsteps were coming up. He used their sound to cover his race up to the next half landing. The footsteps had slowed, a slight panting of someone out of breath floating up the stairwell.

Whoever it was stopped below him, to rap on the door in the way Nuzzale had done. Gibbs went down a step and leaned over the bannisters. The pack was really gathering. In spite of the heavy weather attire the Italian cut was distinct and so was the hungry, hollowed face of the tall, rangy man at Kumira's door. Mario Picale. His black eyes were like jet beads, with the darting quickness of a bird. So now there were four nationalities. Five including himself. With the new arrival came the tiniest unveiling. Picale was a kidnap specialist. A murderer too. Murder was their badge of rank, the entrée to the deadliest, most exclusive club in the world. But Picale was a mercenary, a man of no known aim except money.

Gibbs sank on to the stairs out of sight while Picale knocked again. This was a strange addition. A contradiction. Big money kidnaps. The door opened below Gibbs and when next he looked Picale had gone. He ran down the stairs light-footed and out into the street. The air hit him in a cold blast. He turned up his collar and walked thoughtfully to the next junction, where he waited.

From time to time he walked away from his observation post, changed it, returned to it. The cold had penetrated his bones and he felt he might wait forever without result. However, about an hour later Picale emerged, now carrying a paper bag. Never was Gibbs so careful in following a man. Forty-five minutes later he believed he knew where Picale was holed. At least in the short term. Orta would have organised an elaborate chain of apartments.

When Gibbs got back to his own apartment he found a small pool on the carpet and the dirt box clean. He wiped up, refilled the kitten's saucer, had a starch-reduced lunch and took the kitten to the nearest frozen park where he let it out on the end of a ball of string. When the kitten had stopped rolling and playing and trying to climb up the string and was feeling the cold again, Gibbs put her back into the top of his coat, sought the nearest telephone booth and rang at a time Bannerman had arranged to be in his office. Gibbs went back home, adjusted the fire, decided what time he would wake then went to sleep on top of the bed. When he woke it was dark and the kitten was curled up on his chest. He put it gently on the bed, then prepared its feed.

He went out again. He did a reverse routine to stave off the boredom of following procedure and picked up the cab after a fifteen-minute walk. It had been crouched in the gutter as if mislaid, flag down, lights off. As Gibbs climbed in, the driver said, "They're overworking you, mate. And everybody's out looking for you. Old Bill's chasing his tail."

Gibbs grinned in the back of the cab. It was the first one for a long time and he supposed the driver felt for him. "I'd better grow a beard."

"Naw. They're expecting yer to do that. Been on the news. Always on the bloody news." He turned suddenly, a smile of satisfaction splitting his face. "I got interviewed, y'know. On telly."

"I know."

"'Ow was I?"

"Looking for an Oscar."

"That bad? They paid me, though. I told 'em: I want paying."

It was silence after that. The driver watched his mirrors while Gibbs sat back resting. They parted two hundred yards from where he thought Denise lived. He had a two-way transmitter with him;

the sound equipment he had left in the cab. He sheltered under the tall portico of a house a few doors down. From the deep shadows he waited and watched.

A girl emerged after more than an hour's wait. It could be any girl, for he'd seen very little of the muffled Denise the previous night. The woollen hat with the bobble looked the same. He had to take a chance. He raised his transmitter. "Stand by." And he crossed the street and followed her at some distance. When he reached the intersection he turned round it, tapped on the cabbie's window and climbed in. "She's gone up to look for a cab. Take it slow."

They crawled along, the girl a lonely shadow until she reached the main street. It was five more minutes before she was able to command a cab and Gibbs's driver slipped round the corner and into the main stream after it. It was only a ten-minute drive to an area where the general decay disappeared. There was a middle-class atmosphere about the place. The street wider, street lamps more modern, nearby shops with windows still alight, fashions more elegant.

They went past as the girl was paying her cabbie off. By the time they had come round the block she had disappeared and her cab had gone.

They pulled in. There was a sparse pedestrian and traffic flow, certainly more active than where Denise lived. Gibbs lowered the window, suffered the cutting air, and with difficulty erected his microphone. It took him time to pick up the girl's voice for he had to cover a variety of windows and listen to fragments of some strange talk. But when he did pick her up he had found Denise and Orta too. He closed down because he knew the form. There were certain luxuries Orta could not discard.

Gibbs sat back, for once relaxed. He tapped on the partition which the driver pulled back. "Home, James."

The driver grinned, "I don't know where home is, mate."

"Drop me where you first picked me up." Luxury stopped a fifteen-minute, cold walk from his door. When he finally climbed wearily up the stairs a shivering, agitated Nuzzale was waiting on the darkened landing outside his room.

"Where have you been? I've been waiting for hours."

"I haven't been out for hours. You should have let me know you were coming." Gibbs didn't want Nuzzale inside: he was too aware of the equipment he was carrying, the telescopic rod fastened under his coat and the battery hanging like lead. Yet it was clear that Nuzzale expected to go in. Gibbs unlocked the door using a flashlight. "Get yourself warm . . ." As Nuzzale went in Gibbs hastily slipped the battery from its waistline hooks and lowered it quickly on its straps, leaving it outside against the wall.

The kitten pounced as soon as he was in and the startled Nuzzale backed into Gibbs who had quickly to turn sideways if the Arab wasn't to feel the hard resistance of light steel.

"Where did you get that animal?"

Gibbs closed the door behind them. "Found it. Afraid it might squeal?" He smiled at his own pun but barely felt like it. Getting rid of Nuzzale was a problem. Gibbs turned the fire up and even to do that he had to be careful how he bent down. Nuzzale stood in front of it. "Where have you been?" he repeated.

"Out," said Gibbs bitingly. "Since when have I had to produce an itinerary?"

Nuzzale was holding his hands out to the gas jets, still shivering. He turned his head, dark eyes brooding. "They are looking for you out there. It is dangerous. And that means to all of us."

Gibbs didn't know what to do about his unbuttoned topcoat. He couldn't take it off but he could hardly keep it on if Nuzzale removed his. "I'm not stupid enough to eat in the West End. Anyway the descriptions of me are useless."

"Once you're linked with the missing S.A.S. officer they will have a perfect description. You of all people, a security man, should know this."

"All right, Mohammed, let's leave it there. Just don't take me for a fool. Do you want some white wine?"

"It's too cold for that."

"Coffee then?"

"Okay. Raul wants you to stay in. That I know. That's why you have the T.V."

Gibbs let it pass. The last thing he wanted was a quarrel, but to display any form of subservience would be a mistake. He started to make the coffee and noticed with dismay that Nuzzale was unbuttoning his coat. The Arab was thawing out too quickly.

"Instant. No fresh beans." he said over his shoulder. Then, as if

81

relenting, "As crazy as it sounds I've been out walking. I'm used to these conditions. Worse. I can't stand gas fires, and the room was closing in."

Nuzzale accepted the offering. He now turned round, his back to the fire, his bony hands behind him. A long scarf drooped under his unbuttoned coat. "We have all suffered it sometime. But always we are careful. Always. Our record speaks for itself."

"Now tell me why you're here," said Gibbs. "Not to drink this stuff at this time of night." He handed over a steaming mug which Nuzzale gripped eagerly, long fingers clutching as the heat reached them.

Nuzzale said, "You say you are used to the conditions but you still have your coat on." The steam from the coffee rose in front of him, distorting nose and lips.

"I didn't say I didn't feel the cold. But I *am* used to it. Sometimes I think it's colder inside. Outside one is on the move." Gibbs joined Nuzzale by the fire, sorry now that he had turned it up so much.

"Raul wants to see us both." Nuzzale placed his mug down on the broad mantelshelf, then at last slipped out of his coat, draping it over the end of Gibbs' bed. Immediately the kitten was up, investigating it, wide eyes and needle claws.

"The sooner the better." Gibbs put down his own coffee, moved over to his bed, played with the kitten for a few seconds while it rolled on its back, paws up at his wrist, claws retracted. He managed to get side on to Nuzzale and was able to grip the rod as he slipped off his topcoat. The rod was supported in a slit in the lining so it would not fall out, but it could appear obviously stiff in taking it off or if he stood badly. Holding the coat up by the collar Gibbs meticulously laid it on the spare bed full length.

Observing this Nuzzale said, "Once a soldier, always a soldier. Neat. Why not hang it up?"

"There's no hanger and the coat is too heavy for the tab. Tell me about the meeting."

"Tomorrow. At nine p.m. At his place."

Gibbs could not be sure that it was not a trap. He was not supposed to know of Orta's new address so it must be the old.

"Just us?" He retrieved his coffee from the mantelshelf.

"You don't ask that sort of question."

"I'm sorry. That it? No more instructions?"

"If there are any we will know tomorrow." Nuzzale was staring over at the bed, fascinated by the antics of the kitten. Gibbs followed his gaze and was horrified. The kitten was on his coat and had found the hard shape of the telescopic rod inside. It was clawing away to get at it and, as it did, the shape of the rod could partially be seen under the material. From the corner of his eye Gibbs saw Nuzzale's expression change, his mug stopped halfway to his lips.

8

GIBBS CALLED OUT, "Christ," put down his coffee and rushed over to the kitten. Keeping his back to Nuzzale he grabbed the kitten under its belly, pulled it up to his chest and with the same hand pulled out his Browning, keeping it close to the kitten. With his free hand he rummaged about the coat, quickly erasing the rod line before delving into one of the pockets.

He was about to step back and turn when Nuzzale was at his elbow saying with cold politeness, "Can I help you?"

Gibbs half turned, softly chiding the cat. He raised his other hand, the Browning hanging on one finger by the trigger guard. "Ever been shot by a cat?" And then, "Do you mind taking that for me?"

Nuzzale took the gun, laid it in his palm before putting it down. "I wondered what he'd found. That could be dangerous."

Still holding the kitten, Gibbs moved away from the bed. "You don't like animals?"

Nuzzale eyed the kitten uncertainly. "I don't understand them. You British are too soft with animals. That could have been nasty."

"The safety catch is on. It just shook me for a moment."

The kitten, still playful, wanted to be put down but Gibbs could not risk it. He stroked it slowly while it tried to devour a finger. Nuzzale kept his distance and finished his coffee. Only then did he show signs of leaving when he put on his coat. As he turned to the door he said politely, "By the way, the hair you attached to the door was unbroken when I arrived." It was a begrudging admission of a security he approved. It meant, too, that he had used a torch.

"I know," said Gibbs just as evenly. "I would have known had anyone been in. There was more than the hair."

Nuzzale raised a brow, then nodded slowly. "Goodnight, Ross."

"'Night, Mohammed. See you tomorrow."

Nuzzale did not reply. He glanced thoughtfully at the kitten before leaving. Gibbs followed him out, and stood in front of the battery as Nuzzale went down the stairs.

★   ★   ★

When Leo Roxberg was called in to see Joe Carlin he expected trouble. A special office had been hastily prepared for Carlin who had arrived from Langley, Virginia that morning. What Roxberg didn't expect was to see Eric Brown with him. He could not recall when a top F.B.I. man had sat behind the same desk as the deputy head of the C.I.A.

It was a long library table with drawers one side and plenty of room for the two chairs which the visitors occupied. They both rose and greeted Roxberg affably enough, shaking hands, getting through the preliminaries before taking their seats again and waving him to a solitary chair facing the table. Roxberg noticed that a new green baize had been fixed to the surface. More important, he had not been informed that Eric Brown had arrived from Washington or even that he was coming.

Carlin said, "Mr. Brown is here because security at home could be involved. This is an issue that might affect us both."

Brown said, "Nasty business. About Paul."

Roxberg had been expecting it. "Here of all places. London. Unbelievable."

"Someone must have known he was coming." Carlin had a reputation for quiet appraisal that invariably sounded like accusation. Somehow this one did too, but Roxberg was too old a hand and had too much to lose to be drawn.

"Certainly someone knew he was here."

"That's not what Joe said, Leo."

It was an old technique and they should know better than to use it on him, but at least they were not blustering with it. "I heard what was said. There's no way I can answer that. If someone knew he was coming then they knew Stateside."

Carlin received the ball back with a faint smile. "We're not trying to trap you, Leo."

Like hell they weren't. "I know that, but you're speaking to the wrong guy. Special Branch are handling it, not me."

Brown shrugged faintly. "We've been with the Yard people, of course. What puzzles them is what puzzles us. How did someone know that Craven would be at that spot at that time of day? Almost as if he set himself up?"

"Craven wasn't exactly quiet. He looked the world in the face and took it on."

"Not recklessly, Leo. Not Paul."

Which was precisely what Roxberg himself had said to Bannerman. "I didn't get as far as meeting Craven while he was here. I doubt he would have gone out of his way to meet me had he survived."

Belatedly Carlin offered Roxberg a cigarette and Brown lit it for him. There were several ashtrays on the baize as if laid out for a party. The two visitors adopted a thoughtful silence. They glanced at each other, an unspoken question springing up between them. Perhaps because Carlin thought it would be more acceptable from him than from Brown, he asked confidingly, "Just what the hell is going on, Leo?"

"I don't know what you mean."

Carlin looked at him. "Don't you find it strange?"

Roxberg kept cool. "I don't know what you're getting at. What's strange?"

"Have you been in touch with the Yard?" shot out Brown quickly.

"Naturally. They haven't come up with anything I consider strange."

"When did you speak to them last?"

"Yesterday."

"We've had words with them this morning. There are certain details we're not happy about. They share our view."

"Nothing's been said to me."

"Well, maybe it cropped up since. But then you obviously had no doubts."

It was an accusation again. Roxberg spread his hands. "What is this? Am I supposed to read between the lines? What's going on?"

Carlin glanced at Brown again. "We've been over here five minutes and you ask us that? Well, let me tell you. There were apparently fifteen bullet holes in poor old Paul. We've seen the medical report. There's nothing wrong with that. Four shots missed him and hit either side of the wall. It was a strange sort of shooting. A kind of patchy grouping with deadly accuracy. There were bullets in both lower legs. Through the throat. In the trunk. Widely scattered areas but beautifully grouped. It was the kind of hit that the organisation dreams about. Yet four shots missed. They weren't in a group like the others; they were scattered like four individual shots, two either side of him. What went wrong with an assassin who knew how to put most of a magazine into a man, separating his groups with a very strange precision? A very cool guy, wouldn't you say?"

"Sure. He'd have been cool enough to do the job at all. Are these your own observations?"

"Not initially. There's a bright boy at the Yard who arrived at it himself. It wasn't an immediate observation but a delayed reaction to it. Understandable with the general shebang of Paul's death, the importance of it, the media, the distractions. First things first. Try to close the net. But this Detective Superintendent . . ." Carlin glanced at a note, "Hayes, went back and thought the angle of the chipped stonework might be strange. It was a personal observation and needed expert ballistic appraisal. The bullets were too deeply embedded into the wall to get out with a knife. They needed chipping or drilling out. This puzzled him too because a sub-machine gun isn't high velocity compared with most rifles. So he sent a ballistic team down. By the time they arrived the wall had already been plastered over. Apparently the managing agents for the block saw bad publicity in the gawping crowds that constantly gathered outside to see the evidence of a killing. There was no reason why they shouldn't have done this. There were plenty of bullets in Paul's body if anyone wanted analysis. Hayes hadn't expected it to be done so soon."

Roxberg was fascinated by all this but it was a deadly fascination. Knowing his clasped hands were far too tightly clutched he tried to ease their pressure before one of the others noticed.

Carlin searched the table as if for a glass of water and seeing none continued, "A small thing like that was not going to stop Hayes. He quickly sorted things out with the agents and had his men drill out the holes." Carlin struck the table flat handed, his gaze coming up swiftly to hold Roxberg's. "Wadderyerknow? No bullets. With a strong scent Hayes gets moving real fast. Through the agents he tracks down the workmen. A souvenir hunter had offered them a fat bribe to chip out the bullets and to sell them to him. No bull. The guys admit it. No one can blame them. No one had told them that they couldn't."

Roxberg was frozen. He said awkwardly. "Any description?"

"Of the souvenir hunter? Oh, sure. It won't help."

It was difficult to speak without swallowing first. "It doesn't really amount to much, does it?" He began to unwind. Slowly. Imperceptibly. The others were watching him too casually. Slightly aggrieved he said, "What's the point of all this?"

"The point is, Leo, that it seems that something queer is going on. We thought you might have heard something as you are head of station here. We know you have a close liaison with George Bannerman. George plays things close to the chest but he might have told you something."

"About what, for Christ's sake? What's it got to do with Bannerman?"

Carlin smiled bleakly. "If you don't know that then it's time you went back home. Bannerman's job was to keep an eye on Paul. He didn't do too well, did he?"

"You mean you're sorry Bannerman's watchdog didn't stop it too? That would have satisfied you?"

Carlin held up placating hands. "Okay. Cool it. We all know that there's no real protection against assassination. We all know that Paul was pig-headed. It's just that there are features here that are – a little unusual, say. It's a view shared by the Yard."

"Where's Craven's body now?" Roxberg already knew, but wasn't sure if they did.

"It's been identified and flown back. He's being cremated. There was no reason for delaying it. Maybe it's already done. Right now it's angles we are looking for. If it weren't for the doctor's report it could almost look as if two gunmen were involved. But all the bullets have been extracted bar one which would have involved a major carve up at the autopsy and there was no reason." Carlin sat back wearily, kneading his eyes, "They all match: nine millimetre. Sub ammo."

Roxberg felt his first relief. "So what's all this crap you've been feeding me?"

"There's no need for that. You know the form. We thought you might have an angle."

"I would have told you. Somebody."

"Yeah. I guess so."

It was a try on. There was something they didn't like that they couldn't put their finger on. They were shaking the rug.

"Is that all you wanted me for?"

They looked at each other again, not really satisfied. Carlin said, "You haven't been over here too long have you, Leo?"

"What's that supposed to mean, Mr. Carlin?" He could not bring himself to say, "sir", but his tone was flatly formal.

"You shouldn't be uptight. You've been long enough at the job. It just occurred to me that you've liaised with George Bannerman so long that you might be working for him without really knowing it."

"If you think that then I *should* be sent back. I would like to think that George and I have a working relationship beneficial to both countries. We haven't lost out. The record will check."

Eric Brown was nodding slowly as if in agreement. He would have no idea of what went on between Bannerman and Roxberg. His interest in this was security.

Carlin on the other hand felt there was something he had missed. He said non-committally, "I know the record, Leo. I have no complaint." Suddenly he smiled. "I guess that's it. You got anything more, Eric?"

Brown shook his head. It was no use taking shadows back to Washington. No one would thank them either for raising dust clouds, especially Craven's relatives. They got hold of something solid or they dropped it. The job of finding Craven's assassin was in other hands.

Carlin said resignedly, "Okay, Leo. No hard feelings. We'll be here for another couple of days."

When Roxberg had gone Brown said quietly, "Your boy seemed agitated."

Carlin nodded, toyed with an ashtray. "I'm not satisfied. Something stinks." He looked sideways at Brown. "I wonder if they've used Paul in some way?"

"How?"

"I don't know. It's a gut feeling."

"I don't see how they can use a guy gunned down in the street. *Unless they did it themselves.*"

They looked at each other uneasily. "They wouldn't go that far.

89

Jesus, it'd be war." Carlin held the ashtray like a steering wheel. The prolonged silence was heavy with unspoken doubt. Eventually Carlin added, "I'm gonna poke around some more. If they're riding us, I'll crucify someone."

Brown couldn't resist a faint smile. "Upset for Paul?"

Carlin didn't rise to it. They were back to inter-force rivalry. No one had liked Craven, including himself.

"I'll just dig until I'm satisfied," was all he rejoined.

*   *   *

Gibbs gave the kitten its run out on the ball of string, took it back and fed it. He didn't let it loose because its original state had distressed him. He turned down the fire and fastened an old fashioned guard round it so that the kitten could not get too near or reach the gas tap. For a reason he could not quite explain he slipped his Browning in the waistband at the small of his back rather than put it in its holster.

At Orta's old apartment he gave the special knock. No one had shown him but they were not naïve enough to expect him not to have noticed. He was scrutinised through the spy hole then let in. Orta greeted him affably. Yukari Kumira viewed him blankly from the settee. Nuzzale lifted a hand. Mario Picale gave a brief nod and then ignored him. The only one to show any sign of interest was the flaxen-haired German who came as a shock for Gibbs to see.

Ludwig Mueller, like all of them, was wanted by almost every European police force. In his late twenties, he was the only one who, in normal circumstances, appeared in any way fanatical. He was a man to keep out of sight for he showed his ruthless feelings all too easily. There was an expression in his eyes which remained, no matter how pleasant he was trying to be. Most people meeting him were apt to move their eyes away. His lank hair needed a wash, his off-white pullover a clean. His trousers were crumpled and greasy, his shoes stout but scuffed. He looked taller than his middle height because of his sparse boniness. Orta apart, it seemed that so often extremism went with a hungry look, as if it fed off nerves which in turn encroached into the flesh. He was scraggy and dirty and had a bad, unhealthy skin. It was difficult to imagine him as a German, normally so clean a race.

Running quickly through his mental computer Gibbs came up

with the answers. Mueller had killed a bodyguard and a policeman in Frankfurt during a kidnap. He was later caught and tried for murder, and sentenced for life. Had killed a warder with a six-inch nail fixed into a piece of wood while working in the carpentry shop. Re-tried, but the outcome was academic and a matter of complete indifference to him. Sprung from prison as part of a deal when his free colleague kidnapped a German judge named Manfred Kemper. He had later been involved in Kurt Vogel's killing. In those days he had worn a beard. An electronics expert. That registered last.

Orta said easily, "Ross, do you know everybody?"

Gibbs took it carefully. "I think I know *of* one or two."

Orta introduced him, first names only. And as he did so Gibbs was wondering why he was the last there. Five minutes early yet still the last. Unless there were others to come, but somehow he thought not.

Orta was saying, "Ross came to us on the highest recommendation. He gunned down that pig, Craven." He laughed and the others showed their satisfaction. It was a bizarre introduction but their pleasure at that claim was deep and immediate. Picale nodded approval; the strange sheen in Kumira's eyes glistened; Mueller's drab face brightened, his mania like a beacon. The only one to show no reaction was Nuzzale. He had heard it all before, and shooting down pigs wasn't real news after twenty-four hours when it should be time to shoot the next one.

Orta took up position on the piano stool to face them. They sat where there was room but kept well separated. Gibbs rested on an arm of the settee a foot or two from Kumira.

Gibbs did not speculate on how they had got past immigration. For people like this it had never been a real problem.

Orta lit a long cheroot, blowing blue-black smoke at the stained ceiling. Carefully he said. "We've had too many failures lately."

Kumira smouldered. Picale looked down at his clasped hands as though bored. Nuzzale was non-committal. All he wanted was violent continuation of his own brand of justice no matter at whose expense.

Mueller was the only one who spoke his mind. He said abruptly in good but clipped English, "There is no point in raising it."

"There is every point," replied Orta easily. "To run from failure is to pretend it never happened. To pretend that is to ignore a

91

remedy. We change our tactic. To teach them a terrible lesson. To leave them in no possible doubt that we always come back; that we are indestructible; that our determination and inventiveness are never-ending." The fervour was powerful. He had a good, resonant voice and he spoke with conviction. If Orta were a fanatical revolutionist he was also a realist. He was a man impossible to understand yet one who, in spite of his horrific record, had his feet firmly on the ground.

He had an instinct for knowing when his audience was captive. Picale had looked up. Mueller had the fire back in his eyes. Nuzzale stared hard. Kumira had toned down to a look of guarded acceptance. Gibbs nodded slowly in approval.

"Mario," continued Orta. "You will have guessed that we have a snatch job. Who is better than you at kidnap? There are complications because there are two, and the jobs are separate but must be co-ordinated. Ross, you have an important part in this. You're English. It is an image we will need."

"Good. Who?"

"At the moment the names are unimportant. Within a day or two you will know. You will take your orders from Mario. There is no one here with more experience of this kind of operation. You understand?"

"Of course."

Orta smiled enigmatically. "This is not a kidnap of anyone important."

Even Picale appeared intrigued at that. And disappointed.

"They are children," added Orta. "A boy of fifteen and a girl of thirteen. Children that no one has ever heard of, nor possibly ever will."

*   *   *

The meeting broke up an hour later with Kumira and Picale staying behind with Orta. Once Orta had released his intriguing time bomb little else had been forthcoming. Picale would contact Gibbs, that was all. There was no knowledge of the main objective. Gibbs dared not push his curiosity too far and the others seemed satisfied. Whether this was because they already knew or were used to the gradual release of information Gibbs did not know. He sensed that they knew more than he did, and it left him feeling insecure.

Nuzzale, Mueller and Gibbs had left at ten minute intervals in that order which made it impossible for Gibbs to follow the German, the only one whose location he did not know. In any event, shortly after Mueller had left a moped had fired outside and Gibbs had accepted defeat. They had drunk wine, Orta had played the piano, they had waited. That was one occupation they all had in common: the waiting game.

Back at his apartment the kitten wanted to play, and for a while Gibbs responded. It helped take his mind off things. He rolled the kitten on to its back, rubbed its chest and said seriously, "I hereby name you Cassandra-Cassiopheia XV. Cassandra because you are clearly the daughter of a king; Cassiopheia because you are most beautiful. Fifteenth to make allowance for the passing of time. Cass for short. Okay?"

He continued to stroke the kitten but grew thoughtful. Was Orta using him in a way dissimilar to the others? He had better watch his back: he did not like being pushed to the fringe of knowledge. He put Cass down, sat at the fold-down table and started to clean the Browning. At least no one had entered the apartment during his absence; but it did not remove the feeling of distrust.

* * *

Raul Orta played a little music until satisfied that Gibbs had gone. He swung off the stool and checked outside the door. The only one left in the room was the present occupier, Kumira.

"What do you think, Yukari?"

"About the Englishman?" She was coiled like a cat on the settee.

"Yes." They had worked together before but had never really been close; just two professionals willing to rely on one another.

"He's not one of us. Do we need him?"

"Yes, we do – or someone like him. He did good work in Ireland. And he killed that pig Craven."

"Then why are you in doubt?"

Orta smiled and returned to the piano stool. "A good question. I agree that he's not one of us. He may find it difficult to shake off his army officer image. If he'd come to us as a toe rag I'd have been more suspicious."

"S.A.S. men are well used to being toe rags."

Orta considered the point while Kumira added, "If you're not sure you should get rid of him."

"We need him first."

"He doesn't know anything?"

"No way. That's how we'll keep him by us."

Kumira uncoiled with satisfaction.

"We'll keep an eye on him. When he was recommended for the job I agreed. But our principals are supplying the money, and it was best not to argue." He considered it. "In fairness he's the man for the job."

"But . . ." added Kumira.

Orta echoed her. "*But*. Don't worry. The first sign we don't like we'll kill him."

Orta rose, retrieved his coat from the closet. "I must go." As he put on his coat he said, "I believe he thinks we're holding back from him. Which may force his hand."

As Orta made no move to the door Kumira said shrewdly, "Something else is on your mind."

Orta inclined his head. He wasn't happy about showing his doubts to Kumira, but she was intelligent and was very much the realist. And it meant he could apportion blame if he shared the load. "There was something strange about the Craven killing."

"You mean Craven's arrival was too convenient?"

"Your French improves all the time."

"You think it was – arranged?"

"I'm checking in the States. I'm sure Craven is dead. There's just something I can't accept."

Kumira pointed to the television. "All phoney? All the reports?"

"I wouldn't put it past them. But no. There's something else."

"Anything definite?"

Orta jerked his head up. "No. But I don't ignore this sort of feeling."

Kumira said slowly "May I fire the shot?"

Orta smiled. "Just one?"

"After he's learnt his lesson."

"After you've had your pleasure, you mean."

"It's the same thing."

"Okay. He's yours if he's anybody's."

9

FRAN CHETFORD HELD on tightly to the railings as she went down the ice-bound steps to the basement apartment. At the bottom she slipped, put her hand against the wall to steady herself, then hammered on the door with a gloved hand.

As soon as Cathy appeared she said, "Why didn't you ring? Come in quick, it's like opening a freezer."

The two girls went into the small hall. Fran took off her heavy woollen gloves. "*That's* why," she said. "I can't press the button with these on, and I wasn't going to take them off." They went into the cosy living room.

Both girls had the attractiveness of youth. In their early twenties, they were clear-skinned and clear-eyed, of similar height and slim build. The differences were mainly of personality and hair colour and style. Cathy, the fairer, had long, straight hair and a soft sensuousness about her that men found provocative. She knew it. Because of this she had a certain defiance in her gaze which could hold them at a distance.

Fran Chetford, raven hair short-cropped, held a lurking sense of humour in brown eyes that at times could be quietly sceptical. She took life with a pinch of salt but believed in enjoying it in her own way. That way was not Cathy's, yet the two girls were good friends, a friendship founded on unvoiced emotions rather than anything they had in common. Fran had the interests of most women – clothes, beauty care – but she expanded well beyond that. People, the arts, antiques, wildlife all interested her, and she had an almost insatiable thirst to learn of anything that was going on. She slipped out of an old musquash coat that she had bought third hand from a friend of a friend and rubbed her arms to get the circulation back.

"I can stretch to British sherry or real ground coffee." Cathy stood in the kitchen doorway.

"Coffee, love. Real ground?"

Cathy winked. "I know that look. Present from a friend."

"Not the interpreter wallah opposite?"

"You know him? He's dishy." Cathy's voice came through the open kitchen door.

Fran had settled herself in front of the fire, skirt pulled down over knee-length boots. "Aren't they all. I've never met him but he knows some of the girls at the London School of Economics. I've seen him with Denise Potter, though."

Cathy came in with the cups. "And?"

"Poor Denise."

They sat down opposite each other and as near to the fire as they could bear, as if they both shared the same circulation problem.

Cathy held her head back, gazing at Fran with amusement. "Why?"

Fran relaxed against the springs of the chair. One brow lifted. "If you turned him over I don't think I'd like what I would see. I've never tried L.S.D. and God forbid that I should, but if I did take a taste of sugar with him in front of me I think he'd turn into a great big slug."

Cathy laughed. "You're always like that about people, Fran. Is that one of your long range shots?"

Fran smiled back. "As I haven't spoken to him it has to be. People interest me as much as men interest Denise. But I suppose I could be wrong. He's probably quite nice."

Cathy was still chuckling. "Want me to introduce you?"

⋆   ⋆   ⋆

Ross Gibbs spent a good deal of time at the apartment waiting for the possibility of a call from Raul Orta or from Picale. He took Cass out in the park, let her run with the string then he let her loose. She was at first bewildered at her freedom, then gambolled off, always looking back to see where he was. Cass found many interests until a dog appeared then she fled back to the security of Gibbs who scooped her up, laughing, and took her back to the apartment.

When it was dark he went round to Orta's old address and gave the special knock. The door opened after the usual scrutiny and Kumira stood there in a pastel green happi-coat over blue jeans. There was no expression but cold enquiry.

"Oh," he said in surprise. "I was looking for Raul."

"Raul has moved out." She did not say where; she did not ask him in.

Someone else was in the room. It was something he knew for a certainty without knowing why. "Do you know where he is?"

"If you do not know that I would wait for *him* to contact *you*."

"If I didn't think it necessary I wouldn't be looking."

"I can't help you." There was no friendliness, just an unspoken desire to be rid of him. It was so pointed that he was left with no alternative other than to leave.

He struck back. "I hope you show more comradeship when we're on a job. I don't much care for your attitude."

"You don't have to. As long as the work is done."

It was then that he saw just half a boot; uncleaned, scuffed but with a solid sole. Ludwig Mueller. The boot pulled back. Gibbs met the girl's agate gaze full on. The eyes were like dark whirlpools, the pupils sucking him in. He nodded, turned away.

"Thanks for the help. I'll let Raul know how co-operative you were."

The door slammed behind him; at least he had annoyed her. To have backed down would have shown weakness. All the same, Mueller's presence worried him. As he went down the stairs he knew that he was being cold shouldered. Like the way they had all met before his arrival the previous night. He felt a tinge of fear.

He stood in the portico for some time with his hands in his pockets before descending the stone steps. It was still freezing. Keeping to the same side of the street he walked along slowly, thoughtfully. He did not cross over; there was always a possibility that Kumira or Mueller might be watching.

He walked perhaps a hundred yards into the suffused light from a pub. It was suddenly attractive – the suggestion of warmth, snatches of laughter. He went in and the heat and smoke-fugged air hit him. It was full and he had to ease his way to the bar. The seats behind a long table against one wall were occupied, as were those at the few smaller tables. By squeezing in he managed to order a pint of bitter and edged his way out again to a comparatively clear space. The noise level was high. Everyone seemed to know everyone else. The local. It accentuated his loneliness.

A girl's voice said, "Did you find Mrs. Mayhew?"

At first he did not know the question had been addressed to him.

97

Someone tugged his coat. "Did you find Mrs. Mayhew?" He looked down. The girl in the basement. Hell. With a woollen cap pulled over her blonde hair. There was an attractive dark girl seated with her. He must momentarily have looked blank. Had he seen her first he would have responded more quickly. "Mrs. –? Oh, Mrs. Mayhew. Yes, I did. Thanks for the directions."

Cathy winked at Fran. "She's probably a wealthy widow."

Gibbs laughed. He hadn't realised that she had seen so much of him in her doorway. He knew he hadn't handled it too well. "She's fat, over fifty with five grown-up kids." Why was he fumbling? The dark haired girl who had said nothing was eyeing him amusedly. To cover himself he offered them drinks, grabbed the first vacated chair and squeezed down at the small table with them.

It did not stop there of course. In the friendly, crowded warmth of the Duck and Drake, Gibbs introduced himself as Tony Brooks, son of a Norfolk farmer, up enjoying a couple of weeks in swinging London during the winter freeze. When else could a farmer get away? He bought them more drinks and snacks and learned their names. Did Cathy know Orta who lived so near to her?

He got to like Fran Chetford. He enjoyed her impish humour, her tantalising expressions, but he was aware, too, that from time to time when she thought he wasn't looking, she was watching him closely. Gibbs knew all the tricks of oblique observation and in a pub there are many aids. It worried him.

He kept them there for two hours and none of them was sorry. It was a lively, banteringly witty session, and he made no attempt to detain them.

Eventually Fran pulled on her gloves. "I must go."

"I'll escort you both. There are muggers about."

"Escorts can be costly."

"Not this one. No strings. Cathy's just round the corner so we can take her first."

Cathy could see that Fran was in no hurry to break off with Gibbs and she was both intrigued and warily pleased. They left together and Gibbs took Cathy down the basement steps. Cathy said nothing until she opened her door. "Fran's a nice girl and a good friend of mine. Look after her."

It was strange how the more promiscuous could feel protective towards those who were not. Friendship was often illogical. As

98

Gibbs briefly reflected on this he re-joined Fran at street level. Without the distraction of Cathy a strangeness sprang up between them as if they had suddenly become shy of each other. They were largely silent as they walked along, small talk becoming unaccountably difficult, and the more so as time passed. The longer it was left the more awkward it became. Gibbs knew why he wanted to see Fran home. Now he wondered whether she had a less obvious reason.

When she slipped and fell into him he grabbed hold of her long enough to steady her. It broke the uncomfortable silence. Fran laughed, still clinging to his sleeve and he was grinning at her once she was safe.

"Hang on," he said. "Put your arm through mine. You'll be perfectly safe."

She accepted the chiding with the double meaning and thrust her arm through his. From then on it was easier, their heavily cloaked bodies softly colliding as they made progress along the slippery surface. Now they were talking easily and about almost everything. The physical contact seemed to break down the barriers and they progressed with the easy familiarity of young lovers rather than strangers. A fence, suddenly erected, had just as suddenly been destroyed.

Fran lived only a few hundred yards away, and it seemed that they were there all too soon. They were laughing over something she had said when she suddenly stopped, pulling him to a halt. "This is it. I almost went past."

"I'll take you up," adding lightly, "The steps. I wasn't inviting myself in."

"I know. It would be difficult. I share. Most of us do." Fran shivered, holding her raised collar.

They mounted the steps to the front door with apparent reluctance. He said, "Do we meet again?"

She stopped to face him before they reached the portico. "Why don't you ask me?"

"Would you believe I've almost forgotten how?" It was true, and came as an unwanted revelation. He had buried himself for months. Any liaison with a girl where he had operated had carried real dangers.

"You're out of practice?" She could not believe it.

He could see that she was smiling under the scarf, gently chiding him. He smiled back. "I really need a refresher course. A book of instructions."

"Is Norfolk full of monasteries then?"

"Okay. May we meet again? Please?"

"I'm still studying and you're the one with all the free time. Can you fit in with me?"

They arranged a meeting for the following evening because she was tied up later in the week. There was still a reluctance to break up. Unexpectedly Fran said hesitantly, "Is there a Mrs. Mayhew?"

"Of course there is. What makes you say that?"

"An impression. Right at the outset."

"You don't believe me, yet you'll date me?"

"People are my hobby. Studying what makes them tick. I thought you were telling a white lie. You seem too basically honest to do it well."

He almost laughed. He was trained to lie. Trained to live a lie. He was doing it right now. It was at rare times like this that he despised himself. "Is it important to you? Does it mean that whatever I say you won't be sure?"

"It could be important *why*. Let's go under the portico. I'm frozen."

They went up the last two steps and huddled in the doorway. Although the conversation had taken a strange turn there was no evident strain between them.

"I don't want to be your hobby, Fran." He was trying to keep it light hearted.

"I don't mean it that way. I was watching you in the Duck and Drake. I was puzzled." Then pulling her scarf down from her mouth she added, "I'm not prying."

"You're not sure of me? What do I have to do to convince you?"

She stared up, hunched and cold and fascinated by him. "Tell the truth."

"You mustn't be so positive. That could be insulting. Nothing I can now say will satisfy you."

"You could tell me to mind my own business. I'm surprised you haven't."

"I don't want to do that. I don't want to offend or hurt you in any way." He gazed at her, liking what he saw, wishing that circumstances were different. He thought it out. At a time like this he was a fool to get involved. It was difficult to understand how it had happened. "You want to cancel the date? There's nothing more I can say."

"I dated you because I want to see you again . . ." She hesitated.

"Go on," he prompted.

"It's just that I thought at times you were somehow concerned about Cathy. Even worried."

"I only met her by accident."

"I know. I'm crazy."

"In the nicest possible way. Tomorrow, then?"

Fran smiled a little uncertainly. "How can I resist? You've become a mystery man."

"Trust your judgement, Fran. So far as I can see it's not at all bad." He moved to the edge of the steps as she threw a farewell barb at him.

"That sounds like self-flattery."

It had not occurred to him. He chuckled as he went down the steps.

★   ★   ★

Gibbs hurried back to his own apartment. It was a long walk and restored his circulation. He had left behind him one of those awkward situations one could never plan against. He thought about Fran all the way back. On the stairs up to his apartment he suddenly remembered Cass. He could hear her at the door.

His early warning system was still untouched but there was a note under the door instructing him to ring a heavily inked number that night without fail. That was another thing. Everyone knew where he was but he was not supposed to know where they were. He gave Cass some more milk and went down to make the call.

Mario Picale answered irritably. "Where you be? I try to get you. I stop by even."

Were they simply trying him out? "If you expect me to stay in, Picale, you make bloody sure I know about it. I'm beginning to think I'm with a bunch of bums. Now, what do you want?"

"All right. All right. I was told you be there."

"I can guess by whom. He should have supplied a ball and chain."

"Please?"

"Forget it. Just tell me what you want."

"Tomorrow. We meet at ten in the morning. Your place. Afternoon we work." Picale hung up. Gibbs went back to his apartment. They were still keeping him at arm's length. He was still not supposed to know where Picale was staying.

Gibbs took Cass out on her ball of string. Tomorrow they would kidnap the children. That was obvious.

10

PICALE WAS THOROUGH. He knew his limitations in English and when he was not sure he went over it again and again. He was like a film director insisting on retakes until everyone got it right. This did not surprise Gibbs. What did surprise him was that Ludwig Mueller arrived with Picale.

Gibbs said, "We'll need disguises."

Picale shot him a contemptuous look. Never tell a specialist his job. The Italian opened a grip and produced an assortment of wigs. Immediately Cass jumped on one and Picale sideswiped her viciously. Only Cass's agility saved her. Gibbs leaned half out of his chair, taut with anger. He raised a fist under Picale's nose. "Do that again, you bastard, and I'll break your jaw."

Mueller took cold interest while the others were locked in visual battle. It was Picale who dropped his gaze first. He had seen something in Gibb's eyes he had not seen before. Strangely it seemed to relieve him, as though he had underestimated Gibbs and had just realised his mistake. He inclined his head and picked up a wig, waving it. "Expensive. Hard to find."

"Right. So be more careful with a cat about."

Picale had brought more than wigs. He had beards, moustaches, cheek pads and tinted spectacles. They sorted themselves out. Mueller's lank hair was so long that Picale insisted that he cut it for the wig to sit better. Mueller fingered his hair almost like a woman; his resentment was clear. But Picale would not back down. After a stream of obscenities and a verbal power struggle between the two Mueller finally agreed to have some hair cut off. Gibbs did it there and then, sensing Mueller's burning anger as he snipped away. All three had now been involved in friction. Gibbs could not believe that it was always like this. Who had nominated them? Who had brought them together?

His fair hair already dyed dark. Gibbs now selected a mousy-coloured wig on which his hat fitted if pulled hard down. He selected a moustache to go with it and slightly darkened glasses. These days some people wore them all the time, even indoors. By strapping a sheet round his body he plumped out his build. The topcoat just fitted.

Picale handed Gibbs a folded card. Gibbs opened it. It was a Metropolitan Police identity card belonging to a Detective Sergeant Ward.

"But he looks nothing like me."

"Your finger . . . thumb, eh? stays over picture. It will be enough. Now, some photographs to look at."

He went over everything once again. If it failed it would not be Picale's fault. Both Gibbs and Mueller felt the burden of recognising it. For Gibbs there was nothing to do but wait. For Mueller and Picale there was the right car to steal. The only reason Picale was not doing that himself was that Mueller was more familiar with London, had spent many of his student days there and was at home with a right-hand drive.

*   *   *

Joe Cosgrave, the chief mechanic, was in the cubicle of an office when Bannerman strolled across the concrete, picking his way carefully through the oil patches and broken exhausts.

"Where's Ben?" As though it was his chief concern.

"I thought it better to call you while he's out, sir."

"Why on earth?" Bannerman was unruffled. Joe emerged from the office, wiping his hands on his stained overalls as if Bannerman was going to ask for a fingernail inspection.

"Over 'ere," he said and led Bannerman to the Jag raised on the ramp. The track rods had been removed. He picked up the knuckle from a nearby bench. "That's it. Fits in there." He pointed a well-greased finger. "Worn. That's what caused the skid."

"Are you sure?" Bannerman stooped over the knuckle, refusing to touch it, making certain that his coat did not brush the bench.

"Put it this way," said Joe. "If this was reported to the police I'm bloody sure that's what they'd think."

"What's your point? The thing is worn. Is that unusual?"

"On a model as recent as this? I'd say so. It doesn't look natural to me."

"What on earth do you mean?"

Joe squirmed. He was always uncomfortable with Bannerman. Bannerman could twist whatever he said inside-out without even trying. Already Joe felt a sense of unnecessary guilt. He knew it and it made no difference. He would fumble, and the longer he spent with Bannerman the worse it would get. The odd thing was that Bannerman could be so bloody superior without being snobby. Almost resignedly, Joe said, "It might've been changed. Or it might've been got at."

"Got at? My dear fellow, you've lost me."

"It would need a microscope and maybe a metallurgist to be sure. It's one or the other."

"You mean it's been tampered with?" Bannerman displayed his incredulity and Joe felt inferiority creeping over him like a cool blast.

Sod it, thought Joe, I know machines. "That's what I mean. That's my job." He pulled out a battered pipe that stank of long-burned tobacco and clamped it in his jaws in quiet defiance.

Bannerman said, "You might as well put that thing down," and as Joe returned the knuckle to the bench, added, "This has obviously been worrying you. Have you thought it through?"

"Wadderyer mean? I'm a mechanic, not Einstein."

"Well, dammit, wasn't this car in for servicing? When I picked it up it had been cleared. Ben will tell you. I checked it out with him. Are you saying it should not have been allowed out?"

Joe had been half expecting it. "We wouldn't 'ave looked for something like that on a minor service. No one had complained of faulty steering. And that includes you, sir. You'd 'ad 'er out before."

"Well then. I didn't notice anything. Should I have done?"

That was the crunch. "It might not have played up."

"You mean I was risking my life? This is serious, Joe. It's your job to notice things like that whatever the servicing. None of us can afford to wear blinkers; we're supposed to be professionals." He turned towards the bench. "So that was the cause," he murmured. "A knuckle, you call it?"

It was known in the department that Bannermann had a hobby; his only outside interest. Few had seen it but it was believed that he had one room devoted to a model train layout. He serviced his own engines. It was far removed from twelve-cylinder cars but it did suggest some mechanical sense. Joe did not believe that Bannerman didn't know a knuckle when he saw one, nor of the danger it could cause. "What shall I do?" he asked bluntly.

Bannerman stepped carefully round a tub of distilled water. He looked around distastefully as if the place needed cleaning. He stepped on to a comparatively clean patch and turned to face Joe slowly. He looked out of place. He gazed at Joe thoughtfully, waited until the mechanic shifted his feet uneasily, before saying, "Are you asking me to help you, Joe?"

Joe took his unlit pipe slowly from his mouth. "Help me clear up the mystery, sir?"

"I think you well know what I mean. Are you asking me to help get you off the hook?"

Something snapped and Joe looked down to find that his pipe stem had broken. For a while he gazed unbelievingly; he'd had that pipe for years. When he spoke, his voice wasn't quite steady; he could not match Bannerman at this game. "I'm not on a hook."

"I think you are. You and Ben."

"I found the bloody thing. I didn't fiddle with it."

"You should have found it earlier. Do you realise that there was an accident through your negligence?"

"That's balls. Its been tinkered with."

"You're more positive than you were a moment ago. You're the expert, Joe. You should know. But if you're right, *when*? I took it out after servicing. It could only have been faulty before it went out."

Joe's heart was sinking. He was losing out. He and Ben toiled long hours and were overworked. They needed at least one extra man. He did not know the answers but he was sure that neither he nor Ben had been negligent. They'd never be able to prove it, for they were the logical patsies like an airline pilot after a crash. He shrugged, stuffed his pipe into his overalls then pulled it out immediately unable to grasp that he had broken it as he stared at the two pieces. "You know it's not our fault," he said flatly.

"My dear Joe, I know no such thing. We don't know whose fault it is. Or, indeed, if it is anybody's. All we know is that the damned thing is worn, that it may have caused the problem. Aren't you making too much of it? Aren't you making life difficult for yourself? Inviting criticism?"

"There was a crash, Mr. Bannerman."

Bannerman expostulated, "Good heavens, Joe, we all know how pushed you are. Put it out of your mind. Isn't it possible under sudden, unexpected strain that a trackrod might break?"

Joe did not miss the fact that Bannerman knew about trackrods but not about knuckles. "You want me to report that?"

"Report what you like. I'm simply trying to help you. Don't mention any of it if you'd rather not. The car skidded. Period."

Joe shook his head slowly. He should have known at the outset. It did not pay to be too conscientious. Not with a slippery bastard like Bannerman. He didn't know who'd been driving and knew better than to ask. He felt a fool.

Bannerman said, "Don't look so damned peeved. You've spoken to me. Good man. That's as far as duty demands."

Joe kicked out moodily at a broken radiator. "Whatever you say, Mr. Bannerman." Thank God Ben was out. It was too humiliating.

Bannerman picked his way towards the door. "Joe," he said, "You really do worry too much." As he neared the door he called back, "I'll buy you a new pipe. A really good briar. I'm sorry about that."

And the bastard will, thought Joe as he gazed up at the raised Jaguar. And it *will* be a bloody good one.

★   ★   ★

Mrs. Phyllis Hatton drove the Escort past the end of the long queue of cars parked outside the school. She had long since given up jockeying for position. It merely meant that young Ginny had about fifty yards or so to walk. She looked back down the line, waved to one or two mothers she knew who had been brave enough to step out of their cars and to wait in the cold outside the school gates. The girls were just coming out: perfect timing. Jim, her husband, would have approved of that. She smiled to herself and leaned sideways so that she could titivate in the central rear-view mirror.

There was the usual noise. Footsteps, running and shouting, mothers calling. The same each day. The chore. She didn't mind: it was too far for Ginny to walk home, and Ginny knew where she always parked. The nearside door opened and Ginny piled in, red cheeks puffed from the bitter wind. About to switch on, Phyllis Hatton saw someone tapping on her window: a pleasant-looking young man in rather dull clothes. He was smiling and holding something up. A card. With his other hand he was signalling her to wind down her window.

She gasped as the air struck her. Now she could see him better. A pleasant smile under the moustache. Open faced. He held out the identity card again. *Police?* "Detective Sergeant Ward, ma'am. Can I have a quick word with you."

"Of course. What about?"

Gibbs put the card away, maintaining his smile. He quickly realised that Mueller or Picale might have frightened the life out of her. "You *are* Mrs. Hatton?"

"Yes. Have I done something wrong?"

Gibbs laughed. "Not at all. It will only take a minute. May I climb in? It's freezing out here." He opened the rear door as she released the catch. She turned in her seat to face him. Ginny seemed more interested in waving to some of her friends.

"What's it about?"

"Your husband. You see that blue car further up? On its own. Would you mind pulling up just behind it? It's a plain police car. My colleagues are there."

Agitated now, Phyllis Hatton exclaimed, "My husband? Jim? He's in New York. Has . . ."

"Nothing to worry about, ma'am, really. It's a trivial thing we can clear up as soon as we reach the police car."

Gibbs sensed her sudden suspicion. She turned to face the front and he briefly caught sight of her face. Her mind was starting to work. He had to stop her quickly.

"Mrs. Hatton, there's something I must show you. Just you. Before you do anything would you mind looking over the back of the seat. Not you, Ginny," he said as the girl turned.

He thought then that Phyllis Hatton was about to jump out. Her hand went quickly up to the door catch but she hesitated. She was worried about Ginny, doubtful that they could get out together. She then knew that the opportunity had gone. Gibbs said quietly, "Just look, ma'am."

She turned round, her face away from Ginny and he could see that she was already scared. She had difficulty in looking down immediately behind the seat and she was twisted awkwardly. Gibbs quelled his emotion as he saw her sudden fear and heard her quick gasp. She was frightened but she did not want to scare her daughter. Gibbs was holding the Browning low down and pointing it towards Ginny. He had shielded it with his free hand so that the girl would not see it if she turned. He moved his free hand so that the mother got a better view.

Phyllis Hatton lost colour. She mutely pleaded with Gibbs through soft, hazel eyes but he could not visibly respond. She turned back, and as Ginny began to turn to stare at Gibbs she put a hand out to stop her.

"What's wrong, Mummy?" Ginny was now bewildered, not understanding the fight her mother was putting up in an effort to control her fear. "Why are your hands shaking?"

"It's all right, dear. Really. It's the cold. Let's drive over to that car there."

"There's nothing to worry about, ma'am, if you do as I say." It was the best he could do but it sounded hackneyed. He had seen so much bloodshed, terror, fear, maiming, death, that he had considered himself virtually immune from being affected by it. But he had seen it in context, in a troubled and divided country where people accepted it as a daily part of life whatever their revulsion to it. Here he was witnessing the sudden and unexpected fear of a young mother, a few years older than himself, for her daughter, in a situation for which she could never have been prepared. He suffered his own disgust behind a stony image and was glad that the disguise hid his shame.

She braked erratically but he knew that it was no trick, she was not thinking that far ahead. She pulled up behind the blue car from which Picale climbed. There was nothing Gibbs could do except to repeat: "It will be all right. Just do what he says and there'll be no problem."

"Why?" she implored. "Why?"

But he could not answer her. Picale was reaching for the rear nearside door and he was unlocking it for him. Picale climbed in and produced a gun. He was not as careful with it as Gibbs had been. Ginny started to cry. Picale chose not to hear. "No problem, eh?"

"None." Gibbs was going to ask Picale to be easy with them and found that he could not. It had to go its course. Already he had stayed too long and Picale was glaring pointedly. Even behind the tinted glasses his stare penetrated.

Gibbs climbed out. There was no way he could reassure Phyllis Hatton or her daughter. He avoided the pleading stare, the half-raised hand. The woman was terror-stricken. It was an effect that Picale would always have on people. As Gibbs climbed out he heard a slap, turned and saw that Picale had struck Ginny hard because she was crying. The mother half screamed and he shut the door hurriedly. It was all a matter of priorities and what his target was. He went forward and joined Mueller, sat next to him in the passenger seat. The German had a satisfied grin, his teeth white and even, showing his only acceptable feature.

"So," he exclaimed. "Now I see your value. Good, Ross. You make a fine policeman." He laughed as he pulled out.

Gibbs half turned to see the other car following them. He wondered what the woman's reaction would be once she realised their direction.

The journey was short, about ten minutes. The rear car dropped behind on Picale's instructions and Gibbs, in the wing mirror, saw it stop. Mueller turned the corner and by now Phyllis Hatton would know precisely where they were going. Mueller pulled up some distance from the boy's private school. It was not big, but had fair-sized playing fields attached to it. They were a little early. The boys turned out that much later.

Gibbs rubbed his hands. He was feeling numb at the monstrosity of what he was doing. He shielded his feelings, glanced at his watch. Mueller did the same. They had synchronised their watches a long time ago.

"It is time," said Mueller. He was moving unemotionally towards the school, his appraisal purely professional. He had kept the engine running to keep the heat up in the car. Gibbs climbed out once more, pulled his collar up, hat down, adjusted the glasses. The first sounds of a school dismissed carried across the quadrangle, spread into the streets. Car doors banged, engines started, more cars arrived.

Gibbs stood back from the waiting group at the gate and moved to the other side of the street. Behind him stretched the massive stone wall of a health farm, its ornate gates further along. Plane trees, starkly stripped, stood like frozen sentinels pleading for relief. The boys came flooding out, many of them muffled, making identification difficult. When they thinned out, Gibbs started to worry, thinking he might have missed the boy. Young Tommy Hatton was old enough, and near enough, to walk home. Gibbs glanced back towards the car and shrugged. Most of the cars had gone; there were only two mothers left shivering at the gates.

Then he saw him, with two other lads. They were sauntering, each carrying a briefcase like young businessmen, sometimes swinging them out like children. The elders with all the time in the world, deep discussion putting all matters to right. One boy climbed into a car, a protesting voice escaping from it. The other two gave casual waves as if not caring if they met again and walked seriously away from the gates in opposite directions.

Gibbs waited for the right opportunity then hurriedly crossed the street. Tommy Hatton seemed not to hear his approach until Gibbs called out behind him. "Tommy Hatton?"

Tommy turned like a young executive, eyes enquiring, face fresh, ridiculously young and vulnerable. Gibbs switched on his smile, produced his identity card and the same hollowed words, "Detective Sergeant Ward, Tommy." He turned to wave Mueller forward. "Your mother's had a slight accident. Nothing too bad, but we'll drive you back to see her."

"Mummy's hurt?" The boy lapsed back into childhood.

"Nothing to worry about. We'll have you home in no time."

The boy saw Mueller approach, glanced up at Gibbs and tried to reconcile the two. The young man took over again. He said, "May I see your identity card again, please?"

"Of course." Gibbs flashed it. "Haven't you seen one before?"

Mueller was pulling in. The bloody fool was grinning.

The boy said, "You had your thumb over the photo."

"Really? Just as well. It's a shocking snap. Like a passport photograph."

"I'd like to see it, though." Authority was overtaking age.

"Sure. Let's get in. Here's the car. Get in the back with me."

"I'd like to see it first." Every precaution his parents had taught him was coming to his aid, plus some he had worked out for himself.

"Here we are. In you go. Be home in a jiff." Gibbs pulled open the rear door.

The boy stood there. "I want to see your photograph."

"And so you shall." Gibbs pulled out the card. "Come on. I'll show you inside if you promise not to laugh."

"Now, please."

Gibbs grabbed at him and the boy ran. Gibbs caught up in a few strides, gripping the boy's arm and swinging him round.

"Tommy, you must see your mother. She needs you."

"I don't believe you." Tommy kicked out hard.

Gibbs took the excruciating blow on the shins because he did not want to hurt the boy. Mueller who had run from the car had no such scruples. As Gibbs caught the other arm with the boy struggling furiously Mueller struck down sidehanded on the boy's raised chin. He hit the nerve on the point and Tommy Hatton collapsed at once.

There was no time. They carried the boy between them and bundled him on to the back seat. Gibbs looked back towards the school. There was a small group of boys talking there, stamping their feet, but incredibly none was looking their way. There were still a few cars but the front one was empty, steamed up windows blocking the views of anyone waiting in the cars behind. Opposite, the blank walls of the health farm were stark and silent.

Gibbs crammed in beside the prostrate boy, pushing him to find room. He looked back as Mueller pulled out. Nothing untoward. The boy's struggle had been brief but it could have been very awkward.

The Hattons lived just a few minutes away, a semi-rural area about twenty-eight miles from central London. Picale's instructions were good. Mueller followed the detailed route, one already rehearsed when he and Picale had picked up the cars. He kept to secondary roads and they met little traffic, in parts none. They drove deeper into the country.

The boy began to stir beside Gibbs, who reluctantly drew his Browning. He made sure the safety catch was on, a precaution Mueller would both despise and suspect if he saw. Tommy Hatton sat up shakily, pale-faced, a hand fingering his jaw. He looked sideways at Gibbs who said for Mueller's benefit, "Don't try anything, Tommy. This is real."

The boy drew away to the corner, as far as he could get from the gun.

Gibbs said, "And don't get your hand anywhere near that door catch. You'll never make it. Understand?"

"Yes, sir." The young voice wavered.

"Just do as you're told and everything will be okay. You'll only come to harm if you play up." It was as far as he could reassure the boy in Mueller's presence. To Mueller the boy stood for privilege, the kind he had experienced himself. He found no strangeness in resenting his own successful father.

"Hit him with the pistol if he moves at all." Mueller could speak like that without the possibility of it being interpreted as bluff. Young Tommy Hatton looked very scared then but there was still a resolution in him that time and familiarity with his situation would aid. At the moment his jaw hurt and he was shocked.

They saw the Hattons' car parked where it should be. It was in a narrow country lane, pulled up in an overtaking bay. The snow was still thick here but hard. Driving would be hazardous nevertheless. Track marks suggested that it had barely been used since the heavy snowfalls. The crunch of their tyres made the occupants of the front car turn round. Gibbs saw the fearful stares of Phyllis Hatton and Ginny – pale, expressive smears through the window. Beneath them the exhaust pumped into the clean air. The boy sat up sharply and Gibbs cautioned him again as they drove past and pulled up in front of the other car.

Mueller turned in his seat to point his gun at the boy. He said nothing. There was no need. Tommy Hatton tried to shrink within himself. Gibbs climbed out, put the Browning in his pocket and kept his grip on it. He went back to the Hattons' car. Ginny was now in the back with Picale. Phyllis Hatton had the driver's window down. Before he could speak she said, "Was that Tommy I saw?" She was on the point of tears and despair was torturing her.

"It was, ma'am. He's okay. Nothing will happen to either of them if you are sensible." Gibbs was speaking the lines because of Picale's difficult English, but the Italian had already induced his brand of fear into them. Phyllis Hatton was not in doubt and she was half scared out of her mind. Yet it was important for her to retain hope, which was another reason the shrewd kidnap specialist was leaving it to Gibbs.

Gibbs went round to the front passenger seat and climbed in. "Wind up your window. Fine. Now listen carefully. Try to concentrate, because the lives of your two children will depend entirely on what you do. This is a political kidnap, Mrs. Hatton. It's important that you know who you're dealing with. You read the papers, watch television. You know that there is no degree of bluff. You deviate by one fraction and you won't see your children again. Do you understand?"

"Yes." White-faced, staring straight ahead, gloved hands gripping the wheel as if to break it.

"Don't cry. You must listen. Don't wonder why you are caught up in a political kidnap. We won't explain. Just accept it."

One gloved hand left the wheel and wiped the eyes. The hand remained over her face.

"Are you listening, Mrs. Hatton?"

She nodded, face still covered.

"We are taking the children. They will be safe. Tell the schools they are sick. Are you clear about this?"

"Yes." It escaped as a sob through the spread fingers.

"Make sure that you are." With Picale present there was no way that Gibbs could soften it. And it was better that he didn't. "We can't stop you going to the police. We can only say that if you do we will kill the children. Bear in mind how much we know about you, to what extent you've already been watched. Not all policemen are honest, Mrs. Hatton. One way or another we will know if you've made contact. Don't bring that additional fear on yourself. *And convince your husband.* That too is imperative."

She was shaking her head now, both hands covering her face. "Why?" She pleaded, "Why?"

Gibbs went on, his voice dry. It was not the first time he had seen mothers cry over their children. The frantic grief was always the same. "Your husband will be back tomorrow. We will contact you then and we will want to speak to him. You understand?"

"Yes." More quietly now. The hands came down and Phyllis Hatton had lost most of her looks during the last few minutes. A condensed privation had aged her prematurely.

In the back, Picale was sitting, gun loose in hand, eyes narrowed and indifferent. He had heard every form of plea, had encountered resolve, fear, cowardice. It was all one, did not touch him at any level. He had no respect for courage and no contempt for terror. He merely had an aim, a job to do. He showed no impatience listening to Gibbs; the Englishman was doing it right. This job had its complications, was not a straightforward snatch and, therefore, could not be hurried. Not this part. The woman had to understand, had to act as they needed her to.

Beside Picale, Ginny sat pale and subdued, a red weal across her face where she had been struck. At the moment she had a child's simple belief that tomorrow would come, but she was concerned for her mother whom she had not seen like this before. She wanted to go to her, yearned for her comfort, but the dark-faced man beside her would hit her again if she tried.

Gibbs added once more, "No police. No school suspicions. And no nonsense with the neighbours. You'll know how to handle them should it arise. Just keep it all to yourself, make sure your husband does the same and you'll all have a big family reunion in just a few days. Okay?"

Picale added flatly, as if it offended his professionalism, "And no money. Not a cent. That's good, eh?"

But all it did was to worry her more, to wonder at the motive.

Gibbs and Picale exchanged glances and Picale opened his door. He got out, pointing the gun at Ginny who suddenly let out a wail and reached for her mother as it finally sank in that they really were being separated. Her mother swung round in an awkward attempt to embrace and to reassure the girl. It was essential technique that they remained separated. Build on the pain of separation from the start.

With one hand Picale pulled the girl roughly, with the other he dug his gun deep into the mother's cheek and screwed it. "Try again, I blow your head off. After I shatter the girl." While the mother pulled her head back from the pain, Gibbs quietly removed the ignition keys. He climbed out. Picale was already dragging the girl towards the other car. He stopped once to strike her very hard to stop her screaming and to warn her mother. Gibbs went round to the driver's door. Phyllis Hatton had already lowered the window to shout hollow words of comfort to Ginny.

Gibbs said quietly, "I'll see that they come to no harm. But for God's sake do what you've been told or you'll regret it for ever."

She peered up through reddened eyes, had noticed the change in his voice. He was trying to tell her something but she was too distressed to grasp it. He was dangling the keys out of reach to mislead Picale and Mueller. He could not wait longer. Rattling the keys he said, "When we move off I'll drop these in the snow. Note the place. Find them and drive back home." Very quickly he added as he began to move away, "Just what does your husband do?" It came out as a whisper.

Surprise showed through her anguish. "He's an airline pilot." She could not believe he did not know.

"A pilot?" He couldn't stay, yet he held there a little longer.

"He's co-pilot on Concorde."

11

GIBBS MOVED AWAY fast, leaving her tearful and uncertain. He couldn't help it. Picale had climbed into the back of the car where brother and sister held hands tightly, so Gibbs sat in front with Mueller. They pulled out slowly and Mueller kept to the crown of the narrow lane. There was a suggestion of tail swing and Mueller kept the speed down.

Gibbs said, "This'll do."

Mueller kept driving. "Too near."

"For God's sake, the woman has to find the keys first. Do you want her to freeze to death? We need her."

Mueller compromised. He went on a little further then stopped. "You are too soft," he accused.

"I'm realistic. We have plenty of time." He lowered the window and peered into the wing mirror. Phyllis Hatton was leaning against the bonnet of the car, clenched hands up to her mouth as though both in prayer and aggression. Gibbs put his arm out and dangled the keys. He saw her push herself away from the car and concentrate. He dropped the keys. "Okay," he said, and Mueller drove off carefully, watching in his mirror the running, slipping advance of the diminishing figure of Phyllis Hatton. When she fell and scrambled forward on her knees he laughed outright and Gibbs almost hit him.

The road got worse but the surface was still packed down. Picale was not disturbed by the occasional skid and Mueller did not complain. The German handled the car well. They reached an intersection and turned on to a main road. Traffic again, but very little, and they travelled only about half a mile before turning off.

A large blue Chrysler was tucked into the recess of a farm gate as though abandoned. Ice had formed in crystals on roof and windows. Mueller got out, started the Chrysler after a couple of attempts, sprayed the ice and scraped it off. They all moved over and got into the second car. Mueller pulled out to face the main road, then parked the first car where the second one had been.

They drove on for another ten miles, deeper into the country, eventually turning off again and finally on to double tracks that looked as if they had been created recently by a tractor. It was bumpy, slippery but negotiable. The small cottage, smoke spiralling from its chimney, appeared as serviceable as the approach to it: rough but adequate. It was isolated and well clear of the main road. Creeper had once grown up its stone walls but now hung in dead tendrils around the lattice windows. Icicles and frozen snow clung to the withered branches, giving them temporary beauty as the winter sun brushed them.

The children, still holding hands, were hustled into the cottage where Kumira waited in front of the fire. Without comment, one at a time, she took the children into a room the others weren't invited into until she had finished.

Once inside, they found brother and sister chained to each side of an old-fashioned double bed. They each had a dilapidated armchair they could reach and they were sitting in them now on Kumira's instructions. They had sufficient freedom of movement to get out of the chairs and on to the bed. An oil stove was the only heater but the walls were thick and the single window boarded up. A hurricane lamp was suspended from a hook in the ceiling. It was neither cold nor warm. There was some benefit from the open fire in the next room. The chains were not sufficiently long to allow the children to reach walls or door. The feet of the bed had been crudely clamped to the rough, uncovered floorboards. Vintage Picale.

Kumira was standing beside Ginny. She smiled at the girl but it was hardly reassuring. The strange sheen that covered her eyes had brightened. She stroked the girl's face with the back of her long fingers and Ginny drew back in fear. Gibbs was alarmed as Kumira then stroked Ginny's hair and the girl still tried to avoid her.

"Leave her alone!" It was Picale. The instruction was not for Ginny's sake; what happened to her did not matter to him. His next words explained his reason. "No compli – no difficulties, eh? Not of any kind. You feed her. You take her to john. That all."

Kumira smouldered, but she backed off. Mueller made it worse by saying in a mock American accent, "You're no Fusako Shigenobu, baby. She knows how to stick to the job."

Kumira went within herself, pulling her slight figure upright, making no comment. Gibbs was relieved he hadn't come into it. It was time to return to London.

There were two small cars already at the cottage, presumably clean. Gibbs drove one of these back with Picale while Mueller took the stolen car which he abandoned after twenty miles. He then rejoined Picale and Gibbs who had been following him. Picale, still in charge, instructed Gibbs to drive to his own apartment, after which Mueller took the wheel. It was going to be difficult to find out where Mueller was staying.

Gibbs was depressed as he went up the stairs. Concern about the Hattons was enough, but as he fed Cass he knew that he should not have entered into a liaison with Fran. It was crazy. Yet as he took Cass for a walk he accepted that it was the only thing that could lift him. It might turn out to be a stupid thing to do but it did not stop him looking forward to it. He dropped Cass back at the apartment and went out to pick up Fran, his mood brighter. She had dressed up for him, all trace of the student image removed. It was a beautiful young lady he escorted down the still iced-up steps. And she produced a smile of appreciation from him that had cut through his stark despondency.

They went to a bistro which Fran recommended, and he could see that she was slightly anxious about the cost to him. "We'll go dutch," she said brightly as the waiter took her coat.

"Sit down and shut up. We farmers are notoriously wealthy." He hoped he had enough on him. Then, "Fran, you look really lovely. You remind me of a life I used to know." It slipped out before he could check it. But it was true. Fran's company was timely but unwise.

"What happened to it?" she asked.

"Happened to what?"

"The life you used to know."

He wondered now if he'd ever lived it. Ordinary, decent people. Comfort. Moments like this. He'd already lied to her. A farmer. The nearest he had been to a farm was with a gun and a galium arsenide laser with opto-electrical linkage to pick up conversations from the vibrations of closed window panes.

He grinned. "I don't talk about it. Too painful."

"You poor thing." And then with perception and a slightly challenging look. "Are you sure it's behind you, Tony?"

Tony. Another lie. He was so at home with her that he'd almost looked over his shoulder to see who Tony was. One lie had to be supported by another. "For tonight it is. It's rather wonderful sitting with you like this. Good food, drink, warmth, and *you*. I should be so lucky."

His obvious sincerity confused her a little. She was well used to a line but this was not one. Her appreciation of last night came back. Where was he out of context? With her? Or with another life she could not visualise?

Watching her changing expression he chided, "You still trying to dissect me?"

"Only because I think you're worth it."

"It would take you years to get to know me. I'm one of the great imponderables."

"What an intriguing challenge." She smiled and added, "How's that for man bait?"

They were probing each other pleasantly, as though the easiness between them was born of an eternity of association, but they should now get down to the serious business of finding out about each other.

It was as enjoyable an evening as Gibbs could remember, and because it was he was forced to consider what he might already have lost. He did not have to ask her if she was happy; he could see that she was, and the ebb and flow of deep pleasure passed between them throughout the meal. It was doubtful if either could have immediately stated what they had eaten during the dinner.

Yet throughout it – the smiles, the laughter, the sharp repartee – Gibbs could not forget the abject despair, the instant ageing process he had seen on Phyllis Hatton's face. He could not force it out completely, not even in Fran's company, and the woman's anguish, with her hands tight on the wheel, came to him in subliminal flashes that sometimes made him hesitate, or stutter, or terminate laughter too soon. Once he caught himself shaking his head quickly to dispel the image in his mind. He noticed Fran's quick expression, the fork half way to her mouth, but her lips had closed over it silently, her gaze thoughtful.

She left comment until after coffee. "You want to come back to my place? Or yours?"

This wasn't like Fran. Not so blatant and certainly not so soon.

He was confused: was there something else behind the invitation?

"Don't look shocked. I'm not an old maid. And I'm not a giveaway either. I thought there might be something you'd like to talk about. There's something on your mind. And let's face it, we are very old friends of twenty-four hours."

"It's a wonderful thought, Fran, but I must make a phone call before ten. Anyway, what about your room-mates?"

"They decided you're acceptable. They've vanished."

"So who told white lies then?"

"That was for self-protection."

"So was mine."

"You can call from my place."

But he couldn't. He was wondering how to put it when she added, "I can disappear while you make it. I won't listen."

He thought about it. "I must pick Cass up first. An abandoned kitten."

Fran laughed. "You don't like leaving it?"

"Not for long periods. Sometimes I can't help it."

They collected Cass and went to Fran's place. She had a comfortably furnished bed-sitter and her own bathroom. The interior of the house had been tastefully modernised. Cass took to her at once, female to female, and they went into the kitchen while Gibbs made his call. It was just after ten. Bannerman came on.

"I've got to meet you." Voice low, glancing towards the closed kitchen door.

"Is that wise?"

"It would be unwise not to."

"Developments?"

"Nasty ones."

"When?"

"Tonight. It can't wait."

"Do you know the Ploughman?"

"If it's the one near me, I know it."

"Half an hour. Outside." Bannerman hung up.

Gibbs stared at the phone, then at the kitchen door. Blast Bannerman. He knocked on the door and went in. Cass was on the kitchen counter lapping milk and Fran had the percolator going. She saw his expression. "Trouble?"

"I'm afraid I won't have time for coffee." He saw her undisguised disappointment and said softly. "That's how it is with farmers. Turning out in the middle of the night."

"You have to meet someone? Now?" The percolator began to pop beside her.

"It's my own fault. I knew this could happen but not so quickly. I really believed I had time in hand."

"Is it about what's been worrying you tonight?"

"Don't ask, Fran. I can't answer you."

"I see." She glanced down at Cass, stroked the little head. "And you'd rather I kept this to myself."

"You're a good girl."

"You want me to hang on to Cass until tomorrow? I can drop her in or you can pick her up."

"Thanks, Fran. I'll call you." He went back and made a note of the number then came back to the kitchen doorway. For a moment they just looked at each other then he came forward, held her arms in a grip that must have hurt her and kissed her hard. He stepped back still holding her. "I'm sorry. I told you I'm out of practice. Maybe I'd better get that book of instructions."

"A refresher course, you called it last night. Are you apologising for kissing me or for forgetting the technique?" She kissed him back lightly, warmly. "If the latter, forget the book of instructions. I think I can help."

He went awkwardly to the door, the only time during the evening when he was not sure of himself.

*   *   *

Bannerman had not known where Gibbs had telephoned from, and was annoyed when he failed to appear outside the Ploughman on time. He told Ted his driver, to go round the block, but there was a limit to the number of times he was willing to permit this. Finally he found a dark corner from where he could watch the pub from the comfort of the taxi. When Gibbs arrived, hunched and hurrying, Bannerman tapped the screen with his umbrella and Ted flashed his lights.

Gibbs climbed in panting, whipped off his hat and sat back on the leather. "You didn't give me enough time," he accused, before Bannerman could complain. The engine was running softly, and the welcome heat creeping up Gibbs's legs.

"Help yourself to a brandy," said Bannerman, detecting the other man's mood.

Gibbs knew where it was. He groped in the darkness and poured himself a sizeable slug. As he sipped the brandy Bannerman said, "This is risky, Ross. I trust you weren't followed."

"On a night like this? Deserted streets. Ice. I'd have heard a sparrow move."

"Why so tetchy?"

"I don't like silly bloody questions. We did a snatch job this afternoon. Two kids. Tommy and Ginny Hatton. Fifteen and thirteen. I ask you. Mueller, Kumira as housekeeper, master-minded by Mario Picale, group control Raul Orta which you already know."

"Purpose?"

"I don't know. Their father is a co-pilot on the Concorde flight."

"Which route?"

"As he's in New York at the moment, presumably transatlantic. But I don't know. There are other Concorde runs. They might switch the pilots about."

"Co-pilot? What on earth for?"

"I don't know that either. Orta or perhaps all of them still aren't sure of me. They believe I killed Craven but somehow I'm the wrong image. It could be the S.A.S. tag. They've used me. The way it was played this afternoon they couldn't have done it without me, but they're still keeping things back." He turned to Bannerman in the darkness, "Look, this thing is going to blow in a few days. Orta said weeks, but I don't think they'd keep the kids a moment longer than necessary."

"Will the children be released?"

Consideration from Bannerman? "I have to believe it or I would have opted out, but I may be kidding myself."

"They could identify their captors if they're released."

Gibbs thought Bannerman must have lost his senses. "People like Mueller don't worry about things like that. They're already wanted a dozen times over. They thrive on the fear their reputation brings. If they kill them it will be out of hand."

"I think you're right. I don't like it."

"You should have played my part. The mother's in a hell of a state."

"I dare say. There's nothing we can do to reassure her. Nothing we dare do."

"I know where the kids are."

Bannerman said, "Let me think for a while. Co-pilot. Now that *is* odd. They haven't done this before." He stayed quiet for a while, giving Gibbs time to enjoy his drink.

When Bannerman stirred again Gibbs asked, "Any repercussions your end over Craven?"

Bannerman said, "None that I know of."

"The Americans haven't kicked up?"

"Apart from Leo Roxberg they don't know what we've done."

"Won't Leo tell them?"

"He had no love for Craven. Anyway, he's left it far too late."

"We can't leave the kids at risk. I'll have to start the ball rolling. It may already be too late. I can't trace Mueller, but he's the only one. Four out of five can't be bad."

"There may be others you don't know about. Orta may have reserves up his sleeves. That's why I'm concerned about meeting like this."

"The four are all top names. The very top. It would knock a tremendous hole in the morale of the remainder."

"No. It would incense them. Fanatics are more in fear of ridicule from each other than of death. Destroying them is the only solution. I would like to get more than four."

"Play it by the book and you won't get that many."

"I know. There can be no rules for people like them. There is nothing they understand outside their own fanaticism."

"You're holding out for one man. Mueller."

"He's a very important one."

Gibbs was becoming angry. "You're getting greedy. The Hatton children are on the spot. Something will pop and you'll be left empty-handed. Meanwhile I'm risking my neck."

Gibbs saw the pale shadow of Bannerman's face turn towards him. Bannerman said, "I'm not unmindful of what you're doing, but the timing is all wrong. There's so much missing. Can't you pick anything up?"

"Orta has been with a girl the two times I've tried the mike. There've only been two effective meetings, the one with Orta and then with Picale today. The rest have been getting together somehow, but I don't know where. I've got to rely on my judgement, play it as I see it. They're not idiots."

Bannerman made up his mind. "All right. I'll action it. I just hope you're right."

Gibbs finished his drink, groped to return the glass. "So do I. But if we get them they can't do what they came to do."

"I wonder."

Gibbs pulled the door catch, took one last look at the faint smudge of Bannerman. "I'll need red hot back-up."

"As long as you can make contact you'll have it." Bannerman reached for the telephone.

"It's easier now I have my own pad."

Bannerman nodded sagely. "For your own sake I've had to thin the ground around you. Back-up has been pushed out to long field. You'll need help to take Orta."

"I can cope with him on my own."

"Possibly. But I don't intend that you should. This isn't something you must prove personally. Radio as soon as you have him in your sights. This is too important for games, Ross."

"I know." Gibbs thought again of the Hatton children.

Bannerman patted Gibbs's shoulder. "I know what's worrying you. As long as we take them out does it really matter?"

Gibbs didn't reply. It mattered to both of them.

"I'll see what can be squeezed from Orta."

Gibbs nodded, climbed out and disappeared into the darkness. He called Fran from the first call-box he found. It was a little time before she answered and he was immediately apologetic. "I hope I didn't rake you from bed. I'm sorry."

"I was watching the box. It's all right. Really."

"I don't know when I can see you next. I'm talking in days, not weeks. Can you bear with me for that long?"

"The meeting didn't go too well?"

"No comment. Would you hold Cass for a couple of days?"

"You know I will. Tony, you're not . . ."

"No, I'm not. Nothing criminal. I promise."

"I will see you again?"

"It's important?"

"To you too, I hope. Yes, it's become important. I know it's crazy after so little time."

"No, it's not." He paused, searching for the right words. "Fran, there's not much else I can say. Try to trust me. Even if it's difficult. Hang on for a bit, anyway."

"Is this how it will be? Always?"

"A few days will see it over." If he was still alive.

* * *

He went back to his apartment and noticed, under torchlight, that his warning system was missing. Someone was either inside or had been inside.

He drew his Browning, never without it now. Standing back against the wall he turned the key slowly. The door swung; nothing happened. There was a reflection from the fire. He groped for the light switch, hooking his hand round. The light blazed out across the landing but he stayed by the wall. There was no sound from the room. Lying flat he edged forward, gun out. A clear view revealed that the second bed had been made up, the blankets thrown back as if someone had hastily climbed out.

Gibbs pulled back, moved to the other side of the door. On his knees he peered through the crack between the hinges. He could just see part of Nuzzale's head, the dark eyes watching the door. The Arab was crouched behind Gibbs's bed, gun hand resting on the cover. Gibbs spoke through the crack. "What are you going to do? Blow my head off as I come through?"

"That you, Ross?"

"Who the hell do you think it is?"

Nuzzale rose from behind the bed and lowered his gun. Gibbs rolled round the door, taking no chances. Nuzzale stood a little sheepishly in thick, striped pyjamas. The room was too warm. The fire could only recently have been turned down.

"What the hell are you doing here, Mohammed?"

"Raul sent me. You weren't here. I let myself in."

"Your key just happened to fit?" Gibbs was angry and worried.

"Raul gave me one."

"It's my room, and I don't want you here."

"It doesn't matter what you want. It's a matter of security. Where have you been?"

"Mind your own bloody business. Is that why Raul sent you? To find out what I do with my spare time?"

"For someone wanted for murder you take a lot of risks, and that can affect all of us."

"I know what I'm doing." Gibbs went further into the room. Had Nuzzale found anything? The telescopic rod for his listening gear was hanging down, attached to the side hem of the heavy curtains. The heavy battery was up-ended on the bookshelf with the covers of an old volume of *London Crime Stories* round it. The two-way radio was hooked under the pelmet. He needed all these things right now.

Nuzzale had no intention of moving. And Gibbs didn't want a physical confrontation yet. It was a bitter blow. He had to go through with the arrangement with Bannerman but he was now severely handicapped. He shrugged carelessly. "All right, Mohammed. You've moved in. I'm moving out. For tonight, anyway. I'll see you in the morning."

"Where will you be?"

Gibbs grinned. "Nor far. Where I wanted to be anyway. You've made up my mind for me."

"All you westerners think of is women."

"Do you Arabs think only of men?"

Nuzzale's eyes blazed and he half raised his gun but Gibbs still had him covered. "Don't hand it out if you can't take it back, Mohammed. I couldn't sleep in a room this hot anyway. Cheers." He closed the door and went down the stairs. He hadn't expected it and it wasn't good. He went to Orta's new apartment, walking fast and silently.

The street was deserted. Even the cats had faded into corners for warmth. The street lamps were dull under a moonglow. A dead world, the air so still that tissue paper failed to stir in the gutter. He crossed the street to look up at Orta's darkened window then walked back and mounted the steps. It was uncanny how completely still the whole street had become. Almost all lights were off both sides. It was now half past midnight. Gibbs worked on the front door lock. A heavy set of tumblers sprang quite loudly and he waited before pushing the door.

The hall light was off, and he had to use his flashlight. An old-fashioned grate was at one side but both hall and stairs were well carpeted. The place seemed cared for. Gibbs climbed the stairs quickly. The wood groaned as the temperature dropped. On the second floor he stopped to examine two doors. Which was Orta's? As he ran his beam down the frames he was satisfied that they both were. On each door a broken match-end had been rammed between door and frame quite high up. Gibbs measured the distance from the top by hand spanning. When he looked closer he found another very close to the bottom which could easily be missed. On the hinge side of each door, supported by the central hinge, a piece of paper had been pushed through that would indent when the door was opened. Only the closest scrutiny revealed it. So Orta was cautious, as he would expect, but it meant he was out. Gibbs held the flashlight in his mouth and worked on the lock.

He picked out the piece of paper with the tip of a penknife and a plastic calendar. He held the small piece of paper between finger and thumb as he opened the door. Before entering he retrieved the two tiny match stalks and slipped them in his pocket. Once in, he laid the piece of paper flat on a solitary rosewood table and placed a coin on it to prevent it from moving.

In the limited light the search was also restricted. He had no idea whether Orta would be back, but had to assume that he would be. For that reason he had not quite closed the door so that he might hear any approach.

Orta was still living in comparative luxury compared to the others. His leadership and influence were marked by the comfort of the room and adjoining bath and kitchenette.

Gibbs did not waste time searching for arms. They would be there somewhere, and there was no time to lift floorboards. Instead he searched for any scrap of paper, any form of note that might give an indication of Orta's operational plan. Finding two newspapers he laid them on the table, turned them page by page under the torchlight, searching for notes in the margins, words that might have been underlined. All he found was that Orta did the cross-words. They were incomplete but both had been attempted. Something caught his eye, recognition of an abbreviated word, and he had found in the squares the condensed addresses of the two schools they had visited that day. Had he not already known of them, the shortened versions, a kind of rough phonetical code, would have passed him by. Even Orta did not have an infallible memory. He put the papers back as he had found them.

Encouraged, he searched a bureau bookcase but found nothing of interest except some airline brochures. He opened the small refrigerator in the kitchenette, examined bottles, jars. He searched the bread bin, the half loaf inside it; surprisingly stale, when he probed it contained a small automatic which must have been rammed in when the loaf was fresh. He did not extract it. Orta had saved his life before at the cost of others by having a gun in an unlikely place. It was a standard lifeline for him.

Gibbs glanced at his watch. One thirty. He was more than pushing his luck. Back in the living room he found a small accordion strapped up. It seemed that Orta had to have music available. Gibbs undid the strap, slowly pulled the accordion open. A note fell out from the concertinered section. Times, using an international twenty-four hour system, but so scattered and so many as to be meaningless. Notes on road routes. He studied them carefully. Most of the trunk roads numbered they had used today to the cottage. He tried to memorise the others without seeing a significance. He simply had the feeling that he was trying to remember the past instead of having a glimpse into the future. With great care he replaced the note into the fold he thought it had fallen from, and very slowly compressed the accordion again. A faint hiss of air like escaping gas but no music. He strapped it up again.

For a few seconds he remained crouched on the floor, sweeping the beam round, disappointed and vaguely thinking that he needed new batteries. Where was Orta? It came back to him again and again. The man was so elusive, seemingly constantly on the move. Gibbs was convinced that Orta was too good an organiser not to be available if wanted. So when out he would almost certainly be on business.

Gibbs stood up with the feeling that he had missed something. Yet it would take hours to search the apartment properly. He made sure everything was as he had found it, moved the accordion fractionally where it crossed the carpet when it had not before. Orta would notice something as minute as that; would even have set it up.

Almost two. There was a kind of recklessness about Gibbs as he moved to the telephone, as though he was willing Orta to find him there.

Without his two-way radio he'd have to phone, and he'd seen no kiosk en route. The line was dead. He followed the cord and found a hanging jack plug. Where was the point? He had started to look, not finding it in the more obvious places, when he heard a car turn the corner and slow. He picked up the coin and the piece of paper, went quickly out on to the landing and listened for the heartbeat of the big house. He thought he heard the car move on.

He closed the door and had far more difficulty in locking it than he had in springing it. He simply worked patiently away. If the hall light came on he would go up the stairs. He slipped the paper back above the hinge, careful to get it right in. Then he replaced the broken match sticks.

With the hall still in darkness Gibbs went down the stairs still using the fading flashlight. He slipped through the door. The car had either disgorged its passengers or continued on. He relocked the main door after a quick but thorough survey of the street which he then crossed in a silent, crouched run. He took up position in the doorway opposite.

He wanted to stamp his feet but dared not. Taking off his mittens he held on to his Browning. He had never been able to handle a gun with any form of gloves on. His hands were quickly frozen but he would rather suffer it.

He slipped the Browning in his topcoat pocket, safety catch off, forefinger along the trigger guard. The wait might be abortive. So many of them were. Both cold and tired he conditioned himself for a long spell.

Half an hour later he pulled himself from a semi-torpor and his ears pricked up. A car. And it was near. It pulled into the street on dipped headlights and cruised slowly, tyres cracking the odd ice patch. Gibbs pushed himself further into the doorway. A small Volkswagen like a mechanical bug, scuttled into the gutter. As it pulled into a gap past Orta's place, the crunch of piled frozen snow was quite loud. The engine was switched off, the offside door opene.

The first sign Gibbs had of the driver was the diaphanous veil of breath steaming above the car. The driver locked up. He surveyed the street, even the line of doorways where Gibbs was waiting: Orta. Gibbs kept his own breathing very shallow. Orta moved towards his apartment and Gibbs moved after him.

12

UNDER COVER OF Orta's own footsteps Gibbs went down the steps and on to the street, his gun drawn. Both men were clearly visible, the mooncasts of their shadows distinct and separate. Gibbs had to make up ground without Orta hearing. He lengthened his stride, still to match the timing of Orta's. It would be better to reach Orta before he mounted the steps.

He ran the last few feet as Orta was fumbling for his keys. At the last moment Orta heard him, just the faintest sounds. Gibbs anticipated simultaneously and came on Orta's blind side as he turned.

"Don't move, Raul, or I'll blow a bloody big hole right through you."

But Orta had been in a similar situation too many times. He started with one tremendous advantage. He had absolutely no inhibitions about firing and killing. It gave him a reflex advantage. He simply dropped at Gibb's feet in a shapeless bundle which unwound as soon as it was down. He threw Gibbs in a scissors and fired at the same time.

For Gibbs, trained to the shackling conditions of firing only when fired upon, another set of reflexes were honed. The two men were fighting their own separate wars in the way each was trained. Gibbs wanted Orta alive. Orta wanted Gibbs dead: as soon as possible.

Gibbs felt the scissors rolled quickly as he fell. He didn't feel the wind of Orta's bullet but he heard it and knew that the roll had saved him. He continued to roll as he hit the street and ice ricocheted into his face as Orta's second shot split an ice pack near him. The slivers hit him like needles but he was now behind a car and Orta had to come for him or be contained. He vaguely heard the tear of metal as the shot finished in someone's car.

It was a strange scene on a stark, freezing night under crisp moonlight which reflected prismatically from the crystals spreading on the tops of cars. The two shots had come from a small calibre gun and had sounded like wood cracking. The only sign of life was the two men moving like crouching animals. They were almost like boys playing a game, were it not for the two guns each so expertly held, and the grim, relentless expressions of the two men who held them and who now stalked each other.

Orta had no criticism of his own reflexes; he was annoyed, though, that Gibbs had matched them. It should have been over. There was the danger of the shots being heard. He had to draw Gibbs out and he tried the baiting game. Soft whispers as he tried to judge just where Gibbs was behind the car, or was it now another car: "They didn't teach you too well at Hereford, Ross. You know the trouble? You should have shot me. But it's not British to shoot someone in the back, by jove. Or perhaps you must not shoot me at all. Not done, old boy." All the time he was listening closely above the low cadence of his own voice. He moved slightly to his left: "The only way you'll get me is to kill me. You know that, don't you? And, Ross, if they won't let you kill me I must kill you. You know that too, eh! One of us won't see the dawn."

But Gibbs was now playing a game he knew all too well. He gave Orta no prizes for recognising the restrictions placed on him. He, too, was annoyed that he hadn't settled it at the outset. He listened to Orta's voice, moved two cars down until he had difficulty in picking up the words. The sound still carried like an oscillating sigh. Orta could be musical even in whisper. Gibbs stopped and listened. His hand was welded to the Browning. He reached for a handful of snow from where it had been pushed back into heaps. His hand was so cold he hardly felt it. The snow was hard, almost crystallized. He lobbed it like a grenade and it landed with a thump on a car roof.

Orta was too old a hand at the game of survival. The snowball landed quite near him but did not represent the true sound of movement. It helped him marginally. He considered from the way it fell that Gibbs was further down the street than he had calculated. He moved down the row very slowly on the street side. He was virtually crawling, knowing that his head shadow might be seen through the frost-covered glass. He was breathing low and occasionally into his free hand to stop the vapour rising.

All the time Gibbs was moving further down the line, away from

Orta who had far too much to lose not to follow. One by one he tested the car doors. He stopped, glancing up at the roof of one. He depressed the door catch. There was sufficent give in it to suggest that it was unlocked but it seemed to be frozen. He waited, listened, slipped the Browning into his waistband, then used full pressure, one thumb on top of the other. The lock released but with a loud click.

He worked quickly then. Opening the door was a reasonably silent operation. It was not his intention to get into the car. Instead he stood on the seat, hefted one leg on to the roof-rack and pulled himself up as quietly as he could. But the conditions were against him. The heavy clothes dragged, his hands were numb and the roof-rack was ice-encrusted. There were only seconds, if that. He gripped the rack as if it was a warm towel rail, no hesitation, one sweep of movement. As soon as he was lying flat he reached down to close the door. There was a soft click. Quickly he craned his neck round to watch the results.

Orta came as a suggestion of shadow and movement. Gibbs could see odd glimpses and patches as Orta moved more rapidly, then ducked between two cars and Gibbs lost sight of the fragmentations.

Orta had heard the car door open, not loudly or even distinctly, but enough to identify the sound. His first interest was to locate it and for this he had to remain still. Then came other sounds. Scraping. A foot against metal. By straining hard he then heard the car door being closed and he moved fast down the line car by car, as low as he could get.

On his knees now, he ducked between two cars, came round almost on his belly. He examined the line of doors. He edged along on elbows and feet and saw the crack of a door not quite closed. He crawled slightly past it. Gibbs would be in there.

Orta, facing the front of the car but with his body back from the door, had his head almost level with the base of the door. He reached up with his left hand, depressed the catch Gibbs had loosened, pulled the door open and fired in one movement. The bullet missed the windscreen by a fraction and lodged high in the dashboard. At once he drew back on realising Gibbs wasn't there. His mistake created his first fluster.

Still crouched, he swung round to meet the danger and found the

133

street empty. Orta's breathing became a little heavy. He had been deceived and he did not like it.

Orta was now the more dangerous because he had been out-witted. That shot should have taken Gibbs; he would now have to fire again, and somewhere along the line these shots would penetrate someone's sleep. For the moment he was reluctant to move. He scanned up and down the street, made sure the back of the car was empty, looked up at the line of car roofs but was too near and too low to see Gibbs, who had rolled slightly back. Had Orta then gone to the end of the car he would have seen Gibbs's feet. He did not. He sensed a trap, felt it all around him. He had four shots left. The reflection undermined him; he could not recall when he had needed more than one shot to kill a man.

Holding on to the still opened car door he tried to think it out but pushed himself a little too fast. He pulled himself up slowly on the door, ready to jump into the gap between two cars.

Gibbs, with horror, could now see Orta's head clearly but he was standing too far away. It only needed Orta to look at the roof-rack instead of the shadows around him and he could not possibly miss Gibbs. Although Gibbs had his Browning levelled at Orta's head, Orta now knew that Gibbs would only fire in retaliation. Retaliation against Orta would always be too late.

Orta seemed to make up his mind. He pushed the car door and in so doing stepped nearer the car. Gibbs swung down with his Browning.

Even then Orta received a warning in the time it took the gun to reach him. He swayed away but could not completely avoid the blow. Falling back against the railings he clutched his head, dazed. Orta was still holding his gun, at the moment covering his face, and as Gibbs swung down from the roof-rack, incredibly it came down unnervingly towards Gibbs while Orta's eyes were still half-closed. Gibbs spun sideways and brought the Browning crash-ing down on the other man's wrist.

Orta, too, however was protected by heavy clothing. The blow loosened the gun, but the pain injected quick reflex action from Orta, who now shrugged off the effect of the head blow with an animal instinct for survival. There was no one who could take him. He kicked out viciously and Gibbs's gun went flying. Gibbs dived back and smashed Orta's gun hand against the railings: at last the gun dropped to the road. They locked, now both unarmed. Both men were impeded by their clothes, both produced the extra strength to overcome it.

The fight that followed was savage, violent and remarkably silent. It was a battle where there were no rules other than to destroy the enemy. Every dirty trick ever taught was brought into play and only the fact of the men being so well-covered prolonged it when it must surely have finished quickly for one or the other. For every move there was a counter, and they had both been through the whole gambit of training. How many ways to kill a man and what to do if he tries it on you.

The cold had slowed reactions but the blood flowed just the same: it trickled down scraped shins, from noses and eyes and grappling hands. It was a fight full of hate, of pent-up feelings and the sheer need to survive. Both men had too much to lose and too much to gain to allow the other to be victor. And yet one of them had to be.

Fitness slowly resolved it. Gibbs had kept in condition and Orta had not. They had rolled in the street, struck cars, rolled back again, grappled, risen again and sank to their knees in strain and desperation. They fell back against the railings and Orta took them on his back. As he gasped, Gibbs released him, stepped back with a speed Orta had now lost and kicked hard. Orta convulsed with pain, Gibbs flat-handed him under his nose as the head came down. Orta arched back, his head struck the railings and Gibbs closed in, grabbed the hair and made sure the head struck a second time.

It was over. Gibbs was not counting on how long. While Orta lay crumpled, Gibbs whipped out cord and quickly tied his opponent's hands behind his back. Orta kicked feebly as Gibbs tied his ankles; it was an unconscious reflex action and it was doubtful if he knew what he was doing. A sticker across the thick and bloodied lips and that was it.

Gibbs staggered to his feet, holding on to the railings for support. He let his breath go and wiped his face with the flat of his hand. There was blood all over it. Discipline took a hand. Clear up. It took him a little while to find the two guns. Orta was already struggling, but ineffectively. Gibbs stared round at the blank, silent windows and was suddenly sick. He gripped the railings with both hands and waited until the shaking had stopped. The spasm weakened him, and he needed to lean against the railings to stay on his feet.

He had to move. After the inertia following the tremendous struggle he was feeling the cold more than ever. He shivered and made the effort that could no longer be delayed. Clumsily he searched Orta's outer pockets. No keys. He tried to remember. Orta had his keys in his hand when he had first abortively attacked him. Gibbs moved up the street towards the apartment. He was lucky. The keys sparkled under a street lamp, the black tag clear against the packed snow. Time for a little luck was well overdue, he thought to himself. He picked up the keys and opened Orta's car doors.

He returned to his captive. Orta, grazed and bleeding, was trying to push himself up against the railings. Gibbs said as a back-handed compliment, "The K.G.B. must have put a steel plate in your head while they had you."

He went to grip Orta by the collar and Orta tried to crush Gibb's hand against the railings with his head, and almost knocked himself out again as Gibbs snatched his hand away. He pulled Orta along by the collar. The terrorist fought to the last. He dragged his heels, deadened his weight, kicked out with bound feet and struggled furiously as Gibbs tried to get him into the car. Finally, a weary Gibbs lost his temper and hit Orta hard on the jaw almost breaking his hand, the bones brittle with cold. What was a little more pain? His body was wracked with it. He bundled Orta into the back seat, uncaring how he rested, or if he broke his neck in rolling.

He locked the car doors and went up to Orta's apartment using the keys. It no longer mattered about match-sticks or pieces of paper. He let them fall. He put the lights on, found the telephone point, reconnected, dialled a number, waited. "One trussed turkey at number two pad. Make it quick."

He switched off the lights, locked the door and went back to the car. A door was open; Orta had released the inside catch with hands or feet. He hadn't got far. Gibbs had been too quick. But he'd rolled out, tucked himself behind another car and was frantically rubbing his cords against a metal fender.

"I hand it to you," said Gibbs begrudgingly. "Perhaps you *are* indestructible." He watched the still struggling Orta, who had virtually ignored him. Then the dark eyes swept up full of hatred and silent menace.

Gibbs spoke again, "You want the Browning round your head or do you get back in the car quietly?"

Orta showed his venom and rubbed against the fender. Sickened by his own brutality Gibbs was forced to strike him again and he received the full blaze of Orta's fanaticism before the blow landed. He pulled the body round once again, and bundled it into the Volkswagen. Even an unconscious and bound Orta could not be ignored, and Gibbs half turned in his seat, arm along the back, Browning still in hand, to keep his gaze on the inert, hunched form.

Already the ice had formed on the inside of the windscreen. As it was effective cover he left it there. He resisted the temptation to use the heater. It was remarkable that they had fought for so long without drawing attention. The long winter night had provided its own insulation against sound. His feet were numb and Orta hadn't stirred, when at last he saw diffused lights glow through the frosted rear window. He waited until the car pulled up, then rubbed a little ring in the ice. Bannerman's taxi. He climbed out.

The burly cockney, Ted, was driving. Nobody but Bannerman seemed to know his other name, and there was no need. One fact anyone who worked with him could be totally sure of was that Ted was Bannerman's man to his boots. It was sometimes rumoured in the department that Bannerman had adopted him, or, alternatively, had sprung him from jail or had even spawned him during a student rag day. Bannerman had no need to watch his back when Ted was there.

Ted pulled Orta from the car and held him as if he was a baby. He seemed disappointed when Orta made no move and gazed at Gibbs accusingly. He threw Orta into the back of the cab and was about to close the door when Gibbs stopped him. "I'll go with you."

"Okay, climb in."

"Where're you going?"

"The Hammersmith place."

"Fine, you can drive me back afterwards. I've had a bellyful tonight." Gibbs wearily climbed into the cab, pulling down one of the small flaps opposite the rear seat where Orta was spread out.

It was difficult to stay awake in the warmth of the cab but Gibbs had developed too much respect for Orta's resilience to doze off. Feeling came back slowly and his feet were just beginning to tingle when they stopped.

Ted had driven along an alley between two sets of buildings. The surface was cobbled and slippery as Gibbs climbed out. What appeared to be a garage door faced him but there was no room for the taxi to turn in, barely enough clearance either side of the walled alley. Ted unlocked the door and slid it back on runners. He pulled Orta out and carried him in. At a nod from Ted, Gibbs pulled the door across and then followed the driver over a bare concrete workshop floor, benches and lathes and other equipment neatly positioned, and down some concrete steps at the foot of which was a door.

A modestly comfortable area unfolded. Wall to wall carpeting, a bedroom, kitchen, office, shower room all reasonably, if colourlessly, furnished. And there were two doors with grilles set in with external slide shutters. One door was open and Ted carried Orta in, to drop him on the single bed. The room was self-contained; reeded glass cubicle for shower and toilet, table, chair, easy chair. No loose lamps or flexes, the light centrally flush with the lowish ceiling. A grille set high in the wall provided air-conditioning, the hum of the plant somewhere nearby. Magazines were piled in a Victorian music rack. It was luxurious by prison-cell standards.

While Gibbs leaned against the door jamb, Ted untied Orta's cords and ripped the plaster from his mouth. Gibbs said, "I wouldn't be too casual if I were you. Never underrate that one. He's probably waiting his chance right now."

Ted was searching the clothes, running his heavy finger round the hems and collars and cuffs. He whipped off the shoes and threw them out through the door. There were slippers under the bed.

"Gave you a rough time, did 'e?" he replied at last. Gibbs was impressed with Ted's thoroughness. For such a big, seemingly clumsy man he operated with extreme speed and delicacy. Then he added, still concentrating on Orta, "I was gonna put up a 'To Let' sign. Its been such a bleeding long time since these digs were occupied."

Gibbs smiled and regretted it as he split congealed blood. Ted finally joined him. He stared at Gibbs critically. "You gave it to 'im a bit, didn't you?"

Gibbs said, "Where can I clean off some of what he gave to me?"

"In there, mate."

Gibbs stripped, then showered under piping hot water, turning it to full cold before jumping out. When he was dried and dressed Bannerman was peering through the grill at Orta who was struggling to sit and heaving as if to vomit. Bannerman turned his head as Gibbs came from the shower. "What a stupid risk to take. I told you not to go it alone."

Still rubbing his head with a towel Gibbs said dryly, "When I got back Nuzzale had moved in. I couldn't get my gear. I couldn't contact you in time."

Bannerman still had his topcoat on and he pulled it to him as though it was cold in this cosily warm domain. "He's trained to resist interrogation. All forms. As you are. We don't know how much time we have."

Gibbs nodded thoughtfully as Ted put a mug of steaming coffee in his hands. "If we get the others it might resolve itself." Looking over Bannerman's shoulder, he saw Orta stagger off the bed then look down at his stockinged feet. Orta stared round the room, a hand to his head where Gibbs had last hit him. He glanced at the shower cubicle. Bannerman remarked quite dryly, "Unbreakable glass. You can't damage yourself, dear boy."

Orta cast a restrained look of venom towards the grille. Then, after finding the slippers and pushing his feet into them: "Much too good for a police cell. Am I being entertained by Her Majesty's counter-intelligence? You're wasting your time. It is already too late." He suddenly spotted Gibbs over Bannerman's shoulder. "Did you hear that, Ross? They don't need me. My job's done."

Orta was trying to hide the pain of the fight now flooding through him. "I didn't trust you from the outset. I was instructed to use you." Then, more brightly, "You did a good job for us, though. You will be part of it whether you like it or not."

"Part of what?"

"Don't be a fool."

"I know where the kids are. I'll release them in a few hours. You may as well give us the rest."

Orta laughed. It was spontaneous and real and came intermittently through the pain. "Good for you, *old boy*."

139

Orta's heavy sarcasm distressed Gibbs. His fear for the children increased.

Bannerman, who had been listening to the exchange with some interest, cut it short by slamming the shutter over the grid. To Gibbs he said, "Leave this to me. You do the job you're supposed to do."

Gibbs pointed at the door. "He wasn't bluffing. Those kids are in danger."

"Not while the father is needed."

Gibbs finished his coffee slowly. Sitting on the edge of the desk, warmth restored, he now felt his own pains. He glanced at the desk clock. Four o'clock. He rose wearily. Bannerman said with conviction, "Get some sleep."

"I can't go back to Nuzzale like this."

Bannerman said thoughtfully, "Then I'd better move fast. Or would you rather take Nuzzale out yourself?" To Bannerman it was an academic question.

"No." Gibbs shook his head. "Do it your way."

★   ★   ★

While Gibbs caught up on a little sleep, Bannerman telephoned the Savoy Hotel. It was just after four in the morning.

Vogel came on irritably; the ringing had penetrated a drug-induced sleep. These days he could not sleep without a pill.

Bannerman was gentle with him. "I'm sorry about the hour, but this is your moment of reckoning. You want to go on?"

Vogel cast sleep aside like a blanket. Already he was sitting on the edge of the bed, feet groping for slippers. "I made my decision a long time ago. Do you help me or not?"

"I have two names for you. One I suggest you tackle in about two hours' time. The other you might have to wait for. Perhaps this evening. Mohammed Nuzzale and Mario Picale. Neither was involved in your father's death but both are guilty of similar murders. I'm trying to be fair with you. They are, however, both associating at this moment with Ludwig Mueller, who was directly implicated in your father's murder. We have yet to trace him."

Vogel knew all about Mueller. During his past months of research the other names also registered. "How do I reach them?"

"Memorise the two addresses. There is a special knock. Don't

140

forget it. I will tap it out now. For Nuzzale I have a key. It will be left in an envelope at reception within an hour. Just one thing; close the door when you leave. Now let's go over it until we get it right."

13

ERNST VOGEL HAD an abhorrence of silencers. He was too critical a shot to accept easily any encumbrance that could spoil his outstanding aim. It also made the Mauser unnecessarily bulky in his top coat pocket. The butt hadn't changed, though, and had a very comforting touch to his hand. He hated compromise – there would be none with any terrorist who came under his sights – but with the gun itself, for his own protection, it was necessary. He had not allowed his deep hatred to interfere with common-sense. He used an all-night cab only part of the way. As he walked the rest the cold savaged him: he had lost too much weight. Even the brisk walking could not stop him shivering.

The instructions he'd received were both good and simple. Right from the first tentative feelers he had been left in no doubt of Bannerman's occupation, yet they had never discussed it. Bannerman was the only one in his field who had taken him seriously. And Bannerman had known his father and important political dignitaries. Those facts were his only visible bona fide. For the rest, Vogel had formed his own conclusion, and made his decision. He was fully aware that Bannerman would deny any complicity if it went wrong. Only their very first contact had been public. He accepted that he was on his own without regret or chagrin. It was how he wanted it. The rest was information. It did not matter who supplied it. For this he was grateful to Bannerman. That Bannerman might point him to the wrong man had only once briefly entered his mind. Bannerman would not.

The moon had dipped and the meagre light squeezed back to the harsh pools round the lamp-posts. His isolated footsteps echoed his own loneliness. Yet in spite of the cold, the uncertainty, the obvious danger, he enjoyed a quiet elation. He hadn't felt any form of satisfaction for a very long time.

He avoided an approaching policeman and realised just how furtive he had become. The move had been entirely instinctive and rammed home the depths to which his family's destruction had pushed him. How could life ever be the same? He was closing the door even on its remote possibility. He walked steadily on, checking street names, the number of turnings.

And now he was checking the numbers of the houses. He mounted the steps. He had been informed that the street door was unlocked and it was. Entering the hall he reached for the light switch. It didn't work. He groped his way in total darkness up the first flight of stairs. He stumbled once and cursed his inefficiency. Leaning against the wall he got his breath back, offended by the dank smell. He couldn't see a thing and when he reached the landing he had to find the door by touch. Then the keyhole.

God, he needed light. Obligingly a strip illuminated the base of the door. A light had been switched on inside the room. It did little for Vogel except to show him the exact location. He had to use both hands to get the key in and he failed to do it noiselessly. He pulled out his gun, slipped the catch, got it right in his mind before tapping as he'd practised. Perhaps not quite assured but loud enough. He turned the key, opened the door.

Nuzzale was sitting on the side of the bed yawning. He said bitingly, "If your lust has been satisfied you can make the coffee, Ross." He looked up blearily and his mouth opened. It remained open as he took two bullets through the heart, the force of which pushed him back on the bed, bare feet still on the floor.

Wondering who Ross might be, Vogel closed the door quietly and felt his way downstairs again. He did not feel too much, perhaps a certain disappointment. It had been too easy. The swine should have suffered first as his father had. Nuzzale hadn't known what had hit him. Vogel's father had suffered torture and eighteen days under threat of death. It wasn't good enough. Vogel decided to push his luck and go straight on for Picale. Before he did he made the promised phone call. It was six thirty a.m.

*　　*　　*

At six thirty-five Ronnie Holder and Ginger Adams received precise instructions from Bannerman. Both had been in bed when their respective telephone calls came through. Holder picked up Adams in Lower Regent Street and drove round to Nuzzale's place, parking in the next street. It was seven thirty a.m., lighted windows on in almost every house. The milkman had been; there was a row of bottles in the hall. Unlike Vogel the two men were prepared for the worst and used a flashlight up the stairs. They were glad of the darkness. They let themselves into Nuzzale's room with a duplicate made from Gibbs's key.

Inside they barely took notice of Nuzzale except to ensure that he was dead. Then they started a cleaning-up operation, collecting everything Gibbs had listed through Bannerman, battery, microphone, bits and pieces, clothes. They meticulously dusted out fingerprints on anything that Gibbs could possibly have handled. It was a long job, and by the time they had finished, it was daylight but very dull. They kept the door locked: they could hear people hurrying to work on the stairs outside.

When finally satisfied they piled everything into the grip that Gibbs had used, openly carried the telescopic rod, and chose their moment to leave, locking up after them and leaving Murder Squad with a potential headache as Nuzzale gazed open-mouthed at the ceiling.

*   *   *

Vogel found Picale's apartment without difficulty. It was still dark but there was activity. People were preparing for work, some already mobile. He attracted no attention. The bitterly cold winds and the arctic conditions kept heads down. Nuzzale had been expecting someone even at that early hour; Vogel guessed that he could hardly be so lucky with Picale. This time there was a hall light but he had no key to the apartment. He was rushing it and he had his first doubts.

He stood outside Picale's door realising that it would have been better to wait until evening, to have shot Picale outside in darkness either coming or going. The detailed description of the Italian was quite clear in his mind, even to the way he wore his clothes. Again he pulled out his Mauser. He had not replaced the two rounds he had used, considering that he had more than enough. At this time he felt completely exposed, belatedly accepting that time had passed and that there was a real risk of someone using the stairs. He raised his hand and rapped out the special knock more clearly than last time. He waited, gun out, forearm level, wrist straight.

There was movement inside the room but no response to his knock. He knocked again, louder. He was startled when a voice very close to the door demanded who he was in an atrocious accent. Inspirationally he mumbled "Nuzzale", gutturally; Arabic is guttural.

"Nuzzale?" the voice was in the same place but Picale was suspicious, trying to draw him out.

"Yes. Hurry." Vogel had no idea how Nuzzale had spoken. He'd created his own trap. Nothing happened the other side of the door, no movement and Vogel was listening intently.

"Hold on. I open door. You push hard. It sticks sometimes."

The key turned, Vogel raised his free hand to push the door and he panicked as Picale's punch line registered. Picale wanted him just where he stood. Vogel fired through the wood as the door swung. The wood cracked, splinters flying out. Picale fired as he held his side with his other hand. Both men had fired waist high: both were struck in the stomach.

They crumpled and fell back, strangers staring at each other in pain through the now open door. Vogel was not sure where he had gone wrong. He fired again as Picale did and fell backwards, staggered as his legs went, slipped sideways and crashed down the stairs, dropping the Mauser on the half landing.

Picale had sunk to his knees as if in supplication. His mouth was working; his dark eyes, darker than they'd ever been before, glazed and lost focus as he fell forward on his face, gun still in hand. He never had the satisfaction of knowing that, in death, one of the best pistol shots in the world had joined him.

The first person down the stairs was a typist, a girl late for work and still biting at a piece of toast. Because both men had used silencers she had no warning of what to expect. At first her own larynx was silenced as she choked on the toast but when the nerves suddenly untangled her crust-scattered screams were repeated again and again.

Vogel had despatched two terrorists but he had left a mess behind, and not only that of death and blood. His need for revenge had run out of control, leaving Bannerman with grave problems and Ross Gibbs' life hanging by a thread.

*   *   *

Gibbs did not hear about Nuzzale until Ronnie Holder arrived. The news of Picale and Vogel was to break later through the press in a more bizarre way and cause a considerable sensation. He did not know that Vogel had left them with the job half done. As he could not return to his own apartment with the dead Nuzzale still there he wondered if the Arab's first apartment was vacant. Or was Mueller there?

It was daylight when he left Hammersmith. He could not use his listening gear which he carried with his grip Holder had brought back, so he had to go through the routine at Nuzzale's old apartment of knocking and identifying. When satisfied that no one was inside he used one of several keys Holder had supplied and let himself in. A search satisfied him that no one else was using it at the moment. Apart from a couple of items of Nuzzale's clothing which he recognised, wardrobe and drawers were empty. So Nuzzale *had* been dumped on him purely for observation.

He left his stuff in the grip, hid the battery and telescopic rod, went out into the freezing weather again, caught a train to Chorley Wood station in Hertfordshire and stole a car from the railway parking zone. There were always a few unlocked. He crossed the wires and drove off, inserting the correct coins at the lift barrier.

He kept to the main roads which had been salted and sanded, the snow pushed back to the fringes in huge drifts by the ever-busy ploughs. The worst winter for years, the weather men said.

He took the still frozen track to the cottage and blew the horn so that there would be no misunderstanding. He expected a curtain to twitch as the cottage came in view or even Kumira to open the door but there was no sign that he'd been heard. There was no vehicle outside, and he suffered his first doubts.

Gibbs banged on the door with the disproportionately large knocker and was answered by a hollow echo. No one came. No one called. He struggled round the house, breaking through dead weed and thorn. All the windows were shuttered. He returned to the front, hammered just once more, then went to work on the lock.

The heavy door swung open. He pushed it back and it hit the wall. All doors leading off the low-beamed hall were closed. He could not hurry, the sensation of a trap strong in him. Stifling impatience he moved slowly, a room at a time, Browning in hand. When he'd finished he sat on the draped arm of a chair and put his gun away. The cottage was empty. The bed to which the children had been chained was stripped down. The furniture was covered with dust sheets. There were no food stocks in the kitchen units. No sign that anyone had been there.

It had started to go wrong. He would have been more worried had he known Vogel was dead. Gibbs went round once more, noisily now, uncaring, looking for any sign that would give an indication. Kumira, and perhaps Picale with her, had cleaned up well. There was a telephone still connected, and he called Bannerman to tell him the bad news.

Bannerman took it in his stride. "Picale's work. Careful devil."

"It shows again how little they trust me."

"Not just that. Picale hasn't survived for nothing in this kind of work."

"Have you heard from Vogel?"

"Not again. I hope he'll deal with Picale this evening. Get round to Orta's place. See what you can find." The news of Vogel had yet to filter from Scotland Yard who had a murder squad on the case; as yet they knew nothing of Bannerman's interest, and the media had not yet made releases.

*   *   *

It was one thing applying psychological torture, quite another to get the victim to co-operate. After the torture trials in Strasbourg in which Britain had been found guilty on many counts except the main one, Bannerman had decided to play things close to the chest. The fewer involved the better. He had a mass murderer on his hands who was on his territory planning some form of coup. He was in no doubt that many lives were at risk, not just the Hatton children. If someone wanted to make political capital from what he had authorised Ted, the burly cockney, to do, then they could also answer for what followed if he did not get some quick answers. But the invisible threat did curtail him.

Ted could cope. He wore shin-guards and a box. As for the rest, Orta had already discovered that applying the science of killing on Ted was like practising on a chunk of solid stone. And Ted was beginning to lose his patience. Even now Orta, weakened by his fight with Gibbs and his subsequent attempts on Ted, still showed no inclination to lean against the wall with splayed legs and arms and a short sack over his head.

Ted decided to tie Orta's ankles to the solidly mounted bed and

147

his wrists to a bar that fitted across the room into sockets on each wall. It took time to finish the job. Even putting the sack over the head was difficult with Orta still fighting to the last. Once achieved, the panting Ted stood back and wiped his sweating face. Orta was rolling his head trying to remove the sack. It was now a matter of time – and just how successfully Orta had been trained to resist.

★　　★　　★

The Volkswagen still cowered in the gutter, surrounded by white-fringed empty spaces and frost-covered cars. The deserted car was one of the few reminders of last night's battle. There were dried and frozen streaks of blood down two of the railings, another small patch where the two men had rolled. Gibbs used the keys again, noticing that the match stubs lay where they had fallen. This time his search was more painstaking, and he found the usual small cache of arms, ammunition, explosives and detonators under the floorboards. He rang his report through, suggesting that the cache be left. He did not want any of Bannerman's crowd being caught in the act of lifting; he did not want Orta's people alerted in any way. Before he left he fed in Orta's kitchen, warming canned meat and potatoes and making coffee. Now, at two o'clock, it was his first meal of the day. He took the stale loaf from the breadbin and prized the gun from it: a Beretta .22, really too small for his hand. He put the remains of the loaf back in the bin.

He drove back to Chorley Wood before the traffic started to snarl up and reparked the car. The slot he had taken it from had since been occupied and he had to find another, a fact that would puzzle the owner. The early commuters were already on their way back by the time he caught a train to town.

He went straight to Kumira's apartment and was not surprised when there was no reply. He did not consider the risk too great when he broke in and searched, but he did not expect to discover anything he did not already know. Kumira would be with the Hatton children. In God's name, where? He rang Fran and there was no reply. In a depressed mood he trudged back to the apartment where he had first stayed with Nuzzale.

★　　★　　★

From the night of Craven's death, Bannerman had moved into his Chelsea pied-à-terre. He was at present in his cramped office off St. Martin's Lane. He was essentially a desk man but he made absolutely certain that during any operation under his control he was always available, day and night. If he drove others hard he did not stint himself. Like Gibbs, he had been up most of the night. Without causing alarm he had used ploys to check on the passenger lists of Concorde flights over the next few days.

A trickier job had been to find out the air crew duty roster. As it was knowledge he did not want to request openly, he had obtained it through his security contacts at Heathrow Airport. Even these inquiries were oblique; he did not want it known that it was he who was anxious for the information. He wanted no eyebrows raised, no comment, no enquiry. He simply needed to know when James Hatton would be flying over the next few days.

Because of his back door, double-tracked enquiry it took him several hours where he could have learned it over a phone call. He didn't mind. By the time he received this information he already had the passenger lists for the following five days. It complicated matters, overstressed the work, but gave no indication of any one particular flight that might interest him. There was nothing new in security about checking on possible undesirables under known pseudonyms. Bannerman's security operation cast its biggest cloak of concealment over himself.

He checked the lists and the duty rosters. He then checked information supplied as a matter of course as routine security. What V.I.P.s would be travelling? There was little need to check. The announcement had been made several weeks ago. The British Prime Minister, Mrs. Margaret Thatcher, was travelling in three days' time. She was to have a meeting with the President of the United States of America and would be his guest. That was not all. Herr Schmidt, the Federal German Chancellor was also travelling as a guest of the British Government. Herr Schmidt was arriving for talks with the P.M. the day before the flight and they would then proceed together.

The entourage for each would not be light. Armed security guards do not normally travel on British planes, but to suggest there would be none on this flight would be ludicrous. At the very least each of the two V.I.P.s would have his personal bodyguard.

The check on other passengers would be more than routine; they would be stringent. The flight could be cancelled but both premiers would strongly resist that on the grounds of showing weakness. It was up to security to protect them; it always was.

Bannerman sat back and did a rare thing. He groped in his desk for a cigar. He seldom smoked, and never cigarettes, but when he lit a cigar it was unusual enough to provoke comment. It was the only indication anyone had that he was in any way concerned. At best it indicated total preoccupation. He lit it with some difficulty, his mind elsewhere. When the smoke drifted it was clear, even to himself, that the cigar was ancient and had not been cared for. It made no difference. Bannerman was lost in his thoughts. He was too realistic to ask of himself whether Orta's little bunch would dare to hijack so heavily guarded a plane; they would dare anything. But Orta always planned the detail finely.

Bannerman sat thoughtfully drawing on the cigar, in apparent enjoyment. In fact he was barely aware of it. There was no chance of terrorists smuggling arms on to that particular plane. He made a mental correction. That was an overstatement. Ingenuity had worked before. Yet never on a plane potentially so heavily protected. Co-pilot James Hatton. Now back in England. Bannerman was still not satisfied. Again he studied the passenger list. There were several foreign names, among them two German and one Japanese.

Bannerman reflected so long that his lean frame appeared to be locked in its pose of concentration. The frown over the bony nose deepened and stayed there. Like that, his city image disappeared; his clothes were the wrong prop. By now he had forgotten the cigar and it quietly burned away between his fingers. Finally he flushed it down the toilet. He scooped the dropped ash off the desk into a cupped hand.

He went to Hammersmith and down the steps to pull the shutter back from the grill. Orta was still suspended, his body drooping. Resistance seemed to have deserted him.

Bannerman looked on quietly for a moment before he asked politely, "Are you comfortable?"

The head jerked in the sack. "What day is it?" The words were muffled.

Bannerman was not convinced. "Are you taking arms on board? Who's to collect them?"

Orta laughed. It was so boyish that it was impossible, then, to equate him with a multi-killer. When he stopped he was standing more firmly on his feet. "I'll report you to the European Court of Human Rights."

"And who would take up your case for you, Orta? Which country would allow you to give evidence?"

"There are some."

"I don't need to torture you or even interrogate you. I know what you're up to."

Orta became petulant but there was belief in his reply. "That could be the biggest mistake of your life."

Bannerman closed the shutter quietly. He turned to Ted. "How long?"

"Five hours. 'E's tough."

"Nothing?"

"No. Not yet. 'E'll crack, though."

"But when?"

★   ★   ★

Gibbs snatched a couple of hours' rest about six o'clock. Although it was dark, he could not use his equipment until the streets had cleared and people were sheltered in their homes against the continuing severe freezing spell. He was strapping up his gear when there was a knock at the door. It was so soft he almost missed it. He slipped his topcoat on, buttoned it as the knock came again, a little louder. "Who is it?"

"Fran."

He had finally managed to contact her to tell her the change of address because he didn't want her anywhere near Nuzzale.

He opened up, embarrassed. She was wearing a cloak, the hood leaving just the oval of her face. In one gloved hand she carried a basket. "Don't I get asked in?"

Gibbs opened the door wider. "I'm sorry. Of course."

"I'm not holding you up? Are you going out or have you just come in?"

"Going out. I didn't expect you." He didn't want to take his coat off with the equipment underneath.

151

"I can see that. It's Cass."

"What?"

"Look, I *am* holding you up."

"I can think of no pleasanter delay. What's happened to Cass?"

"She's in the basket."

Gibbs peered down. He could just see the tiny tulip ears and the pink nose. Between them two enormous eyes stared up at him. A miaow of welcome reached him and Cass put a small paw out from the blanket that cosseted her. He smiled and some of his tension went. "From rags to riches," he said, "Cass has never had it so good."

"Do you want me to leave her here?"

"Could you keep her for another couple of days? I don't want to take advantage . . ." He could see she was biting her tongue back over something.

"You've been in a fight," she blurted out.

He'd forgotten the cuts and bruises. "A drunk. Big one."

"I don't believe you, Tony."

He hadn't even asked her to sit down and suddenly he felt it was too late. "You're psychoanalysing me again."

"Not this time. You're not the type to get in a drunken brawl."

What attracted him to her so strongly? All his training screamed a warning, yet she made nonsense of it. She was trying to cover a concern for him that was ridiculous after so short an acquaintance. All the warnings were there and Fran was standing quite still in front of him silently begging for some enlightenment. His recent life had been one of distrust of anyone outside Sergeant McKechnie and the occasional link-up with other colleagues. He could die for a mistake.

Fran put the basket on the table and Cass climbed out to jump down and brush against Gibbs's legs.

Tiredness and the conditions of work were getting at Gibbs. He used this as part excuse for what followed but he knew, at root, that it was nonsense. He had huge reserves against privation.

"Can I trust you?" It came out as a cold, clinical question.

Fran faltered, aware there was about to be a profound change in their relationship. She could not predict for good or bad but it had, illogically, become of desperate importance to her. She kept her head, sat on her natural feelings. "To what point? I won't help you do something wrong. And if you do I'll not get involved in it." It had been very difficult to say.

Gibbs said, "Good girl. A cry of assurance would have been too emotionally motivated and I would have had to lie to you again." He shrugged. "I don't know what you call 'something wrong'. Many people would interpret what I'm doing as wrong. Certainly most of it is against the law. But I'm not a criminal, not in the accepted sense."

Gibbs took off his coat and threw it on the bed. He unstrapped the rod and battery and saw Fran's expression change. She hadn't known what to expect, certainly not this.

"Sit down, Fran. I'm afraid I can't even offer you a drink, though I reckon you'll need one." He pointed to the rod and microphone. "Listening gear. It can pinpoint a single conversation from an apartment block." He watched her closely. "I'm telling you this not only as explanation but to convince you that you mustn't come here again. For your safety's sake."

Only then did she sink on to a chair and she chose a straightback, just the edge of it. She pushed her hood back, shaking her hair out. "Are you a detective?"

"Sort of." He saw her gaze go to his hands. When he looked down he saw the bluish, broken skin around the knuckles. He made no attempt to move them out of sight. Fran must make up her own mind. He had qualms as he realised the size of the shock he had thrown at her and which was but a fraction of the truth. She could not possibly have conceived any of this and because she showed it so obviously he was reassured.

Fran clasped and unclasped her hands. At the moment she was bewildered. "Tony Brooks. Norfolk farmer. I don't know you at all do I? Is that really your name?"

"No. I wouldn't be telling you this if I didn't believe there was a fair chance that we could remedy it when this is over."

"*This*? You haven't told me anything."

"That's why I asked for your trust. I can't tell you more. I didn't want you thinking all sorts of peculiar things."

"Oh, Tony, what can be more peculiar than this?" She gestured helplessly.

"Have I your trust?"

"What are you detecting?"

Ross considered it. It made no difference. "Terrorists. Don't ask me any more."

Fran rose slowly and was glad that he took her extended hands. "I'll *have* to trust you. I want to. I don't know what else I can do."

He held her close and they rocked together. Over her shoulder he said, "I must strap that stuff back on."

"I know you have to go." But she was gripping tight as though to stop him. "Will you be in danger?"

He stroked her hair. "Stop right there. That's part of the trust."

She pulled her head back, their faces close. "How can it happen so quickly?"

"I don't know. It doesn't matter." He cupped her face and below them Cass was intertwined between their legs.

"How long will it take?"

"Days at most."

"But you don't really know?"

"No. There's no way. Have faith." He pushed her gently back and reached for the gear. As he did so his jacket opened and she saw the butt of the Browning. Her hands went up to her mouth; she was confronted with the brutal violence the gun represented; the job that he was doing. She watched him leave in silence.

14

GIBBS WENT BACK to Orta's apartment. The note was still in the accordion and he took it to the table where he flattened it out. From the haphazard figures he could at least arrive at the original route they had taken, or at least the last, important part of it. Was it possible to get sense out of the remaining odd jottings which were presented almost as doodles? He searched the bookshelves, found a series of sectional maps, spread two of them on the table and studied the meagre findings.

Over an hour later all he had were two vague possibilities plus the faintest of pencil marks on one of the maps. He had used the area of the first cottage as the centre of the web; trying to reconcile the other road numbers in conjunction with it. There seemed no obvious connection as none of the road numbers emanated from the cottage area. It was possible that they did not have to, that the route from the cottage to the trunk and secondary roads was left as a matter of personal choice. The pencil mark could be no more than a smudge, for there was nothing precise about it: it was just the sort of mark one might accidentally make while opening a map with a pencil in one's hand. He folded the map back, made his own road references in the margin, then left. His transport lay before him, almost crusted over by now, body and windows opaque white.

Before he could open a door in the Volkswagen he had to heat a lock. There was a de-icing spray on the driver's shelf and he sprayed round the windows, scraping and wiping. Starting the car was another problem but gradually it jerked to life, choking erratically, the engine turning despairingly slowly. The ice was already reforming as he sat there and the car shook around him in a series of death throes. He waited until the engine was thoroughly warm before he moved off. It was another ten minutes before the heater began to be effective and the little car filled up with warmth. He drove out into the country, the folded map and notes on the seat beside him.

The next hour was spent in driving on treacherous roads, and the search did not begin until he was thirty miles out. The only strategy he could follow was to apply a painstaking pattern by entering every country lane that led from the arterial roads mentioned on the jottings. It was a hopeless task but he had one extremely helpful if time-consuming aid. The listening gear was on the back seat, and on approaching any isolated house he would stop, use the directional mike and learn something about its occupants quickly. The real problems began the nearer he reached midnight. People were going to bed, more houses were in darkness, and his own approach was more obvious, with the engine noise and headlamps. He found himself stopping more often, advancing for longer distances on foot. Time began to drag, and his processes of elimination slowed down.

There was a cross-over point where he began to fall into a crude rhythm. He was still searching while not at all sure that he was even remotely in the right area. Yet a feeling of being one with the job overtook him. The familiarisation of what he was doing ceased to feel hopeless when in theory, after so much time on it, it should be the opposite. He simply became used to exploring the increasingly empty roads for isolated dwellings, stopping the car, getting out, carrying the gear, setting it up patiently listening. Lighted windows had long since gone. At two thirty in the morning it occurred to him that even if he found the kidnap centre, with those in it asleep, there was no way that he could know.

He kept on. The job had to be finished to his satisfaction if only to eliminate a whole area. He was not cold any more. The car was warm, the walking kept his circulation going and the only time the cold began to bite was during the listening periods. The moon was helpful and so were long vistas of snow. They combined to give him appreciable vision with minimum use of the flashlight.

He found the children at just after four in the morning, the hour of deepest sleep and lowest heartbeat. The approach had been difficult. The house was off a track which could easily have been missed between the overgrowth of two massive hedges. The double tracks led from a small country lane which itself ran from a narrow minor road that was two miles from the major road. It was well tucked away.

A tile-hung farmhouse; its white-canopied roof had been Gibbs's first sighting of it. With the snow packed on top it was either well insulated or under-heated. The children proved it to be the latter. He picked up snatches. They had woken shivering in the morning and were huddled together for warmth. The faint rattle of the thin steel chains that bound them cut across their low-pitched dialogue. They were complaining of the cold, worrying about their mother. With the tremendous resilience of children they had already got used to their plight and, although afraid, believed in their future freedom.

He back-tracked down to the car and continued on before stopping to look at the map. The pencil mark had turned out to be no more than a smudge but had served its purpose in prompting him. He marked up the exact location and drove on. It was five miles before he found a telephone kiosk. The pale glow of it stood out isolated and forlorn on the corner of a lane. It gave him certain satisfaction to ring Bannerman at five-thirty in the morning to tell him he'd located the children. It was then that Bannerman told him of Picale and Vogel's deaths. It left the job less than half done. And Orta was still holding out, though weakening. The big question now was how would the others react? Where did it leave the children? And Gibbs himself?

* * *

He appeared far removed from the urbane, uniformed figure who conveyed so easily the confidence of long experience to his super-sonically travelling passengers. The scattered strands of hair over Jim Hatton's head were untidy, as few as they were. His eyes were bruised from fatigue and worry. He had climbed from bed at four-thirty, cold and shivering, and had switched on the central heating to stop his developing cold.

Phyllis Hatton found him on a stool stooped over the kitchen counter, a hot cup of tea untouched in front of him. "You won't sleep on tea," she said as she joined him, reaching for the pot. "And you won't stop shivering without your dressing gown." She poured herself some tea and said, "I'll get it for you." And left the kitchen.

Hatton didn't reply; he barely turned his head. When his wife returned she had to force him into slipping on the dressing gown. She sat beside him again, facing the dining room she could see through the slatted wooden screen at the back of the counter. They had planned it together, had seen it develop with the concerted pride and thrill of creation. Their dream home had become an empty, cold box full of unwanted secrets. She said once again, "Are you going to tell me?"

He turned his head then, hollow eyes focusing on her with difficulty. Suddenly he put his hand out and held her face. She leaned towards him, once more fighting back her tears. She had cried so much that she had considered herself dehydrated, but the sobs were never far away. They had no counsel but each other, and that was shadowed by the same grief. She rested her head on his shoulder and he leaned his head on hers. "Tell me, Jim You're torturing yourself."

"He said tell nobody."

"How can he know? He couldn't have meant me. I'm part of it."

It was an argument she had used before going to bed, when he had returned after the telephone call, haggard and nervous. The early hours had taken their toll. He sat upright again, stirred the tea, sipped it. "I think we're mad not going to the police."

They had been over that before too. Phyllis Hatton did not reply. They had sorted out their emotions. What was most important? The children. What was best in their interest? The police, or playing the safer game of compliance? Where did their confidence lie? In truth they had none. They did know that they had been specifically warned not to go to the police, that the children would die if they did. And that was really it. The police would be able to give no guarantees. And the children were in the hands of terrorists. That word had a deadly, meaningful, well-substantiated ring. There was never, ever, compassion with terrorists when it came to a choice of lives or cause. Their only possible chance was compliance, and both knew that that was no guarantee either. On record, terrorists had kept their word once demands had been met. Equally they had kept them when demands had been ignored. Both Ginny and Tommy Hatton were under threat of death. It always came back to that, no matter how long they discussed it. They did not want to take any risk that might endanger their children.

"Tell me, Jim. Darling, *please*."

At this time of morning things were always worse, but nothing could *actually* be worse. With great determination Jim Hatton had fought off the need for a drink. When Phyllis had first confronted him with the news he had been tempted to fortify himself, but self-discipline was part of him, and was in every good pilot's make-up. Never drink before a flight. Keeping his head clear hadn't solved a thing, but it had helped him face the matter logically. Again he put his hand out to his wife. "I'm making it worse for you, aren't I, Lis?" He had always called her that.

"It can't be worse. God, how can it? You're just presenting one more problem to worry me sick."

He bowed his head, then squeezed her hand, still undecided.

She said quietly, "If you go on like this they'll stop you flying. You look ill, Jim."

Immediately he stiffened with fear. God, they couldn't stop him flying. His children's lives depended on it.

"They want me to take something on board."

15

SHE GRIPPED HIS hand fiercely. "Not arms?" A scared whisper.

"I don't know. He told me it could be attached snugly to my own case, or replace it. It could contain arms. But I'm guessing, Lis. I have no idea."

"Won't you be searched?"

He shrugged. "It would be easier for the flight deck crew to get something on board than anyone else. We'd hardly hijack our own plane."

"Is that what they intend to do? Hijack Concorde?"

"How the hell do I know? For God's sake." He covered his face in his hands then drew them away with a long sigh. "Sorry, Lis. I just don't know. With Thatcher and Schmidt as passengers you can take it that no one else will get anything on board that shouldn't be there."

They were silent, still clasping hands. "Wouldn't you be in danger if they take over the plane?"

"I don't think so. They've blown up planes but not with people on board. He told me that no one would be harmed."

"You believe him?"

"Stop pushing me, Lis. What do you want me to do? Tell him to go to hell? I *have* to believe."

"You'll lose your job, darling," Her lips trembled. "They'll send you to prison."

He moved his head as if in agony. "You do understand the alternative?"

"Yes." She was biting on a knuckle, turning her head away.

"There must be mitigating circumstances. I know I'll lose my job. There are others." Then, with false, unconvincing good humour. "It'll mean I'll be home more. I don't think they'll send me to prison."

She gained control of herself, then turned to him red-eyed. "Will it be easy to get it on board?"

"It can be done. Because of the importance of this particular flight nothing will be easy, the main attention will be on the passengers."

"What was he like, this man?"

"Muffled up to the eyeballs and wearing a hat. He also had a gun in case I tried to throttle him. I had to leave the car at one end of the street so that he could see me approach. He was in a doorway, stepping out when I reached the corner. A German or Austrian, although the accent was difficult to pinpoint behind the scarf. I pick up the case at Victoria Station later today. We fly tomorrow."

"You couldn't follow him?"

"Do you think I didn't want to? He warned me what would happen to the kids. By the time I reached the car he was long gone."

*   *   *

"I'm sorry I'm late. I've had rather a trying time." Bannerman showed signs that even he needed sleep.

Sir Henry Winters inclined his head, indicated a chair the other side of the desk. He eyed Bannerman coldly. He had endorsed much which he had found distasteful, for he was no fool, and understood the vital necessity of intelligence; as a sailor he had earlier benefited from it. But close to it had a different flavour. He could not quite dispel the impression that he should be in the wardroom addressing his officers with a gin and tonic in his hand.

Bannerman had that impression now; that he was just about to receive a lecture. He was somewhat surprised when Winters said, "You know I'm retiring in summer? The end of June."

Bannerman, legs crossed, elbows on the arms of the chrome framed chair, made an arrowhead of his fingers. "Really, Sir Henry?"

"Do you see yourself in my job?"

Bannerman, so attuned to the devious, was forced into hesitancy by so direct a question. "I really haven't considered it."

"Don't take me for a fool, George. You've considered it."

"With respect, I don't think this is the time to discuss it."

"Your contempt for me won't help."

Bannerman stiffened. "I've never expressed contempt for you."

"Not expressed it. Shown it. Little touches along the line."

"I'm sorry you think that." Bannerman was about to get up when Winters waved him down again.

"That's not what I really wanted to see you about, although it *is* connected. The Americans seem to think Craven didn't die by shooting."

"We know that he didn't. How did they arrive at it?"

Winters looked uneasy. "I don't know. They're unhappy."

"Who?"

"I had a visit from Joe Carlin. He smells a rat."

"Has he some form of evidence?"

"The evidence of a long, suspicious nose."

"Leo Roxberg wouldn't have told him."

"Perhaps Carlin is not satisfied with what Leo had to say. Why don't we just tell him what happened?"

"We can. When it's over. There's too much at risk for the Company suddenly to get on its high horse. They won't like it. One angry tongue can cause disaster."

"Possibly. Carlin was obliquely suggesting that Craven was killed in some other way."

"Why doesn't he search the ashes?"

"That's not funny, George. Did you meddle with the car?"

"What precisely are you saying, sir?"

"That it's not beyond you. Not where Craven was concerned."

"The car was passed out to me serviced. It was sent straight on to Craven." A touch of anger would be expected.

Winters clasped his hands. He stared warily at the desk. "Carlin has been more than nudging us over this. They are agitated and dissatisfied, and if they keep on at Leo they may get the truth. There'll be repercussions. And they'll want someone's head."

"Let's hope Leo holds out. Gibbs is in the hot seat." But Roxberg knew only what Bannerman had told him.

"It's too late for me to quarrel over it, but if you were stupid enough to kill Craven you'll pay the price. I've no brief for Nuzzale or Picale but you should have warned me that you intended to use young Kurt Vogel."

"He used himself. It was all he wanted from life. The world will see it as revenge. Which it was. I'm only sorry that he got careless. It leaves things dangerously poised."

"I'm inclined to think you did kill him, George."

Bannerman unwound his long legs. "Sir Henry, you are accusing me of murder. This is monstrous."

"Possibly."

"Why don't you check with the pool mechanics?"

"I have."

"I don't quite know what to do about this. I'm stunned."

"I dare say."

Bannerman straightened. "Obviously this has to be cleared up. I hope we have time to do so before you retire."

"Don't be insolent, George. Don't try it on me. Did you weigh Ross Gibbs against Paul Craven?"

Bannerman rose swiftly. "Had I done you might have been right."

Winters shrugged. "I'm too old, too weary to care. I didn't really want this job in the first place. I can certainly now see why I was needed. Unfortunately you might pull others down with you. Have you discovered what Orta is up to?"

Bannerman thought carefully before he replied. "No. Short of torture I'll get nothing from him. Which is why it's so important to keep Gibbs where he is."

"Torture's a hot number after Strasbourg. Don't add that to your list." Winters added thoughtfully, "You can't hold him indefinitely. You have until six. By then you must get Special Branch to arrest him or get him out of the country unnoticed."

"If we arrest him it's public knowledge and Gibbs is in trouble. It comes back to that every time. Kumira and Mueller are still loose. And most likely others we don't know about."

Winters looked at Bannerman intently for a moment, then said, "Can you see them doing much damage without Orta, Picale and Nuzzale?"

It was the most difficult question of an unpleasant session. Was Winters being devious? The straight stare said no. Yet it could be a trap. Bannerman took his time; he would be expected to. "If Kumira and Mueller are still around then it's for a purpose. If they find out we have Orta they'll go flat out to succeed and to get Gibbs."

Bannerman left Winters to think about it and, back in his own office, he sagged a little. He was both weary and wary. Winters wasn't quite the fool he thought. And it was clear, too, that to some

163

extent he had been protected against the suspicious probes of Joe Carlin.

He went through the Concorde passenger list again, picked up the direct line and dialled. "Just how much longer do you need for that run-down?" He glanced at the list. "There's barely half of them cleared and we're short of time." He picked up a pen, ticked at names on the list, made one or two marginal notes. He made a quick calculation. "That still leaves nineteen unaccounted for." And then, "Are you saying that there are four untraceable? Booked through different agents? *All* paid cash?" And the names? Welsch. Julich. Harb. Kawar. He cupped the phone and considered the names. Possibly two Germans and two Palestinians. Four? For a heavily protected plane? "Keep at it. Put more men on it."

Bannerman sat back. He put a red asterisk beside each of the four names. There was a link between them: untraceability and cash. The right initiative would permit a small team to succeed even with armed bodyguards on board. But still he wasn't satisfied. He reached for his scrambler, pressed buttons. It was a little while before he was answered. "Ted. Have you got anything?" Bony fingers tapped the desk, a sound that Ted picked up and which informed him that Bannerman was having a rare fit of agitation.

"Yeah. I got it on tape. Do you want to come over, guvnor, or do I give yer the gist?"

"You mean he cracked?"

"I mean 'es told me something."

"Let's have it."

"They're getting the co-pilot to take arms on board. They're to be picked up there."

"Did he say how many would be on board?"

"I've gotta think. Shall I run the tape? No, wait. Four. I think 'e said four."

"How is he? Orta?"

Ted considered it. "Like a jelly. An unhealthy bugger."

"Unhealthily tough, wouldn't you say?"

"Yeah." Begrudgingly. "You want me to go on?"

"Do you think you can get more?"

"If there's any more to get. No resistance now."

"Give him another three hours if he can stand it. If there's nothing more forthcoming I want him prepared for Special

Branch." Bannerman did not want Orta too disorientated before an official arrest. He lowered the cradle then released it, pressed more buttons. "Ronnie, I want you to get round to James Hatton. This is what I want you to do and I'll make the arrangements for you."

*   *   *

Ronnie Holder suffered no reaction to wearing the uniform of a captain of Pan American Airways. He had, in his time, worn some strange garb. He agreed with Bannerman that simulating local tradesmen or the post office engineer were out if suspicion was to be minimised. One house couldn't be singled out like that. On the passenger seat beside him was an ordinary brown paper bag with the top of a bottle of whiskey protruding. He drew into the street, made a show of lowering his window and checking door numbers before pulling up outside the Hatton house. Holding the parcel like a baby, he looked around, stamped his feet from cold but managed a wide grin as he rang the bell. As soon as the strained, puzzled face of Phyllis Hatton stared up at him he called out affectionately, "Hi, Phyllis baby. Long time no see. Where's the old man?"

Phyllis Hatton's stare was blocked by Holder who stood straight in front of her waving the bottle he had pulled from the bag and she then was drawn to the boldly printed notice on the bag, held so that she could not miss it. PRETEND YOU KNOW ME. At that stage she well knew that Holder was connected in some way with what had happened to her children. Holder kissed her cheek affectionately as he went in, an arm squeezing her shoulders. A nervous James Hatton came hustling from the kitchen.

As soon as the front door was closed Holder demanded, "You alone?" When they nodded in silence he said, "Good. You have nothing to fear from me. Now where's the case they want you to take on board?"

As Phyllis Hatton gasped her husband said, "Who the hell are you?"

"I'm not a Pan Am pilot, for sure. Can we leave this hall? Let's say I'm security, Mr. Hatton. I wouldn't say no to a coffee." He wanted to give her something to do.

Hatton led the way into the drawing room, still full of disbelief. "Have you an identity?"

165

Holder showed him a card, he wasn't sure which one. "Look, I know about the kids. We know where they are." It was important to establish rapport but it had the opposite effect. Phyllis Hatton who had overheard came bustling back from the kitchen with tearful questions and emotional demands for their return. Holder back-pedalled, "We know where they are, Mrs. Hatton. They're okay. Really. Their release has to be handled very carefully. You understand? It's tricky but there's no real problem. We might have them by tomorrow." He withstood the barrier of disbelief, gradually quietened by the drawn-faced pilot.

To cut through the emotion Holder said, "I've little time. Where's the case they want you to take on board?"

Suspicion set in again. Holder quelled it by producing instruments from his pockets and a small detector from the bag. "De-fusing gear. Can you give me a room? It's better that you stay clear."

They gave him a spare bedroom upstairs where there was a table with some aircraft models made by young Tommy Hatton. Holder moved the models to the bed then hefted the case on to the table. The case was black, thick leather, thicker than a document case and heavy. Holder treated it with the utmost respect, leaving it lying flat, studying the rim of the lid and chrome lock and the two hinges first with the naked eye and then with a magnifying lens.

The case was unusually sturdily made but with the weight it was carrying it needed to be. The lock was large, the hinges thick and long, the hide well finished. He took his time: there could be no hurrying this job. Well qualified for what he was doing, he had been trained for defusing all manner of bombs and booby traps under an Army demolition expert in Ulster, one of a small group of incredibly brave men. For a few moments he lost confidence and hopefully wished his old instructor was with him but that particular Major had been blown to bits by tackling one bomb too many while suffering severe fatigue. Holder pulled himself together and continued, the coffee he had brought up with him going cold on the table.

Satisfied that the case wasn't booby trapped he unlocked it, relieved when nothing happened, and lifted the lid.

For a while he stared at the contents. The interior was custom designed, with compartments and clips, to hold a small armoury.

In the lid were three neatly placed Colt automatics with three spare loaded magazines. In the body of the case was one more automatic, two American grenades and four detonators, each separated in its own cavity. A coil of instantaneous fuse wire and a quantity of plastic explosive in its own compartment. There was one old-fashioned box of fuse matches.

Holder treated each weapon as if it were individually booby trapped. Once out of the case he unloaded the magazines, cleared the breeches and disarmed the grenades. There was nothing he was prepared to do about the detonators except to remove them. They were of no noticeable weight. He went to the head of the stairs and called the pilot.

A white-faced Hatton stared at the haul then got his personal priorities right. "If I don't take the case on board they'll kill the children."

Holder agreed. "You *must* take it on board. It's just possible that somewhere along the line they may want to check it. It's unlikely that it could happen." He picked up the plastic explosive. "This fits in here. After I've gone I want you to send your wife out to buy some kid's plasticine. Make it up like this and put it in. The cavity dictates the size. The guns and grenades have been disarmed. Have you any aluminium foil?"

"I suppose so. In the kitchen."

"I can't replace the detonators. Roll the foil on its dull side. Get the size right to match these. It's makeshift but should pass a momentary inspection."

"You want me to do this after you've gone?"

"Yes."

"I won't be able to lock it."

"I'm going to teach you now."

Hatton got back to his main concern. "None of this is going to help our children. It could even make it worse for them."

"Your children will be all right. We'll spring them once the passengers are on board."

"Like hell you will. I'm not taking that sort of . . ."

"Leave the hysteria for your wife, Mr. Hatton." It was like a whiplash. Holder thought Hatton would strike him but the pilot held on.

"I'm sorry."

167

"I'd have reacted the same way. We dare not spring the kids before the plane is loaded. It will be a giveaway to the terrorists that we're on to them."

"I don't give a damn about that. I want them back."

"And so do we. We'll get word to you before you take off." Holder watched the haggard face. "Look, once you know they're safe you'll be laughing. Four men are going to try to hijack Concorde with useless arms. It'll be your turn. The nearer to take-off the better chance the kids have. These killers must believe they're ahead of the game."

Hatton nodded slowly, observing the logic but emotionally unconvinced. He rubbed his forehead. "You'd better show me how to fix the lock."

"Yes. Did you have any instructions about the case?"

"Apart from getting it on board? I was told to keep it away from heat. To keep it in a cool place."

Holder smiled wryly. "Not difficult in this weather." He stared thoughtfully at the detonators.

★   ★   ★

Ross Gibbs arrived back at the apartment just after six fifteen a.m. He found a parking slot a block away, not wanting to be connected with the car. He still hadn't traced Mueller. All he could do was to go back to Kumira's country hideout as soon as it was dark, in the hope that Mueller would contact her.

He cooked a solid breakfast and ate slowly, wondering how he could use the daylight hours. Bannerman was up to date on the details so far. All he could usefully do now was to get some rest. He climbed into bed and fell asleep almost instantly.

The rapped signal on the door woke him like an alarm. He sat straight up, hand reaching under the pillow for the Browning. Incredibly it was dusk. He could barely see around him, a dark greyness in the room like fog. He found his watch. He had slept for almost nine hours. Quickly climbing from bed he slipped his socks on before padding over to the door for the light switch.

"Who is it?"

"Open up," said Mueller.

Gibbs held back against the wall, leaned forward and turned the key. "Okay."

Mueller came in, stared angrily at the levelled Browning before closing the door. Gibbs lowered the gun. "Can't be too careful."

"What's going on? What are you doing here?" The voice was full of hate and spite.

Gibbs kept the Browning at his side. "What do you think I'm doing here?"

"You should be at the other place. Nuzzale should be here." Suspicion was oozing from Mueller. Something had badly upset him. Gibbs had the impression that if he put his gun away Mueller would draw his. Gibbs said, "You'd better speak to Raul. He's the one who plays musical chairs with us. Mohammed and I have switched places."

"I could get no reply from there. Nothing." Mueller was roaming the room like an animal with a scent, his scuffed shoes dragging at the worn carpet.

"Something's upset you?"

Mueller turned, eyes blazing. "Raul's missing and Picale's dead. You don't know?"

"I heard about Picale on the radio. Some rich crank. It's a pity. A waste. But how the hell would I know if Raul's missing? You think *he* tells *me* his movements? I've been hanging around waiting for instructions." He sat on the arm of a chair. "Do you know how Picale was found?"

"That's the big question."

"Well, don't look at me. I didn't know where he was staying. I'm the last one anyone tells anything to. And sit down, for God's sake." But Mueller kept prowling and Gibbs felt his neck prickle as the German passed behind him.

Mueller was unsettled. Nuzzale and Raul missing, Picale dead. "Kurt Vogel killed Picale. I shot his father through the back of the head. He babbled for mercy for days. Everyone thought he was strong. He cried before I let him have it." No mention of the torture. It wouldn't have mattered to him. The German swung round suddenly facing Gibbs. "I don't trust you."

"Do any of you?"

"That sounds like you're not one of us."

"I'm a realist. My aims are the same but you all hate my S.A.S. background. If it helps I don't like you either."

Mueller wasn't insulted. Suddenly he straightened as he made

169

up his mind. "I'm going back to Nuzzale's pad. I'll open up."

"Why, for God's sake?"

"I don't know why. But that's what I must do."

"I'll come with you. Better than waiting."

Mueller didn't dissent. He saw the advantage of two and he wanted Gibbs in sight.

Muffled up, they walked round. It took some twenty minutes and neither spoke a word during that time. Gibbs gave the signal on the door. He put his ear to the wood, inviting Mueller to do the same. Mueller said, "Keep watch," and knelt to the keyhole.

They found Nuzzale where Vogel had left him. Mueller showed some relief as if he'd been expecting the worst and being right helped in some way. Gibbs kneeled on the bed, went through the motions of checking. He closed the now sad brown eyes. "He's cold. It must have been done some time ago." He turned round to say, "What's going on, Ludwig?" and faced Mueller's gun. He looked at the gun then at Mueller's eyes. "What's that for?" Gibbs kept his nerve. "You think I should join him?" But he was afraid of Mueller's expression. Mueller was confused and uncertain, and squeezing a trigger had solved so many problems before. It was an easy way out and he was on the point of taking it.

"*You* should be here. But Nuzzale is instead, and he is dead."

"You think I shot him?" Gibbs was still poised awkwardly on the bed.

"I think I don't know you at all. Don't move."

"Why should I shoot him? Did I shoot Picale too? And why didn't I shoot you in the back as we came in?"

Mueller was standing against the closed door, his shorn hair untidy and dirty, the unhealthy skin pale. The eyes were steady and indifferent. Gibbs could see that he was about to fire.

Still kneeling awkwardly on the bed Gibbs said, "I've got a knife on me. Why don't I dig the slugs out and you can compare them with mine?"

It was the sort of callousness that Mueller appreciated. He said, "Why should he be shot?"

"Perhaps Kurt Vogel did it. You say he did Picale."

Mueller acknowledged the possibility but did not lower the gun.

"I'm going to fall over if I stay like this. Put that gun away."

Gibbs climbed off the bed carefully, making sure Mueller could see his hands all the time. He added, "You sure Raul's missing?"

"I've tried his place several times."

"Were you supposed to meet him?"

When Mueller didn't answer Gibbs said, "You know Raul. Maybe he has more than one pad."

Mueller lowered the gun reluctantly. "Perhaps. I don't like the feel of things."

"Does it affect the operation?"

Mueller's expression was veiled. "Nothing will affect the operation."

"Is anyone going to tell me what it is?"

"If Raul hasn't told you no one will."

"Thanks for nothing. We'd better leave here. Lock up."

Mueller nodded. He had no feeling for Nuzzale's death but he didn't care for its circumstances. It meant they were under observation. Or had been betrayed. He scrutinised Gibbs again, vacillating considerably on what he should do. Mueller didn't know how to handle the situation which suggested only one answer: remove the problem. Gibbs, who arrived at the conclusion a fraction before Mueller had, flung himself at the German as Mueller's gun arm came up again. Gibbs grabbed the gun and broke the trigger finger in the trigger guard before Mueller could fire. Mueller screamed as Gibbs wrenched the gun and it flew on to the bed by Nuzzale's dead hand. Without the gun Mueller was useless; he had no physical strength and was holding the hand with the snapped forefinger, his hatred of Gibbs complete.

Gibbs drew the Browning. "Stay there Ludwig or I'll kill you." He moved over to retrieve Mueller's gun and in that time Mueller was through the door and gone, leaving it open.

Gibbs followed quickly, closing the door without using his fingertips. There was no time to lock it. He went down the stairs two at a time.

If Mueller lacked physical strength he had no shortage of speed and guile. A worried Gibbs searched in each direction, but Mueller had gone to earth.

16

"Do you intend to let the case go on board now its contents are disarmed?"

Ronnie Holder watched Bannerman across the desk, surprised at his reaction to the question. There was no sense of victory about Bannerman. At the moment he looked like a loser. Instead of answering he said, "I'm worried about young Ross Gibbs. He's floating loose and I dare not raise him on the box at the risk of it buzzing at a dangerous moment."

"Why doesn't he come in? There's nothing else he can do. He set up Picale and Nuzzale and personally gave us Orta."

Bannerman was still thoughtful. "He wants to run down Mueller and he's worried about the Hatton children."

"You didn't answer my question?"

"Oh?"

"About the case of small arms."

"There's no trick about the arms? Second fuses, that sort of thing?"

"None. They *are* harmless."

"Do you really believe that four characters who we already have in our sights are going to try to hijack Concorde knowing there'll be armed bodyguards? The moment they check in they'll be under surveillance."

"They don't know that."

"Don't they? They'd expect more than a routine check of passengers on a flight carrying top V.I.P.s yet they've drawn attention to themselves by obscuring themselves and coincidentally all paying cash. You don't find that odd?"

"You mean they're decoys?"

"I don't know what I mean. It's too easy." Bannerman showed irritation.

"Perhaps they think they've been clever."

"They *have* been clever. I wish I knew how."

"But it checks with what Orta has coughed."

"Orta's tough. We've been pushed for time."

"You think it's not these four? They're a smoke screen? That might mean the arms case is too."

"You're getting warmer. But we're no nearer. That's one reason I'm glad Ross is roaming. Ted's putting Orta under the blanket again. Let's hope it produces something quick. I think we're being conned."

*　　*　　*

Orta's world was floating. Even the surrounding blackness was moving, like a heavy swell on the sea at night. The sea thickened and darkened until it was total. Now it was oil and the universe was made of it. Opaque, liquid, suffocating and constantly moving, and with it, under its heavy pressure, went his head. His feet had left the floor, the bonds on his ankles no longer painful. His arms were numb but there was still feeling in the wrists, which were held to the solid bar above his head. He tried to concentrate on the bar for it was reality. But he could not see it nor feel it. He reached with his fingers but they had disappeared painlessly and he had nothing left with which to grope. He was floating in the oil now, but below its surface, and he could not understand why he hadn't drowned as he drew the thick sludge into his lungs. He heard himself gag. It must have been him because he could not see or feel anyone else, yet the sound had come from outside this black world, a strange relay from outer space.

Intermittently the pain in his legs and lower back returned. At such times he knew he couldn't stay up any longer yet his bound hands would not let him sag. The cramp in his calves was excruciating. When the pain was there he could almost reason. The agony of it pulled him from the black sea of oil but he badly wanted to sit down. Yet the pain was his saviour. It was largely this that made him hang on and, conversely, was by far the worst to endure.

Through his haze the rough cockney voice would reach him, the same questions, over and over. And he supplied the same answers when the hood was lifted and the light blinded him. Sometimes he did not hear his replies but by the voice that came back at him he knew that he had, and that they were still the same. But he was reaching the point of total confusion. His will was flagging, the gaps growing longer between concentration and intermittent accidents. He knew what he had to do but his words were becoming impossible to control. His replies had become instinctive instead of planned and instinct would, in the end, let him down as his mind crumbled. Once that happened it was over; for him and for the rest.

Orta dug into the very depths of resistance. He made a last, incredible effort to recall all he had been taught. The lessons he had learned at Patrice Lumumba had never been this severe. Theory, even when followed by practical application, could only go so far for fear of destroying the mind to a point of permanent psychological damage. Right now they wanted to destroy him if by so doing he would produce the truth. He fought on, knowing that in the end he would lose and that he could resist for little longer. He conjured up the many considerable hates within him and was surprised to find himself struggling against his bonds. That was a mistake. The appreciation took an age to reach him.

Light and questions again. He couldn't recall the hood being removed. He must have answered for someone said, "Okay. We'll tidy you up for Special Branch." Strong hands helped him to the bed. His cords must have been untied but he had no feeling in his legs or arms. It was his body only that sat on the bed, ill-balanced and in danger of falling. He fell back and a suggestion of feeling touched his legs as someone lifted them on to the mattress. He was exhausted and unclear about what happened to him, yet somehow he knew it was over. For the moment anyway.

Orta was too disorientated to know for how long he had been tortured but with release came the seeds of a fight back. Terribly slow at first, once he could grasp a fraction of what had happened momentum increased considerably. The will strengthened with realisation. How had he done? The cockney seemed satisfied.

Orta pushed himself to the side of the bed feeling both mentally and physically depleted. The fight with Ross Gibbs he could have borne but for the psychological treatment. He started deep breathing, concentrated, got the detail of the room back in focus. He felt Ted watching him through the grille but didn't rise to the bait, keeping his head down, gaze averted. He stopped breathing exercises immediately.

Ted said, "'Ave a shower and get yourself tidied up. When

you're ready I'll give yer back your shoes. Don't make me come in, sonny."

Orta had intended to refuse although he knew that physically there was no way that he could cope with the cockney; the man was granite. Mention of the shoes changed his mind. The fight with Gibbs had been so fast, close and bloody that he'd had no opportunity to use what they contained against the S.A.S. man. This was different. He made a show of reluctance, gave a passable cowed impression as he stripped and moved dejectedly to the shower cubicle. The shower freshened him. For the last few seconds he ran it ice cold to endure another kind of torture. By the time he was dressed he felt considerably better.

Ted, watching him through the grille, said, "Comb your hair and I'll throw your shoes in. When they're on, stand with legs and arms wide against the wall. I'll shoot you if I don't like anything you do. Okay?"

Orta liked the burly cockney's friendly aggression. The man meant what he said no matter how he said it. When the shoes came in, already examined for hollowed out heels and soles, Orta had difficulty in drawing out the short, fine needle from the instep flap. His fingers were unsteady and it was vital to avoid the tip. It took a little time, and as he sat on the edge of the bed he half turned his back as if fumbling to get his shoes on.

Ted, still watching, misinterpreted the move. "Don't think I'm coming in to 'elp you on with 'em mate. I'm not that stupid."

Orta could hardly feel the needle between his fingers. Its use was twofold; to commit suicide in an impossible situation or to get him out of trouble if it could be used. To palm it was impossible without risk of a scratch. He positioned it between two fingers. Too fine to feel in such a position, he had to hope it remained there.

"Over by the wall, cocker."

"Filth. Torturing bastard."

"'Ave it your way." When Orta was against the wall, legs and arms splayed, Ted went in, gun in one hand, a pair of handcuffs in the other. He approached Orta warily, having developed a begrudging respect. He was afraid only that Orta might make it a little difficult for him; he had no doubt of the outcome. He reached up to pull one arm down, snapping the bracelet round the first wrist. He pulled down the second arm and Orta struggled. It was minimal resistance but during it Ted felt a prick on his hand which enlarged to a brief unbearable agony before he felt no more.

*   *   *

It took three separate calls to reach Bannerman by telephone. Gibbs said irritably, "Is this what you call back-up?"

"You took yourself off, dear boy, and I didn't want to risk breaking radio silence. I've restricted your calls to me personally."

"Why? Don't you trust the others?"

"You sound distressed."

"I had and lost Mueller. Now I'm completely blown."

"You'd better come in."

"I'd like to push around the apartments some more first."

"That could be dangerous."

"Anything from Raul?"

"An on-board drop of arms. Dealt with."

"You don't sound satisfied."

"I'm not. Look, I want you on that plane."

"Take-off?"

"Thirteen twenty-five."

"I'll pick up Kumira and the kids before midday. Their father should know they're safe before take-off."

"No. I'll get some men on to that. You concentrate on the plane."

"It'll be crawling with guards. What can I do?"

"I don't really know. But I want you there."

"Gut feeling?"

"I hate that expression. I don't want Hatton told about the children. I want everything as it is. If there's a leak certain people might cancel. I want them. All of them. He can be told when it's over."

Gibbs was unhappy. Bannerman hadn't seen Phyllis Hatton crumble nor seen the children's fear. "Which side of the pond do you expect *that* to happen?"

"I don't know."

"You seem to be groping" – a fact that worried Gibbs more than anything else. It wasn't like Bannerman.

"There's a missing factor. You might pick it up."

"It all sounds dicey to me. You're playing with two heads of State. Why not cancel the flight?"

"It's been suggested. The P.M. won't wear it. She won't stand down in face of threats and nor will Schmidt. They take the view that we should be capable of protecting aircraft". He paused. "I'll arrange for your tickets at Heathrow. Collect at enquiries. A visa'd passport will be in the same envelope. Whatever you do, don't miss the flight."

Gibbs said, "Okay, but leave me with radio silence." He hung up before Bannerman would interpret his intention.

★   ★   ★

Bannerman weighed Gibbs's cryptic instruction and decided there was nothing he could do about it. He didn't like the arrangement, but a precipitous action from him could be disastrous. He rang Ted and received no answer. He held on for a very long time before quietly replacing the receiver. The special taxi was with Ted, so Bannerman called for a pool car and drove round to Hammersmith. He pulled up in the narrow, cobbled alley opposite the double doors and noted the small red light glowing above them. His qualms increased to fear and emotion hit him for the first time in years. Ted had always been special to him, the gruff cockney the complete antithesis of himself.

Unarmed, Bannerman climbed back into the car and called Ronnie Holder on the radio. "Bring an armed team and something for me."

It was half an hour before four men arrived and Bannerman had sat watching the red light as if hoping it would go out. He wasted no words, simply telling Holder bluntly, "Orta must be loose and he could only manage that by killing Ted." Holder realised what it had cost Bannerman to be so matter of fact; he gave Bannerman an issue gun.

They went through the routine procedure. An offshoot from military street-fighting technique, they covered the doors, opened them, went through the garage workshop and down the stairs. They worked fast and well and reached a now open door at the foot of the stairs.

They found Ted in the unlocked cell; a big scruffy heap that would pour out a harsh cockney voice no more. His pockets had been turned out in Orta's frantic search for keys. The double street doors had presumably been closed after his departure as a delaying tactic.

Bannerman knelt by Ted, moved as he had been only once before over his stepson Steve – for which Craven had paid the price. His emotion ran deep behind a rigid, almost callous expression. He put his hand out and lightly touched Ted's shoulder several times. The agony before death still showed in the drawn-back lips, the staring eyes. Bannerman closed the lids and rose.

With Orta loose Ross Gibbs was in grave danger. Bannerman took the risk of trying to raise Gibbs on both car radio and Ronnie Holder's hand set. Gibbs was either refusing to respond or was out of range. They left Hammersmith, and back in his office Bannerman made arrangements for Ted's body to be removed. There was little else he could do now except wait, but he was more certain than ever that he lacked vital information. He sat behind his desk, depressed and worried and seeking the clue that he had somehow missed.

17

ROSS GIBBS WAS uneasy. He had no objection to flying to New York, although if he could find Mueller it might solve all their problems. The idea of leaving Ginny and Tommy Hatton with Yukari Kumira while he went off to the States was unacceptable. He knew Kumira too well. If she found herself in trouble she would retaliate on the children without thought. There were other things, too, that he was unhappy about. Bannerman's untypical uncertainty: not to be told his role, yet. Gibbs had played undercover far too long. Now he was about to step out of line.

He went round to Fran as soon as he believed she would be home. She noticed his grimness as soon as she let him in. Cass made a fuss of him but Gibbs couldn't raise himself to play.

"Something's wrong. Sit down, you look bushed."

He shook his head. "Can't stay. Near crisis point. I may want you to do me a favour later tomorrow. I won't be here. I'll be away for a few days."

"Still not breaking the law?"

"I wouldn't ask that of you. The opposite. I know it's asking a lot on short acquaintance."

"Acquaintance? You want a hot drink?"

"No thanks. I've no time. I can't tell you now. You'll curse me for that but I won't see you again for a day or two. Anyway I won't tell you until I'm sure. I'll phone. Okay?"

"All right." Fran didn't like the look of him; he seemed feverish.

"It might be in the middle of the night."

She smiled feebly. "To check up on me?" She shrugged apologetically. "Weak joke."

"I'm sorry Fran. This time tomorrow it should all be over."

She wanted to ask more, but he had enough problems, whatever they were. Even during the few days she had known him his face had drawn in. She watched him unconsciously rubbing the swollen contusions on his knuckles.

"You *will* be all right?" It was a silly question and she knew it, but she could not prevent herself.

He smiled. "No problem. Do I get a kiss?"

★   ★   ★

Raul Orta went to a safe house and shaved off his beard, the skin pasty beneath. He had no intention of staying long. He rang the remaining apartments knowing that some were now anything but safe, until he tracked down Mueller. The two men sat in the freezing cold in St. James's Park which they had almost to themselves. They walked on the iced path curving between two totally white swards, luminous in the dark.

When they had brought each other up to date there was one common conclusion. Ross Gibbs would pay for his treachery. They had no doubt now that he was connected with the deaths of Nuzzale and Picale, whoever had squeezed the trigger.

Immediately more important was that fundamentally nothing had changed for them. Orta's plan was working as he had intended. Mueller was ready and was now the key. "I'll break in tonight," he said.

Orta, after his harrowing experience, was cautious. "They'll be watching the place."

"Of course. But more from the point of view of front door callers and keeping an eye on Hatton. There is plenty of cover at the back and four o'clock in the morning is a good time. They won't expect it; not a break-in."

Orta felt his legs weakening. His wrists were sore. He said nothing of this to Mueller. "I hope you'll operate as if the place is surrounded."

Mueller confirmed that he would. The risks were higher now that they were on the run. Yet everything was still under control, the prize more attractive.

When they reached a call-box they both somehow squeezed inside while Orta rang Kumira. He hung up after a brief exchange and the two men stepped outside. Orta pounded his hands from cold. "She rang Hatton on cue. Made the kid scream. There'll be no trouble from him."

Mueller was disturbed. "Hatton's line will be tapped."

Orta smiled grimly. "I'm banking on it." He looked at his watch.

"It looks as if that S.A.S. bastard hasn't found the new kidnap hideout. Kumira's had no problems."

"Should we go down there?"

Orta considered it. "Let's check your gadgets first."

★   ★   ★

Gibbs drove slowly. There was time, and the minor roads hadn't improved. The freeze-up was unrelenting but at least further snow had held off. He reached the tracks leading to the kidnap cottage at about eight thirty. It was pitch dark, stars in their trillions but no moon yet. On his own this was not something he could rush. He had risked picking up the listening gear to establish the presence of Kumira and the children. The youngsters had eaten and were complaining about the tinned food; tea when they preferred coffee, and that had been rolled over to them in a vacuum flask. When they referred in derogatory form to the "Chinkie", he knew they were talking of Kumira. They were too young to draw a distinction between the physical appearance of the Japanese and the Chinese. It seemed that Kumira was still alone. A radio or television was on.

Gibbs sat on his haunches, microphone as near as he dared. The children started to talk of home and their parents and then, unexpectedly, Ginny burst into tears. Tommy tried to reassure her with the young man image Gibbs had already seen. Gibbs packed his gear and took it back to the car. He removed his topcoat, as cold as it was, and kept a grip on the Browning. He had read Kumira's dossier many times. What she had done to some of her earlier associates was chilling; what she had done to her enemies was also on record. It would be better for him not to forget.

He took the track back to the villa as if he was stepping on glass. Everything was brittle with cold. He crossed the frozen, snow-stiffened grass in slow motion. As he drew nearer he could hear the very faint sound of the radio. Kumira obviously had Western tastes in pop music.

He kept clear of the children's room. If they heard him their reaction would be unpredictable. The only lights came from two windows close together. Possibly the same room. The curtains were drawn. He continued round the house, trying to locate the

181

kitchen. With all windows covered it was a little difficult until he found the drain and the sink outlet pipes. The dripping water from the pipe had frozen into long icicles. He examined the door and the small window beside it. He thought it out. The most likely places for someone to go would be the kitchen or the toilet. Yet the only other room available was next to the children's.

★   ★   ★

Nursing kidnapped children was not easy. After a while they could try mischief or yell, cry, and shriek. They could throw things, too, if a little discipline wasn't applied. It was a pity it was the girl who had started the tantrums. She was pretty, rosy-cheeked as damp climate children are. Clear skin and big eyes. Yet ugly when crying and her face contorted with fright and anger. She had to be punished severely, and that had left her less attractive. The boy had tried to protect her, so he too had received wounds. Both now were settling down better. The girl was over her petulance and was behaving herself more, the weals on her young face were already healing, her prettiness and brightness almost restored.

Kumira's mind kept going back to Ginny and the boy. Her job was immensely lonely and boring. She was a prisoner as they were, forbidden to leave the house. The only difference was the lack of shackles and the freedom to move in the small confines of the cottage. She could accept the discipline of it but it did not make her like it. She had been miscast by Raul Orta who should have used her more actively. She did, however, accept the need and in a scheme so grand would rather play this part than none.

The biggest scare had come when she heard over the radio of the gunning down of Picale. That had been a shock, but Orta had consoled her, told her to hang on. His second call had suggested that he might come down with Mueller.

She had tried reading but had grown restless. There was enough food for three more days and that was more than enough. One small foot tapped to the beat of the music coming from the transistor. Her energy was beginning to overtake her mental stalemate. She badly needed something to do. Getting up, she paced the small room, then danced round the austere furniture in lithe and graceful movements. The only jarring note was the suspended automatic pistol from the belt at the waistline of her heavy woollen dress. Suddenly she stopped gyrating and decided to make herself some jasmine tea.

★   ★   ★

Gibbs was peeling back the lead latticework with a commando knife when the lights went on in the kitchen. He froze immediately. A tap was turned on and he moved back cautiously. There was nothing he could do but wait. Kumira was humming softly to the music that filtered into the kitchen. Without his topcoat Gibbs shivered, but he did not want to be hampered by it. Afraid of dropping the knife because of numbed fingers he eased it back into its waistband sheath.

The ten-minute wait was an eternity to him but the lights went out again. He heard the internal kitchen door close and rubbed his hands to restore the circulation.

Opening up the lead he removed four small panes of glass, laying them carefully down away from himself. He bent the lead frame carefully to avoid cracking the remaining glass.

He took off his jacket to get an arm through the small gap and lifted the curtain to move articles on the window ledge. He turned the key, waited, put his jacket back on, and opened the door. His eyes, well used to the darkness by now, quickly located the inside door and he took up position where it would open. He waited, gun raised, for perhaps two minutes.

From the faint light strip under the door he assumed that the kitchen led straight to the room where Kumira was. The radio was more muted here, giving the impression that it came from a room further along. He had now been in darkness for some time. From the moment he opened the door the glare would hit him. He found the handle, did not turn it. Placing his ear near to the wood he tried to pick up Kumira's position. There was a faint chink of china. Was she sitting down drinking her tea? He burst through the door in one frantic movement.

Kumira rolled back off her chair, the cup flying, tea splashing the wall. Gibbs did not follow up but threw himself sideways as she fired through the back of the chair, tufts of cotton waste bursting through in a tight group. A spring burst in the chair and tore through the fabric. The shots went through the open doorway and there was a rending of metal as they hit the cooker, some whining off. In the next room Ginny started to scream while her brother repeatedly shouted for help.

Gibbs heard the click and moved quickly round the chair. Kumira was kneeling, removing the empty magazine with haste.

"Drop it," said Gibbs, "You'll never make it."

"You'll have to kill me. Filth."

"That won't be difficult."

Suddenly she flung herself at him. Slight and agile, aided by unbelievable fanaticism, she hurled herself from the floor throwing her gun at his head as she did so. Gibbs backed, ducked and fired twice. Kumira collapsed just in front of him, a surprised look on her face. She showed no sign of pain. Her thigh was bleeding, her dress rucked well above her knees. For a moment she looked down stupidly at the wound then rose, one hand against the wall. She sneered openly at him. "Two shots at zero range. You only hit me once."

He didn't rise to her taunt; it was all she had left although even that could be a dangerous assumption. With his spare hand he removed twine from a pocket. "Turn round."

She laughed openly then spat at him. "Try it." Her eyes had lost their opaqueness; they were bright with hate. He stepped forward at which she took the weight on her good leg and leaned over to claw at his eyes. He brought the Browning down hard on her wrist and broke it. She collapsed again, now with a cry of pain. She gazed up at him, her feelings mixed. "I'll kill you so slowly for that," she whispered at him.

"Turn round," he said tonelessly. Her expression was lost again and she was with her private thoughts. She turned slowly, now obviously in pain. "Hands behind you back." The broken wrist was already swollen, an ugly shape as her hands came behind her. Gibbs came forward with the greatest respect. Kumira still had one good hand and two legs: she was more than capable with all three. He dummied behind her so that she turned the wrong way as she tried to unbalance him, and he clipped her hard behind the ear.

The children were still shouting but Gibbs ignored them as he quickly tied Kumira's wrists and ankles. The only concession he made was to bind her arms above the break. He searched her roughly, found the spare magazine in her belt and removed it. The keys to the children's chains were in a bag on a cheap, whitewood sideboard. He picked up her gun and pocketed it.

He went to the children's door, opening it without taking his eyes from the prone and curled Kumira. Even when nearly unconscious she was not to be underrated. He groped for the light switch inside the door, then pressed it. Tommy and Ginny were sitting upright in bed, white and scared and clutching each other.

"I'm sorry I frightened you," Gibbs said. "I had to take care of Chinkie." He pointed. "She's tied up and won't hurt you any more." He could see he'd done little to ease their fears. "I won't hurt you. Honestly. I know you recognise me but you'll be safe now. I'm not one of the gang any more. Okay? I'm going to get you home."

"*When?*" Tommy, putting tremendous effort into his young man image.

"As soon as I can. In the morning. Will you trust me?"

They were silent, still clutching each other. He couldn't blame them.

"If I take your chains off and put them on Chinkie, would you trust me then?"

Tommy nodded slowly. Gibbs said, "You'll have to give me a hand, Tommy. To chain her up. She's a bad one. Will you do that?"

"Yes." Still not sure.

"There's a reason why I can't take you back immediately. It affects your father. You wouldn't want him to be harmed in any way, would you?"

"No." A chorus.

"I want a promise from you both. When I release you, don't try to run away. There's nowhere to run to. We're miles out in the country and you'll freeze to death. In return I'll promise to get you back to your mother. Come on, let's hear you."

Tommy had to nudge the doubtful Ginny into it but they promised.

It largely depended on the common sense of Tommy. Whatever he did Ginny would follow. As Gibbs unlocked the chains he said, "Tommy, whatever I did before there is no way I'll do it again. I'm relying on you. You're going home. Don't muck it up."

185

The two children each rubbed the ankle which had been manacled. What finally resolved them was seeing Kumira trussed up. They were afraid of her. Gibbs carried her into the bedroom, laid her on the bed, manacled her ankles, using both chains, and then undid the cord, retying her wrists across her belly. The broken wrist was swollen and misshapen. He tore a sheet and bandaged the wounded leg. The children were searching for their coats and gloves. As he helped them he said, "She won't hurt you again." With Mueller still loose they had to move fast.

They found their coats under the stairs and were putting them on when the chains rattled. The children involuntarily shuddered. Gibbs went to the door. Kumira's bound hands were searching for something in her hair. She was so intent and so much in pain that she failed to notice him. Her hands came down with a probe between them. As he stepped into the room and reached to take it from her she tried to stab him with it and came close. After that the pain in her wrist slowed her and he grabbed her again, got a grip but had to fight for it while she bit his hand. He called out, "Tommy, I need your help."

Tommy came in reluctantly and stood just inside the door. Kumira was heaving about the bed and even shackled posed a threat.

"I'm going to hold her while you search through her hair." He held up the probe. "She just produced this and would have tried it on her ankle locks. Don't be afraid. I'll see that she doesn't hurt you."

Gibbs grabbed a handful of Kumira's hair, jerked her to a sitting position, then pulled her head right back. Holding her hair with one hand he gripped her jaw with the other, putting pressure on the nerve centres. He let go the hair and gripped her neck. She was in a vice. She tried to claw his hand away but he increased the nerve pressure until she stopped. "Okay, Tommy. Take your time but make a good job of it."

The boy gained confidence as Gibbs held her still. He unwound the jet black hair and, at Gibbs's instruction ran his fingers over the scalp. There was nothing more. Gibbs offered a wink to Tommy who seemed to enjoy the chance of getting back at Kumira. "Okay. Back off."

Tommy stepped back and Gibbs let Kumira go and even then she tried to take a bite at him. She started mouthing in Japanese so vehemently that saliva trickled over her lips.

Gibbs said to Tommy, "Thanks. You did a good job there." He waited for her madness to subside. She finally fell back, legs straddled, small breasts rising. She wiped her mouth, slowly regained her breath and stared up at Gibbs in a malevolent attempt to will him to death.

Gibbs observed quietly, "You need a doctor for the leg and the wrist. You've lost blood even if you seem to operate without it. I can do one of two things; get a doctor or release you so that you can get your own. A patched-up freedom. If you tell me now where Mueller is."

She laughed at him. It took an effort, her face was covered with the sweat of pain.

"We've got Raul. Nuzzale and Picale are dead. All we want is Mueller."

She seemed puzzled, then hid her feelings. "I don't want your doctor. It does not worry me to die. Filthy traitor."

"We know that the co-pilot is taking arms on board. We know that they will be picked up by someone in flight. Nothing is going to work for you. I'm giving you a chance to get out."

Kumira stared at him blankly, the sheen back over the dark eyes. Her lip quivered and she burst out laughing. She turned her face away, almost choking from laughter and broke into a spasm of coughing. She recovered slowly, turning back to look at him, fighting to hide her feelings.

Gibbs noticed the sense of triumph in her eyes before her expression glazed over again. He was sickened, and the cold struck him as never before that night. She was trying to suppress her laughter again. Oh Christ. She was biting her lip now, trying to avert her gaze but wanting to witness his agony of mind. And then she was talking, baiting, swearing, hardly pausing for breath: it struck him coldly that she was trying to keep him there.

He gave one last glance at the still taunting Kumira and rushed back to the children. "Come on. Out. *Now*."

They were ready. Their excitement should have communicated itself to him, and in a thoroughly preoccupied way he did notice it. Yet he could not enjoy it with them. A sense of horror had caught him unawares, and a pattern was falling into place in agonising slow-motion. He took their gloved hands, one each side, as he hurried them down the track to the car, their breath rising like morning mist.

"*Run*." Gibbs set the pace, dragging the children with him, heading for the road. "*Run*." A fierce urgent whisper. With one tugging at each of his hands his fear reached them.

He had parked the car round the curve of the road beyond the track. It was further to go but it wouldn't be seen. He bundled them on the back seats and drove off without lights, using the reflection from the packed snow. He headed away from the main road, relying on a sense of direction to map a course. It was impossible to hurry. The minor road hadn't been cleared; again and again he felt the tail swinging and he performed quick corrections.

His intense and near-reckless driving frightened the children. Their incessant babbling in the back was an added distraction he could have done without. They had been through enough without him shouting at them to keep quiet, so he suffered their noise. He said, "I'll ring your parents when we see a phone."

They stopped at a call-box and Gibbs phoned Bannerman, who answered as if he'd been waiting with hand on receiver. When Gibbs told him he had the children Bannerman exploded. "You damned young fool. Orta's loose, and if he finds out the children are safe it changes everything. He'll expect us to inform Hatton and for Hatton to tell them what to do with the case."

"Orta loose? How?"

"Get round here fast and I'll tell you. You've ruined everything."

"No. You have Kumira's voice on tape. Get a girl down who can imitate her. She'd better come with an armed team. If Orta and Mueller go to the cottage they'll be caught. If they ring, the girl can reassure them. They'll only want to know the kids are safe and that I haven't been there."

"Get an impersonator at this notice?"

"She can play the bloody tape on the way down. A team could be there in ninety minutes."

"And if Orta calls during that time we're done. I don't know what will happen; how they will react."

"I'm not apologising. The kids come first."

"Get round here and stop doing my job. On no account contact the Hattons. You understand?"

Gibbs went back to the car. He'd stuck his neck out and he knew it. But both Orta's and Mueller's revenge could well have been taken out on the children. He steadied himself, saying disconsolately over the back seat, "I can't raise them. No one answers. They might be out, they might have taken sleeping pills. I'll take you to a friend."

They didn't like that, but he could not evade a direct order. They were beginning to distrust him again. "Look," he said uneasily, "I'll take you past the house. It's on the way, but I can't risk stopping. It might be watched. Just to show you. Okay?"

The house lay in darkness. It was a new development, no street lights. He drove on and found himself nervous of any approaching cars. There was little traffic at this time of night, which made it worse, each one ominous.

★   ★   ★

He knocked Fran up with some reluctance. When she stood at her door in housecoat and slightly tousled hair he wanted to hold her. She was relieved to see him and surprised to see the children holding his hands. She laughed, finding it hard to believe. They went in but it was Cass more than Fran's friendliness that won the children over. The kitten had uncurled from a blanketed basket that Fran had bought her and was protesting at the unexpected light.

All Fran could do was to accommodate the children in armchairs, but even that was luxury after the chains. Gibbs left them almost before she knew he was going but he couldn't wait. He gave Fran a telephone number together with instructions.

★   ★   ★

Bannerman was in a heavy woollen dressing gown and looking his age. He had cooled down a little, begrudgingly admitting that he'd got a team off against the clock. He had a filter pot going and both men fought off fatigue with strong, hot coffee. Gibbs thought that some of Bannerman's authority had disappeared along with his clothes; his chief looked tired and vulnerable. The weakened image went as he recounted Orta's escape and Ted's death. His tone was soft and reflective. Somehow Orta would pay. "We took another look at the arms case, Ronnie and I. Thorough. Used probes and detectors. It's harmless."

189

"But you're still not satisfied."

"No. Frankly I don't know what to tell you to look for once you're on Concorde. Except the obvious. There's another thing that concerns me. The phone tap revealed that Kumira called Hatton, put Tommy on just long enough for identification then plucked a scream from him before hanging up."

"He didn't mention it in the car."

"He was probably too relieved to be free. There's more than the obvious reason for the call. Hatton hasn't told us of it. He doesn't know his phone is tapped though he might expect it to be."

"You think there's another approach to him? Not by phone?"

"It could well be. He's terrified for his children. We don't know it all."

"Have you tried contacting him again?"

"I don't want to. I want him to go ahead. We will, of course, do a final check of the case in the briefing room.

There was nothing to do but wait. Gibbs drank another coffee, cleaned the Browning, and replaced the two rounds he had used, while Bannerman watched. Sleep was not contemplated by either of them. There was too little time.

★   ★   ★

The sky was slate grey when he drove down to Heathrow airport. Snow clouds were swelling up from the east, squeezing out the paling stars and blocking the moon. Traffic was already heavy and miserable, hunched together; dipped headlamps fighting the gloom. He'd topped up the tank. He stayed in line in the under-pass, the neon strips pointing the inevitable way in arrowhead perspective, and followed the signs to Number 3 Terminal. Already he could hear the whine of the big jets, and through the lifting murk see the lights of a moving aircraft. He walked back to the terminal from the car park.

They hadn't made his ticket out at the enquiry desk. The instruction was there and so was the sealed passport, but the flight was still several hours away. He hung about impatiently while the ticket was completed, and when he had it was surprised to find it in his own name. He checked the passport. Brand new with two hundred dollars inside. He discovered that he was an actor. Against the issuing office stamp on page four, just below the initials of the issuing officer, was the small code that identified his real vocation. He hadn't expected it to be left off, but he had no other way of proving his status. A United States visa had been stamped. He was holding a first class ticket on Concorde and was beginning to look like a wino who had slept rough and had fought for the position under the shelter.

He was there too early, of course, but it gave him a chance to watch arrivals while sipping doubtful coffee. After a time he prowled restlessly, keeping his eyes open for Bannerman.

At ten thirty he spotted what he considered to be the arrival of a security team. They scattered through the concourse, reading newspapers, magazines; one sat beside him on the balcony from where there was a wider view. Special Branch men reinforced by an armed section of the Metropolitan Police. He made no attempt to identify himself; the process was too involved and there was no point. These men would not be travelling.

His uneasiness grew as he waited. There had been something missing all along. The aircraft should be sealed tight with the huge security force they had working on her. Yet doubt persisted then grew and he started to roam again. He thought back to the beginning; every meeting, every conversation he'd had with Orta and his team. He recalled every single word that he could, and still he was convinced that he was missing something.

If the link did not lie with words could it rest with events? He chronicled them carefully and came up with nothing. Time was passing and his fears grew. The Hatton children entered his mind and he tried to cast them out; they intruded yet would not go away. It was no time to be concerned for them; they were free and would recover from their ordeal. And then behind their fading image he could see their darkened house. He stopped walking and someone bumped into him. Why had he stopped? He recalled the house again, deep shadows, no street lights. He felt close to an answer yet still could not see one.

The house. The Hattons. The case. He looked around him, seeing little, anxiety building up. He should be doing more, but what? Every possible check had been made. His restlessness increased and he decided to make enquiries about the flight crews. Immediately he found a barrier, and himself under suspicion. It was some time before the duty officer found a security man who

191

understood the passport coding, and that turned out to be Ronnie Holder.

"Where's Bannerman?" Gibbs asked once they'd detached themselves from the concourse melée.

Holder shrugged. "Briefing room. What's the problem?"

"I want to see him before the co-pilot boards."

Holder smiled. Both men, while talking, were searching, probing arrivals, anyone. "Bannerman's had the aircrew sealed off. They may not know the protection they're enjoying but they've got it anyway."

"Tell Bannerman I must see him."

"My brief is clear. And it's not chasing after him."

"It's vital."

"He'd have my balls off if I slipped up on instructions and something went wrong."

"Something might go wrong if you don't."

Holder caught Gibbs's tone. "You'd better tell me." When Gibbs hesitated, he added "Don't you know or don't you trust me?" He grinned, "You've been in the cold too long."

Gibbs made up his mind. "I was with Kumira a few hours ago. She was hilarious at the suggestion that arms were being taken on board. Bannerman knows this – he's just as worried. It's a late thought, but what about the case itself?"

Holder nodded agreement. "George had the same idea. When we went the second time we examined the case. The hinges were over-large and we thought they might contain detonators – thought the case itself might be made of plastic explosive. Didn't he tell you?"

"Not like that; just that you took a second look."

"The case is a special job all right. Heavy for its size, but it's made for a heavy load. Anyway it's clean. If we missed anything there couldn't be enough explosive to burst a soap bubble."

"Where's the case now?"

"Either on board or in the briefing room. You don't think we did the job right?"

"Don't be bloody silly. If you say it's clean, then it's clean."

"But you don't like the idea of being on board with it?" The remark was from genuine concern.

"I must see Bannerman before I board."

"Okay, I'll fix it. Won't solve anything. The plane is being searched from high tail to droopy nose before any passenger gets near her."

"Is there any problem getting my Browning on board?"

"The bodyguards will insist on issuing you something with pancake bullets. Heavy stoppers but won't pierce the hull."

"I'll check in after I've seen Bannerman."

Bannerman had left the briefing room just after the crew had left for the aircraft. It would not be exceptional for them to board earlier than usual with such important passengers. Gibbs caught up with Bannerman as he was coming down the stairs.

"What's the problem? You should be on board."

"There's plenty of time. The case gone?"

"With Hatton. We've filled the Captain in. Had to. We examined the case again in the briefing room." They reached the bottom of the stairs and sought a quieter position away from the ever drifting crowd.

"A third time?"

They stood by the huge windows looking out over the apron.

"Had to. Hatton scared the life out of us by giving a ride to a student thumbing a lift."

"When was that?"

"On the way to the airport this morning. We never lost sight of him. Nasty fright, though."

"Odd to give a lift to a stranger with what Hatton has on his mind."

"Very odd. Claims he needed a distraction, anything to take his mind off things."

"And the case is still clean?"

Bannerman placed a hand tolerantly on Gibbs's shoulder. "I've been through it as you're doing. The student was picked up later. He's as clean as the case. I'm just as uneasy. It's almost as if they wanted the case to be examined."

"Keep us occupied?"

"Perhaps."

"What about the cash-paying passengers?"

"Welsch, Julick, Harb and Kawai. They haven't checked in yet."

"Do you think they will?"

Bannerman was frowning. "It worries me. You're thinking who might be top of the waiting list if they cancel or fail to check in?"

"They've certainly occupied a lot of your time."

"Yes. So will the first four on the waiting list."

Gibbs was watching Bannerman closely. "So it's all sewn up. Nothing more to worry about." It was meant neither sarcastically nor as serious observation. Gibbs wasn't sure how he meant it. But the strained silence from that point and the expression of both men clearly conveyed that neither believed one word of it.

Morosely, Bannerman observed, "The case was taken on board with the full knowledge of the Prime Minister and the German Chancellor. They know what we are trying to do. We've had to assure them that the case is harmless, of course. They want the pack caught as much as we do." Bannerman was almost talking to himself as if rehearsing lines he had tried many times before. "I agree that the concentration has been on the case. I've had the plane isolated on the apron. I want no crowding in corridors. Every passenger will have to walk in the open and each one will be under close scrutiny."

"Is that the only reason you've left it out there away from the buildings?"

Bannerman's face changed, its lines seemingly deeper as though the skin was contracting. "All right, Ross, you've convinced me. I deplore the loss of opportunity but we'll compromise for safety's sake. Have a look at it when you're on board and if you're not satisfied get the bloody thing off. Let's see what happens from there."

18

GIBBS BOOKED HIS seat position. A block had already been marked off for the V.I.P.s in the front section immediately behind the coat spaces. He established that the forward boarding door would be used exclusively for the same party. He missed the arrival of Mrs. Thatcher and Herr Schmidt simply because he was already in the embarkation lounge, and when their motorcade drew up they were quickly escorted into a private and guarded V.I.P. lounge. Even though he did not see them at that stage the ripple went round the airport building like a growing whisper. Heads turned; tongues wagged. The buzz grew. And the buzz was right. For those who did not like flying there was satisfaction. This was one flight when all would be well. Most people had seen the array of tanks around the airport perimeter.

As Holder had predicted, Gibbs's high velocity Browning had been taken from him and replaced with a .38 revolver loaded with pancake bullets. The bullets actually contained lead shot in a canvas bag rolled into a cartridge, finally appearing a little longer than a normal .38 slug. On firing the bag would spin down the barrel leaving it at more than a thousand feet per second. The spinning motion flattened the bag to coin size within two feet of leaving the barrel, which slowed it down after a hundred feet to only a hundred and ninety feet per second. This deceleration prevented it from passing through the target. It was lethal only at a range of fifty feet.

Holder had arranged a special pass for Gibbs, which precluded a search at the boarding bay. He was guided to the rear door entry, handed over his boarding pass to the smiling stewardess and hurried up the aisle between the two rows of double seats. As soon as he passed the centre cabin staff seats and the slide raft packs he was stopped by two security men. Holder's pass was useful but they still didn't like it. They searched him, his pancake gun doing more to convince them than either his card or coded passport. They let him through reluctantly but there were three more men by the forward embarkation doors.

The V.I.P.s were not yet on board. They were invariably first or last, separate from the other passengers. Gibbs went through the tedious routine of being checked again and was then allowed through to the crew's approach. Past the coat spaces, the toilets, the galleys. Two uniformed men were talking in the space between the life raft pack and the passage leading between the double banks of electronics. They turned almost hostilely as he approached. At once he saw that one had four gold sleeve rings: the aircraft Captain. The other, with one gold ring less on his sleeve, pinched face and absence of colour, had to be Hatton.

"Your children are safe. Tommy and Ginny." There was no reason now why Hatton shouldn't know.

Hatton sagged with relief and the Captain put out a hand to steady him. "Are you sure?" Hatton asked. He rubbed the side of his face as if he had toothache.

"I released them myself. They're okay."

Hatton gave a sloppy grin. He simply hadn't expected it. He looked down at the cabin seat but if he intended to sit he changed his mind. He leaned against the wall instead, vast waves of relief sweeping through him. "I must tell Phyllis."

Gibbs said, "Don't worry. Your wife will be told."

"Thanks. Thank you. I don't know what else to say. This is Captain Godfrey."

"An unenviable start, Captain. Where's the case? I'm off-loading it."

"Thank God for that. Jim's been under tremendous strain. It's with the crew's handbaggage."

"Can you bring it out here?"

When he had the case Gibbs laid it flat on the floor and knelt beside it. Black leather covered the whole frame. He looked up. "Can we have better light than this? I don't want to take it into the passenger cabin."

The Captain produced a flashlight. Gibbs raised his radio. Bannerman came on at once. Gibbs said, "I've got the case here on board. Before I bring it off I want a quick verbal check. It can't be booby trapped if you checked in briefing."

"Go ahead."

"Bottom left hand corner of lid has a nick in the skin. Metal showing a fraction.

"Check."

"Colour black, no other marks on body. Handle has a tiny fold of leather. Chrome off one end of each hinge."

"Check. They're examination points."

Gibbs lifted the case, scrutinising it all round. "I'm opening lid." He checked the arms, was satisfied that they were harmless. It took time, and Bannerman's impatient breathing could be heard as Gibbs clicked in, then out again. The two pilots watched impassively. Hatton said tentatively. "It hasn't left me. It couldn't have been got at."

Gibbs, still kneeling, looked up wearily. "You slept with it under your pillow?"

Hatton said nothing.

"Took it around the house with you? In the bedroom at night?"

"No one has been in the house except your fellows."

"You mean you sat up all night to make sure?"

"I'm sorry." Hatton gestured.

"So am I," said Gibbs, still checking. "I know you've suffered."

"I just want to see the back of the damned thing," said Captain Godfrey tersely.

"A moment more," Gibbs raised the radio. "Can you give me the number on the guns?"

"Don't be funny, laddie, they've been removed. Aren't you through yet?"

Hatton interjected again. "I can promise you that its been with me since it was re-checked in the briefing room until brought on board."

Gibbs ignored him, spoke into the radio. "Last leg. Checking the interior packing. Colour of baize lining?"

"Red."

"Areas of examination?"

"Top, near pistol cavity. One small hole under baize. Another in the corner at eight o'clock from the lower grenade. Also one above . . ."

Gibbs listened then said, "I'm cutting baize out. Stand by." Once he had a knife blade inserted he ripped the cloth pack in patches. It had been well glued, and his face beaded with sweat as he struggled in the confined space under the sometimes wavering light. When he had enough off he spoke to Bannerman again. "Your probe points check. They seem okay. What was the substance?"

"It was some papier maché stuff. Quite hard. I hope this is the lot."

Gibbs probed very carefully with the knife. And again. "Was it hollow?"

"No. Solid."

"Paper maché right through?"

"I've already said so."

"Well *it's not papier maché now*. Not right through."

"Good God! Look here, hold on Ross. I'll check with Ronnie."

Gibbs sat back on his haunches wiping the sweat away. He rose slowly, flexing his legs as he stood beside the two pilots.

"What does all that mean?" demanded Godfrey.

"It means that the case hasn't been switched and nor have the arms. But the internal moulds for the arms has." He turned to Hatton. "What about the student?"

"The one I gave a lift to? He sat in the back. The case was on the seat beside me. There's no way he could have done it."

"Then it was done at your house during the night."

"You were supposed to be watching the house."

Gibbs made no comment.

Hatton went on, "Why wasn't it discovered in the briefing room? They examined it; pulled back parts of the baize."

Gibbs wiped his face wearily, "They'd done it twice already. They checked the areas they'd checked before. The probe points have been duplicated on the new interior which was already made and waiting to slip and glue into the case. Did you check your windows next morning?"

But Hatton had been too preoccupied with the danger to his children. The call he had received from Kumira during which Tommy had spoken and screamed had terrified him; he hadn't even told his wife.

Bannerman came on breathlessly. "Ronnie bears out what I said. Are you sure you're right?"

Gibbs didn't reply directly. "You'll have to leave it with me. I want radio silence just in case. Anything desperate, use the control tower."

Captain Godfrey was agitated as Gibbs closed the case. "What does all this mean?"

"It means that the whole of the moulding is explosive. I can see no obvious detonators. There's not enough time to dismantle and it's far too dangerous to rush."

"Then get it off my bloody plane quick. I'm having no bomb on board."

"It's not so simple." And as the Captain was about to exert authority, Gibbs added, "Bear with me, Captain. The idea is to blast this plane from the air. My guess is that it was meant to happen on take-off when the whole horror of it would be seen and recorded by film crews for world distribution." Gibbs saw their shock; they were shattered. And at last he knew why Raul Orta needed Mueller.

"Before you say that's all the more reason for getting it off quick, listen. Somewhere out there is a fanatic with high powered binoculars in one hand and a box with a button in the other. There is no time to find him. If he has the slightest doubt he'll press the button and cut his losses. I've met him, I know him. If anyone walks off this plane with anything remotely resembling this case he'll detonate it and still take most of the plane, if not all. People will die. Not as many as a planeload, but far too many. Can we get it off on a catering or fuel truck?"

"They've gone. We can't leave it on board, for God's sake!"

"And we can't take it off, obviously."

Behind them the plane was filling up. Captain Godfrey said. "We must offload the passengers immediately."

"You'll kill most of them if you try it. Mueller has his finger on the button. Rely on it. The slightest deviation from normal routine and he will press it. He will have studied that routine day after day. Anyone leaving this aircraft with anything more than a newspaper and up she goes."

Having been told that it was planned for his plane to be blown to bits with everyone on it, Captain Godfrey produced a creditable coolness. This was part due to shock and part to his professionalism – he would be as cool during a major crisis in the air – but he felt his authority slipping away, being eroded by a security man who looked as if he'd been pulled through a treadmill. At the moment he and Hatton were overdue on the flight deck. Flight checks had to be made. They were late for them and the chief steward had signalled that the V.I.P.s were on board.

Quietly he said, "I have our Prime Minister, the German Chancellor and a hundred or so other passengers. They are my responsibility. *I'll* decide what best to do."

"Of course, Captain. You'll agree that when the bomb explodes we want no one near it. That's not easy to achieve. We're under a microscope. The only absolute certainty is that the bomb *will* explode. May I make just one suggestion before you decide?"

*   *   *

To substantiate the belief that the case was to be picked up during flight Hatton had been instructed to place it at the rear end of the electronics bank in the space before the life raft pack on the starboard side. It was not intended that he would ever get that far. Gibbs went down to the rear galley. He had to squeeze his way past passengers who were still sorting themselves out in the aisle, the heavy bomb case in his hand. Captain Godfrey raised the senior steward on the intercom and gave specific instructions. When the plane was full the security men already on board left, handing over to the bodyguards who had embarked with the V.I.P.s.

It was a crucial moment. Gibbs knew that Mueller, wherever he was, would be particularly alert at this stage, watching who, and what, disembarked. He would be dying to send his deadly radio wave. A little later the engines were being run up and the doors closed. The senior steward joined Gibbs in the rear galley as Concorde taxied forward, slowly, elegantly. The chief steward's cabin staff was checking on seat-belt fastening. At the end of the taxi lane, the aircraft strained against the increased power of the engines, awaiting clearance to rotate. The great craft turned gracefully facing parallel to the main airport buildings. It was the sight of the day. All eyes would be focused on the take-off of this supersonic giant. Cameras whirred, the winter sun highlighting the aircraft as it taxied towards the runway.

Gibbs nodded. The chief steward hurried to the rear door facing away from the airport building complex and pulled it open. The Captain, knowing what was happening at that precise time, made it easier for him and idled over the turn. He braked, ran up the engines to a shrieking roar and rolled. Gibbs made sure the momentum was right before flinging the case as hard and as far as he could. He didn't see it hit the runway. The Captain had taken Concorde as near to the verge as he dared. The case landed on one corner and bounced in an ungainly roll as Concorde roared on.

Everyone felt the explosion. The roar of it and the massive red-flamed spread of it was seen only by those outside the plane. But the shock waves caught the tail end and the aircraft slewed, before the Captain made a quick correction. The aircraft lost speed as he throttled back, by now some few hundred feet from the point where the bomb had been detonated to one side of the runway, a crater blasted into the concrete, spreading to the grass verge. Mueller had pressed the button a fraction too late.

The plane was brought round slowly and began to taxi back for checks on possible damage. In fact there was none apart from the runway being closed off. Minus Ross Gibbs, the great plane took off uneventfully some three hours late.

*   *   *

It was four hours since Gibbs had left the madhouse of the airport behind. Police and security men, newspapermen and passengers had formed a noisy jostling barrier, and he was glad to break free. Camera crews on the spot had a field day and others arrived as the news broke loose. The story started hitting the headlines as he arrived back in town. Mueller had not been caught and Gibbs doubted now that he would be. The German had done his job and would go to earth. Raul Orta was different: he had always shown himself to be revengeful. This was the time, if ever Gibbs was to do it, to put himself in Orta's shoes. Orta had almost pulled off mass murder. He had even fooled Bannerman: few men had done that. Gibbs could not see Orta scuttling back to his Middle East eyrie with his tail between his legs. The terrorist was not short on courage; he would not be satisfied until he had killed Gibbs. And he would know too that Gibbs would feel the same about him. Orta was a man who planned – so what had he planned now? Where would he expect Gibbs to appear? There were a few possibilities, perhaps one in particular.

It was dark when Ross Gibbs caught a cab to Nuzzale's old apartment. Someone had taken the hall light bulb again. He felt his way slowly up the stairs, pausing now and then, listening, peering into an empty blackness that was unnerving. This was no time for qualms. From the half-landing on, he advanced almost on hands and knees. He reached his own front door, kept low as he produced his key and lightly fingered the door to locate the lock. He inserted the key by touch, a fraction at a time, his controlled breathing louder than the faint sound of metal. He turned the key slowly.

He waited for some time, crouched uncomfortably against the wall. If he had feared the turn of the lock, then so had Orta if he was inside the room. It was freezing cold yet he was hot. He wiped his forehead with the back of the hand that held the Browning he had retrieved at the airport. After several minutes he prostrated himself and reached up for the door handle. He turned it softly, eased the door open an inch, sufficient to clear the lock. He lay flat and waited again.

Pushing himself back, his feet touched the bannister and he stopped. He reached for the door and pushed it back hard. From the darkness of the room a series of flashes sprayed over him, the whine of bullets above his head. No other noise, apart from the crashing of shots into the wall behind him and into the wood of the staircase.

He kicked hard at the bannisters, thumped the floorboards with arms and legs and gave an agonised groan. He raised a leg again and let it fall then lay still, both hands stretched out in front of him, holding the Browning. Nothing happened for a while. It would have been the easiest thing in the world for him to have returned fire by aiming straight at the flashes, but he had it fixed firmly in his mind that he was dealing with Orta.

When he saw the suspicion of movement at the side of the door he knew he had been right.

Suddenly the room light came on and Gibbs was bathed by it. The temptation to roll from the light patch was tremendous but he stayed still, holding position. He had made sure that he had pushed the door flat against the wall. Orta could not be behind it. Facing him, held in a portable vice, was the gun that had been triggered, probably by an extension rod, to fire centrally at the open door, stomach height.

Gibbs made no move. He now knew for certain that Orta was there but the terrorist had to show himself to find out if his own

202

ruse had worked; he did so in typical fashion. Orta hurled himself across the room, too quickly for Gibbs to fire accurately. But at the first sound of movement Gibbs anticipated well, lowered both gun and head before Orta flashed across. Orta had a fleeting glimpse of a prone body.

It needed all Gibbs's nerve now. He did not move his body a fraction but immediately Orta had reached the other side of the room, he raised gun and head again, angling his aim. This time Orta crept back, crouched, gun in hand. His reflexes were excellent as they'd always been, but Gibbs was too finely coiled to be beaten now. He out-thought Orta to the last split second; the difference between hitting Orta with a bullet before Orta could fire. And he struck him again as the terrorist sank to his knees. Even then Orta tried to raise his gun, his gaze vehement. Gibbs coldly fired twice more and Orta fell back, his gun falling from his hand. Only then did Gibbs rise and step carefully into the room.

Raul Orta lay on his back in a spreading pool of blood. A Colt .45 fitted with a silencer was near him. Gibbs advanced cannily, ready to fire his last rounds. Orta was dead, the soft lips open.

In the apartment above, pop music was pounding out, and Gibbs was only now aware of it. Whether it had been on all the time he wasn't sure. He rang the police and left, pulling the door closed with the light still on, leaving behind the acrid smell of cordite. He ran down the outside steps, looked at Orta's Volkswagen where he'd parked it, shrugged and decided to walk. He tried to concentrate on Fran and little Cass whom he had saved. But it would be some time before even such honest, warm-blooded, loving attractions would thaw the deadly cold that had frozen him both inside and out.

★ ★ ★

Sir Henry Winters offered Bannerman a cigar and a cognac. They had been talking for a little while with reasonable goodwill. Winters said, "You nearly slipped up, George. Saved by young Gibbs."

Bannerman shrugged, tasting the cognac without comment. "One can sometimes be too close. If Gibbs had walked off with the case he would have gone up with it."

"And the plane and crew and the nearest passengers."

"But not the P.M. or the Chancellor." Bannerman was always the realist.

"What do you intend to do about Gibbs now?"

"Give him a long rest. After two years underground in London-derry and now this, he's earned it. Anyway, he's taken up seriously with a girl. Let him enjoy himself."

Winters watched the trailing smoke of his own cigar. "You think a good deal of Gibbs, don't you?"

Bannerman's gaze misted. "He reminds me of someone; has the same qualities."

"Steven, the stepson you lost?"

"Yes."

"Through Craven?"

Bannerman didn't answer and Winters guessed that nothing would induce him to.

"Your wife blamed you for that?"

"Did she?"

"All right, I'm treading on private ground. But it gave you no right to do what you did. None."

"What did I do, Sir Henry?"

"Does Leo Roxberg know?"

"He knew I would use Craven or anyone conveniently dead."

"But not that you killed him?"

"He killed himself."

Winter paused. "The Americans want your blood."

"Not for the first time. Do you intend to give it to them?"

"I certainly deplore what you did. Intensely."

"What you *think* I did. Let's look at the result. Four dead terrorists. Kumira strangled herself with her chains. A planeload of people, mainly V.I.P.s, saved from a horrible death to have been watched by hundreds of people. It would have been the terrorist coup of all times. A big chunk of the pack is destroyed, their motives discredited. Craven played a most important part. Without him I think we would have lost this one. Don't you?"

Winters drew on his cigar, his expression suddenly bland. "Without who?" he asked.

Bannerman rose wearily. He didn't go so far as to smile. "Thank you, Sir Henry. I *will* need protection."

"We naval chaps are good at smokescreens. But for God's sake don't ever try it again."

★   ★   ★

Fran reached across the table to touch his hand. "Is it over?"

He had bathed and changed, but his clothes were still shabby. Tomorrow he would go shopping with her. "It's over. For the time being."

Her hand stiffened on his. "There'll be more?"

"Not like this one, I hope."

"It *was* to do with the business at the airport. Someone resembling you was described by the news reporters."

"It could have been anyone, Fran."

"But it wasn't, was it?"

He smiled. "I'm not allowed to say. Where've you left Cass?"

"I haven't. She's in the bag at my feet."

He squeezed her hand. "Thanks for understanding. Choose the best dishes. This dinner is on a friend, though I sometimes suspect he's my enemy." His expression changed. "One more sleepless night won't kill me."